**Praise for the Novels
of Juliet Blackwell**

The Haunted Home Renovation Mysteries

Murder on the House

"A winning combination of cozy mystery, architectural history, and DIY with a ghost story thrown in . . . this well-written mystery has many different layers, offering something for everyone to enjoy." —The Mystery Reader

"Juliet Blackwell successfully blends house renovation and ghosts in . . . this delightful paranormal mystery."
—Lesa's Book Critiques

Dead Bolt

"Juliet Blackwell's writing is like that of a master painter, placing a perfect splash of detail, drama, color, and whimsy in all the right places!"
—Victoria Laurie, *New York Times* bestselling author of the Psychic Eye and Ghost Hunter Mysteries

"Cleverly plotted, with a terrific sense of the history of the greater Bay Area, Blackwell's series has plenty of ghosts and supernatural happenings to keep readers entertained and off-balance." —*Library Journal*

"Smooth, seductive. . . . Fans will want lot more of the endearing Mel." ers Weekly

"This is a gre try that is developing th dation for a strong serie our cozy, this will deligh re."

s and My Musings

continued . . .

If Walls Could Talk

"A riveting tale with a twisting plot, likable characters, and an ending that will make you shudder [at] how easily something small can get totally out of hand. [It] leaves you wondering what you just saw out of the corner of your eye ... a good, solid read."   —The Romance Readers Connection

"Ms. Blackwell's offbeat, humorous book is a fun, light read.... Mel makes a likable heroine.... Overall, a terrific blend of suspense and laughter with a dash of the paranormal thrown in makes this a great read."—TwoLips Reviews

"Kudos and high fives to Ms. Blackwell for creating a new set of characters for readers to hang around with as well as a new twist on the ghostly paranormal mystery niche. I can't wait to see what otherworldly stories Juliet has in mind for us next!"   —Once Upon a Romance

"Melanie Turner may well be one of the most exciting, smart, and funny heroines currently in any book series.... There's enough excitement to keep you reading until late in the night."   —Fresh Fiction

The Witchcraft Mysteries

Tarnished and Torn

"Blackwell has another winner with the fifth installment of her Witchcraft Mysteries ... a great entry in a really great series."   —Romantic Times

In a Witch's Wardrobe

"Funny and thoughtful."   —The Mystery Reader

"Another engrossing story by an author with marvelous storytelling skills."   —Lesa's Book Critiques

"A really entertaining read.... I look forward to the next installment."   —Cozy Crimes

"[Blackwell's] writing is creative and wickedly imaginative."   —Once Upon a Romance

"A wonderful paranormal amateur sleuth tale.... Fans will enjoy Lily's magical mystery tour of San Francisco."   —Genre Go Round Reviews

Also by Juliet Blackwell

HAUNTED HOME RENOVATION MYSTERIES

If Walls Could Talk
Dead Bolt
Murder on the House

WITCHCRAFT MYSTERIES

Secondhand Spirits
A Cast-off Coven
Hexes and Hemlines
In a Witch's Wardrobe
Tarnished and Torn

HOME FOR THE HAUNTING

A HAUNTED HOME RENOVATION MYSTERY

Juliet Blackwell

AN OBSIDIAN MYSTERY

OBSIDIAN
Published by the Penguin Group
Penguin Group (USA) LLC, 375 Hudson Street,
New York, New York 10014

USA | Canada | UK | Ireland | Australia | New Zealand | India | South Africa | China
penguin.com
A Penguin Random House Company

First published by Obsidian, an imprint of New American Library,
a division of Penguin Group (USA) LLC

First Printing, December 2013

ISBN 978-0-451-24070-5

Printed in the United States of America
10 9 8 7 6 5 4 3 2 1

To Bee Green Enos,
Amiga verdadera.
We will always have the snuggery!

Acknowledgments

Every book published depends on the time, talent, support, and hard work of many people. Thanks are due, as always, to Kerry Donovan, Jim McCarthy, and Kristin Lindstrom for being such advocates for me and for my work. Also, to all the copy editors, artists, and assistants who made this book a reality.

I thank the Rebuilding Together organization and its clients for teaching me so much about organizing volunteers, as well as for giving me so much hands-on construction experience. Special thanks go to my cocaptain, Shay Demetrius, Bruce "I'll Do It" Nikolai, Suzanne "Safety" Chan, Anna "Tool Czar" Cabrera—as well as to the dozens of volunteers who showed up for work weekend—for all their energy and hard work.

As usual, my sister Carolyn was an indispensable reader/cowriter for this book. She and I shared many a laugh over the sibling rivalry in *Home for the Haunting*, though our own relationship is one of unflagging support and true friendship. You are such an important part of my writing. I can never thank you enough.

Thanks, as always, to the ever-encouraging writing cabal: Sophie Littlefield, Rachael Herron, Nicole Peeler, Gigi Pandian, Victoria Laurie, Mysti Berry, Adrienne Miller, Cecilia Gray, Lisa Hughey, and L. G. C. Smith. What would I do without you? To my neighbors and all the members, near and far, of the Mira Vista Social Club: J. C. Johnson, Pamela Groves, Anna Cabrera, Mary Grae, Karen Thompson, Susan Baker, Jan Strout, Bill Logan, Brian Casey, Claudia Escobar, Kendall Moalem, Wanda Klor, Antonio Jimenez, and Gomez Gomez for their unflagging friendship.

To my father, who is the inspiration for Mel's dad; and to my sister Susan for all her support. And thanks to my son, Sergio, for making me so proud to be called Mom. And finally, *merci à* Eric for putting such a song in my heart.

Chapter One

You know your job is tough when you find yourself escaping into a Port o' Potty for a minute alone.

The blue outhouses are indispensable on a jobsite and, like the old joke about growing old, are a darned sight better than the alternative. But they're not normally a place I choose to spend much time.

Today, however, I found myself lingering within one. Warmed by the early-spring sunshine, the bright blue potty reeked of hot plastic and a sickly sweet air freshener but offered me a few minutes' respite from the steady barrage of questions and demands from the dozens of eager but unqualified volunteers I was directing.

"Mel, was I supposed to apply a coat of primer before painting?"

"I think I stepped on a rusty nail. Is that bad?"

"Mel, there's this thing inside that's marked 'Biohazard.' What should I do with it?"

"Where's the dust mask/safety glasses/respirator/first-aid kit?"

"Is this mold toxic? Do I need a lawyer?"

"Um . . . Mel? You should probably come see this."

Running a renovation project involves answering a lot of questions, and since I renovate houses for a living, I'm accustomed to fielding rapid-fire inquiries about building details, design issues, and bureaucratic snafus. Usually, though, I work with professionals who know which end of a miter saw is up.

Today's project, I now realized, was as much about wrangling a horde of well-meaning volunteers as it was about home repair.

A few months ago, in a burst of charity inspired by a champagne-fueled New Year's resolution, I volunteered to help a local organization that renovated the homes of the elderly and the disabled. It is a wonderful cause, and seemingly tailor-made for me, Mel Turner, the general director of Turner Construction. I figured I would show up a few weekends a year, tools in hand, go where I was pointed, and do as I was told. By the end of the project, my conscience, and someone's house, would be ship-shape, and I could relax for another six months or so until the next project came along.

As with so many of my life plans, it didn't exactly work out as I'd anticipated. Ashley, the perky and deceptively shrewd recruiter at Neighbors Together, took one look at my business card and appealed to my vanity. Merely volunteering my labor was a waste of valuable and *rare* expertise, she suggested. Wouldn't it be a better use of my talents if I agreed to be a house captain? That way, Ashley insisted, *"You can more fully experience the joy and unique sense of accomplishment that comes from giving of one's self, working with a homeowner in need, overseeing the project from beginning to end, and supervising the eager volunteers.*" I think she probably knew she had me there, but, not willing to leave anything to chance, she finished with "*Imagine turning a loving grandmother's house from a daily nightmare into a warm and safe home sweet home, as only someone with your impressive skills can.*"

I'm such a patsy. I fell for it.

I spent the next several months inspecting the project house, prioritizing repairs and improvements, and gathering materials in preparation for this project weekend, when a group of volunteers descended upon a modest two-bedroom cottage on a quiet street in San Francisco's Bernal Heights. The scene was reminiscent of an old-fashioned barn raising: folks swarming over the place like ants as neighbors strolled over to watch and kibitz. The untrained volunteers would accomplish an astonishing transformation in one short weekend because even though most had never held so much as a paintbrush, many pairs of hands could be turned to good effect when directed by a house captain who knew her business.

And this house captain had been up since four a.m., organizing food for the volunteers, gathering tools and the blueprints for the wheelchair ramp, checking on the arrival of the Dumpster and the Port o' Potty, and running around town picking up last-minute supplies.

And if all that weren't enough to occupy my mind, I was also focused on ignoring the big, abandoned house next door . . . where pale, flickering faces kept appearing in the windows, their breath leaving foggy traces on the panes of glass.

Ghosts. Again.

Why does every interesting building in San Francisco seem to be infested with ghosts?

Ignore them, Mel.

I knew they weren't figments of my imagination. Like it or not, I seemed to have a knack for attracting souls from beyond the veil. Besides, Dog kept staring at the house, too, barking up a storm.

I had found Dog, abandoned and starving, on a construction site some months ago. Despite my initial reluctance to accept more responsibility, we wound up adopting each other. It wouldn't be so bad, I thought: He could ride around with me during the day, come to jobsites and hang around, be my constant companion. Mel's best friend and all that. But then it turned out Dog got carsick, and had a tendency to wander off when I wasn't watching. He didn't play ball, catch a Frisbee, or fetch sticks. He wasn't much of a dog, really, as dogs go. My whole family adored him.

But, like me, he appeared able to see—or hear, or maybe smell?—ghosts.

This morning, Dog's barking got so bad I had to confine him to the car. The canine lovers in the crowd kept visiting with him through the half-open window, sneaking him snacks, and glaring at me for being mean. Luckily, as an experienced general contractor, I wasn't fazed by dirty looks.

And, in any case, the ghosts next door were *not* my problem; not today. Today I had three dozen volunteers to coordinate and put to work before their enthusiasm flagged, plus a house with peeling paint, a warped roofline, and a sagging porch to repair and spruce up, a wheelchair ramp to build so the disabled homeowner would no longer be a virtual shut-in, and one weekend to do it all.

Which explains why I was hiding in a plastic outhouse. I needed a moment to steel myself to ignore the neighboring spirits.

"Sooo," my friend Luz said, catching me as I emerged from my ignominious Port o' Potty break. She was clad in the bright yellow T-shirt of the "Tool Czar" because, by gosh, if I'm going to sink into the quicksand of do-good volunteerism, I'm taking my friends and family down with me. In fact, after my father razzed me one time too many about "giving away" my services, I had goaded him into signing up himself. As the (unofficially) retired founder of Turner Construction, Dad brought a wealth of construction know-how to Neighbors Together, and Ashley had swiftly appointed him house captain for the renovations of the sweet rose-covered bungalow across the street—a project that appeared to be humming along quite nicely, darn it all.

We had a friendly rivalry going: Team Mel vs. Team Bill, Turner vs. Turner. Whoever finished first won control of the television remote for one full week. If Dad won, he swore he would watch repeats of *NCIS* from dusk to dawn. If I won, I vowed to keep the normally blaring television turned off.

The stakes were high.

I had also strong-armed my friend Claire, a landscape architect, into running a yard crew. She was gleefully barking orders to a group of New Age Berkeley types planting a drought-friendly garden of native California grasses and flowering bushes. My buddy Stephen, a clothing designer by aspiration and a barista by trade, was the project's health and safety coordinator. I considered it perfect casting: Stephen was a world-class hypo-chondriac who fussed over the smallest splinter with a wad of gauze and Neosporin. He also roamed the jobsite slapping gobs of sunscreen—donated by a civic-minded local drugstore—on necks and noses. Although it was only April, the sun shone fiercely on the jobsite, which meant reminding everyone to keep hydrated as well.

"The frat boys have arrived," Luz said, nodding toward the street, where half a dozen young men in UC Berkeley T-shirts and Bermuda shorts lounged against a huge SUV. Others were stretched out on the dry, brown, sorry excuse for a lawn, apparently napping.

"Oh, good. They were supposed to be here two hours ago."

"Yeah, well . . . ," continued Luz, "I hate to be the one to tell you this, but half of them appear to be hung over. Drunk frat boys—what're the odds?"

"Isn't the fraternity here to do community service because of an alcohol infraction?"

She grinned. "Gotta love college students."

"If half are hung over, what about the other half?"

"Still drunk."

"Let me get this straight: You're saying my dad's assigned the engineering students, the Eagle Scouts, *and* Turner Construction's finest, while *I* end up with drunken frat boys and a sorority of girls more interested in fashion than construction?" I washed my hands with the hose in the jury-rigged stand on the lawn and clamped my mouth shut to keep from repeating one of my father's favorite sayings: *No good deed goes unpunished.*

"And this surprises you how, exactly?" asked Luz, lifting one eyebrow. "He's a crafty old coot, your dad."

She was right about that. While I had been busy wasting time working for a living, Dad had cozied up to the Neighbors Together point person and nabbed all the skilled volunteers. I'd been so consumed with bringing to conclusion several of our company's paying projects that I hadn't noticed when he had also convinced our best construction workers, even my stepson Caleb, to join his team.

I'd been lucky to get Luz. She was my best friend, but she and my dad adored each other, and at times I suspected he liked her better than he did me. Fortunately, my semi-sort-of boyfriend, Graham, was out of town. I'm not sure I would have liked the outcome had his loyalty been tested.

"Hey, Mel?" Monty Parker, the homeowner, rolled up to the front door, two large, scroungy-looking dogs of dubious ancestry attached by leashes to his wheelchair. After a motorcycle accident had paralyzed the forty-one-year-old a few years ago, he had lost his job and couldn't afford to maintain his home, much less build an access ramp or make other necessary modifications to adjust to his new circumstances. That was where Neighbors Together came in.

I felt for the man, but my stomach clenched at those two little words: "Hey, Mel?" I'd heard them so often the past few months. *"Hey, Mel? What do you think about building a small deck out back when we make the ramp so I could sit outside and watch the world go by?" "Hey, Mel? I hate to ask, but would you change these light-bulbs?" "Hey, Mel? I heard maybe some of the other families are getting new linoleum for their kitchens." "Hey, Mel? My dogs could really use a flea bath; think you could put a new tub in the bathroom?"*

Today, Monty was trying to be helpful by relaying

questions from the volunteers. But he was driving me crazy. Not for the first time, I wondered why my father got sweet Ms. Etta Lee, who was accommodating and grateful and baked him fresh cinnamon cookies, while I was stuck with the needy, grasping Monty.

"Hey, Mel? The folks fixing the kitchen sink found a problem," he said. "Maybe dry rot? Hey . . . are those boys taking a nap on the lawn?"

"Not for long, they aren't," answered Luz.

"Tell the kitchen crew I'll be right there," I said to Monty, then spoke to Luz in a low voice. "Whatever you do, don't let those frat boys near the power tools."

"They're on the schedule as the painting crew," said Luz, flipping through the sheaf of papers on her over-stuffed but organized clipboard. "We're slated to finish the exterior painting today. Not sure the boys are really up for that. How about we leave it to the sorority girls— they're not quick, but at least they're sober—while I find something else for the boys?"

"Any ideas?"

"Well, I was thinking . . . Monty has those two big dogs. Before we can do any work out back, somebody needs to clean things up. What do you say I put the frat on pooper-scooper duty? Make them the Kaopectate Krew."

"You, madam, have a mind of rare and infinite beauty."

"So true. You should tell the promotion and tenure committee."

"How's that going?"

The committee was ruminating on Luz's promotion to full professor of social work at San Francisco State University. Luz was a dedicated teacher, a brilliant scholar,

and an astute judge of human nature . . . but her inter-
personal skills could stand some adjustment. When it
came to tolerating fools, Luz had about as much finesse
as a demo crew.

"Let's just say I'm considering applying to be a sorority mother. According to the girls, there's an opening at
their house. Anyway, after the fraternity finishes doggie
doody duty, I thought I'd get them to clean out the old
shed."

"Great. Keep an eye out—Monty says he has no idea
what's in there, so there may be something we can repur-
pose for the renovation. Could be a real treasure trove.
Be sure to explain to them what constitutes hazardous
waste, since they're also likely to find some old paint or
gasoline cans."

"Will do," Liz said, then turned toward the fraternity
members. "Yo, boys!" she bellowed, and I saw more than
a few wince. "On your feet and follow me! Fall in!"

If the gig as a sorority mother didn't work out, I
mused, Luz could always join the Army. She was a natural drill sergeant.

I heard Dog barking again.

Before I could stop myself, I glanced at the house
next door. There, in the window, was a ghost of a woman,
her pale countenance as clear as you please, spectral
breath leaving traces on the windowpane. She looked
straight at me, as though yearning, seeking . . . something.

Ignore it, Mel. You've got dry rot to deal with.

What does it say about my life when *rot* was a pleasant alternative?

Chapter Two

In today's world, in San Francisco at least, it seems most folks can barely figure out how to reglue the little felt pads to the bottoms of their chair legs. Asking them to re-roof a house was out of the question. Which meant that the volunteers with actual handyman skills were like gold.

Two such volunteers were working diligently under the kitchen sink while a tall woman standing nearby handed them tools and offered suggestions.

"Hi, I'm Mel, the house captain. Thank you so much for being here today—we really appreciate it."

"I'm Hubert, but I go by Hugh . . ." said the first man to extract himself from the cramped cupboard under the sink, where he was accessing the pipes. Though he seemed polite enough, Hugh's eyes did not meet mine; instead, he looked at everything in the kitchen but me, as though his thoughts were somewhere else.

"Mike," said the other man with a nod.

None of us offered to shake hands—plumbing doesn't lend itself to that kind of customary greeting.

"So, what did you find?"

"I think . . ." Hugh said, speaking deliberately, "that there was perhaps a leak under the sink, a slow leak . . ."

"I'm Simone," said the woman, who then proceeded to finish Hugh's sentence for him. "It's a leak that's gone unnoticed, or simply not fixed, for years. Water appears to have gotten into the subfloor."

That wasn't good. Drips led to wet wood, which in turn led to dry rot, an oddly named condition that could spread through healthy wood like a cancer. I inspected the subfloor and instructed the volunteers to remove the wood back to the studs. I was relieved to see that the joists were not affected. Once the dry rot had been removed, they could repair the leaky plumbing, replace the framing and floor, and lay down protective laminate over the plywood. Monty's kitchen would be good as new.

"Sounds just peachy," said Simone. "Unfortunately, Hugh and I have to leave for another engagement. At least we figured out the extent of the problem, but we won't be able to stay and help fix it."

"No . . ." said Hugh, his gaze focused on the on the sink. "We won't."

I nodded, my jaw clenched in frustration. We asked volunteers to commit to at least one full day of work, but there really wasn't anything we could do if they refused.

"I think I can handle it," Mike said. "I'll need a couple of helpers, though."

I thanked him for stepping in and corralled a couple of unskilled but willing volunteers from a local high school's service club who said they didn't mind getting dirty. With luck, they would be helpful and learn something about home repair.

From overhead came the sound of loud banging and a crash, but I wasn't too worried. I knew the leader of the roofing crew. He was a stickler for safety, and he was working with a handful of semiskilled workers from the local fire department. Still, I thought I should probably check, just in case. On my way outside I looked in on the progress being made in the master bedroom by the painting crew. A church group was cleaning the surfaces and taping off edges meticulously. I appreciated the effort, but experienced painters knew better than to sweat using too much blue tape or plastic sheeting. Still, the cardinal rule of directing volunteers was to let them work at their own pace. It was good of them to be here at all, and for many it was their first time on a worksite.

"Mel, do you think someone could get those children to stop singing that little ditty?" asked a middle-aged woman on a ladder. "It's very . . . disturbing."

I listened. Through the open window came the notes of a song I remembered from childhood. "*Lizzie Borden took an ax . . .*"

But although the notes were the same, the lyrics had been changed:

Sidney Lawrence grabbed a knife,
Killed his daughter, then his wife . . .

I glanced out the window and saw a group of tweener kids walking past the big house next door.

"Let me see what I can do," I said, thinking to punt to Luz, who had a natural authority that young people responded to. But she had her hands full handing out shovels and plastic bags to the frat boys, so, though my time would have been better spent on construction, I headed out to chastise some children.

"Hey, guys," I said as I found the little gang of mini-hoodlums: slouching, wearing baseball caps and over-sized clothing. Four boys and one girl. They couldn't have been more than eleven, still dewy and plump with youth. "Can it, will ya?"

"What're you doin'?" demanded the apparent ringleader. He was short and chubby and wore glasses.

"What's it look like we're doing?" I responded in the same tone, waggling my head a little. I had helped raise my stepson, so I wasn't intimidated by this age group. The kids, predictably, responded to my challenge.

"Looks like you makin' a mess," the ringleader said.

"Yeah. *Big* mess," echoed another.

"Of course we're making a mess. Can't make an omelet without breaking a few eggs." I winced as another of my father's favorite expressions left my lips. Did people even *say* such things anymore? Or was I now the epitome of lame, one of those grown-ups who still used words like "groovy"?

"We're making our community a nicer place to live. Better than hanging around singing about murder. What's *that* about?"

"It's 'cause of the Murder House," the ringleader said, as the others looked at me as if to say, "What else?"

"Murder House?"

"That one right there," he said, gesturing to the large Art Nouveau house next door. It stood silent and menacing, flanked by tall palm trees whose spiky fronds waved serenely in the breeze. Years ago, it was in vogue among California's wealthy residents to plant palms around their posh homes. Today, a row of mature palm trees often signaled the site of a fine historic building. This house was different from the small bungalows surrounding it, I noted, but that wasn't unusual. Historic neighborhoods often boasted one fine house among many smaller ones, which were built later when the original owners sold off the original acreage, parcel by parcel.

Don't ask, don't ask, don't ask, a little voice inside my head kept saying.

"What about that house?" I asked.

"Long time ago . . . ," the ringleader said dramatically.

"Yeah, long ago," another child chimed in.

". . . a man murdered his family in that house. His *whole* family."

The other children nodded.

"Kids, pets, even the pizza delivery guy."

"Yeah," the girl continued. "One of the kids tried to escape—"

"He climbed out the window!" a redheaded boy missing two front teeth added.

"Yeah, he fell!" the girl continued.

"And broke his neck!" the ringleader concluded. "Everybody died!"

"Not everybody," the girl said. "The boy got away."

"And a girl got away."

"A boy and a girl got away."

"Yeesh," I said, hoping they were exaggerating. "Lizzie Borden only killed two people, and we thought *she* was bad."

"Who?" The kids stared at me.

"That song you were singing? We used to sing it about Lizzie Borden."

They gave me a skeptical look.

"You sayin' it's a remix?" the ringleader asked.

Modern music loved to piggyback on the old stand-bys. Why not kids' rhymes, too?

"Never mind," I said. The last thing these kids needed was another grisly tale to excite their imaginations.

"What are your names, anyway?"

"I'm Kobe," said the ringleader.

"I'm Kaitlyn," said the girl.

"Ryan," said the redhead.

"I'm Mel. Nice to meet you all. Now I better get back to work."

"It don't look like you're workin'," said Kobe.

"That's because I'm the supervisor."

He looked at me askance. "You're sayin' supervisors don't gotta work?"

"Oh, we work. We work plenty. But it's a different kind of work. Instead of doing it all myself, I tell other people what to do. I coordinate things."

"You mean you order people around."

"Okay, yep, I order people around. Plus, I get paid more. Not on this job, where nobody's getting paid. But in real life, the super does less work and gets paid more."

The kids seemed mesmerized; apparently, this had never occurred to them.

"That's why you have to stay in school," I said, launching into a public service announcement. "That way you get the good jobs and get paid more."

Okay, it was a bit simplistic, but overall it was a pretty good assessment of how the world worked.

"So tell me more about the house next door."

"Not much more to tell, 'cept it's haunted now."

"Mmm," I said. "So you say there was a man and a woman? How old was the daughter?"

Shrug. "I dunno, not a kid."

"A teenager?"

"I guess."

"What did she look like?"

He looked at me askance. "Geez, lady, you seem kinda into it. Prob'ly there's a YouTube or somethin' if you're that curious."

How could I explain that I wasn't some gruesome thrill seeker, but was only trying to identify the ghostly face I'd seen in the windows? But he was right—it would be better to just look it up online. A murder-suicide was bound to have made the news.

"When did all this happen?" I asked.

"Dunno. Long time ago. In the eighties. Can we have a bagel?" he gestured to the table laden with food donated by local businesses or baked by volunteers: bagels and cream cheese, Blue Bottle coffee, chips, energy bars, cookies. Luz and Stephen had not only begged and cajoled any number of local businesses into donating food and drink but had also organized a schedule of cookie drops. Folks who wanted to contribute but couldn't dedicate the whole weekend baked cookies and dropped them off every hour, on the hour. My team might be falling behind on the actual construction, but we were hands down the best-fed group in the program.

"Or cookies!" suggested Ryan.

"The food's for the volunteers. You have to work for it."

"What we gotta do?" asked Kobe.

I eyed him and his motley crew. Technically, only those fourteen years and older were allowed on the jobsite, and strictly with a release form signed by their parents. But there was a lot of debris in the front yard of the house that could be tossed into the Dumpster. . . .

I glanced at Luz, who was signing out a circular saw. Luz hadn't known a monkey wrench from a Phillips screwdriver when she started, but she was a quick study. And since she's naturally bossy, in addition to being Tool Czar I had her check everyone in, get them to sign waivers, and assign them to work teams.

She saw me pointing, pursed her lips and shook her head.

"Tell you what: You guys check in with that nice lady over there"—I pointed to Luz—"and she'll give you T-shirts and work gloves. You clean this yard up for me, put all this stuff into that Dumpster. Then you can help yourselves to snacks."

They looked at one another, and Kobe shrugged. "'Kay."

"Hey," I said to their backs as they descended upon a grumpy-looking Luz. "No more Murder House rhyme— you get me?"

"We only sing it when we go past the house," Kaitlyn said shyly. "It's so the ghosts of the people who died won't get us. But that's not the worst."

Don't ask, Mel. Don't you dare—

"What's the worst?"

Kaitlyn hesitated, glancing around as if fearful of being overheard. I leaned toward her and she whispered. "The ghost of the *dad* who *did* it."

I blew out a breath. Try to do a good deed and what did I get? A drunken fraternity, a bunch of hoodlums in training, and ghosts next door. I was willing to bet my dad didn't have ghosts next door to his project house. Of course, if he did he'd never know it. My sensitivity to ghosts came from my late mother.

I walked Kaitlyn over to where the other kids were encircling Luz and donning bright purple T shirts.

"Hel-*lo*," Luz said, her gaze meeting mine over their heads. "No one under fourteen, ring a bell?"

"They'll stay here in front. They're going to clean up all that stuff; then they get snacks, same as the other volunteers. And then, when they're fourteen, maybe they'll come back and help us out, and maybe learn some skills, like building a handicap ramp. Right, guys?"

"Why I want to build a handicap ramp?" Kobe demanded.

"Because it's better than flipping burgers," said Luz, still glaring at me. "Watch and learn, you guys. You could do worse than a construction job."

I noticed a blond frat boy peering through the window of the neighboring house—the Murder House—his hands cupped around his face to block out the light.

"Hey, Peeping Tom, let's leave the neighbors alone, shall we?" I called out.

"Sorry," the young man said sheepishly. "Didn't mean to be so nosy, but this place is incredible; it's like a time capsule. Look at those lines—that's Art Nouveau. You don't see a lot of that in this area."

"Architecture major?"

"How'd you know?"

"Not a lot of people know much about Art Nouveau."

"It's one of my favorite styles. I'm Jefferson, by the way."

"Nice to meet you, Jefferson. I'm Mel Turner, the house captain for this project."

"Aye aye, Cap'n."

I had to smile. "I'm fond of the Art Nouveau era, myself. But that's a topic for another day. Today we're restoring this fine example of twentieth-century cottage architecture. You guys arrived late, so how about you make up for lost time and get to work?"

"Sure thing. Just tell me what to do." Jefferson was a good-looking guy, tall and strong, with pearly white, straight teeth. Someone had made sure he took his vitamins. And now that he was shaking off the hangover, he appeared polite and accommodating.

I wondered how he would handle it if, while he was pulling his Peeping Tom act, a ghost had peeped back.

"Check in with Luz over there. She'll put you to work."

I looked around for Monty and spied him on the porch. It was his usual perch, overlooking the crowd, except when he hid inside, reading.

One of the things I had immediately liked about Monty were the wall-to-wall bookshelves—stuffed with volumes—lining his living room. Many of the clients I dealt with had adorned their living spaces with nothing but giant flat-screen TVs and sound systems worthy of a professional rock band. Even in the finest homes, entertainment systems had replaced libraries. Book lover that I am, this hurt my feelings.

"Monty?" I called from the side of the house. "What do you know about the house next door?"

"My house used to be its carriage house, or something like that," said Monty.

"Uh-huh. But it's unoccupied, right?"

"You could say that."

Okay . . . I guess I should follow up on the Murder House once I found a little free time. I wasn't getting involved, though. No way. I would just ask Monty what he knew, and then I would move on.

Our main goal today—besides the roof and now under the kitchen sink—was to build the wheelchair ramp, which would allow Monty easy entry and exit, both for safety and to improve his quality of life. I had asked Stan Tomassi to lead this part of the project. Stan worked for Turner Construction and was himself in a wheelchair as the result of an accident on the job. In typical Stan fashion, he had collected all the materials needed, including "lumber" made of recycled pressed polymers, and early this morning had gathered around him several eager beavers to explain to them what the job required.

Stan made a point to encourage women to join and learn as well. He checked them out on the power tools, demonstrated how to read simple drawings, and helped them lay out the project. At the moment, a newly empowered group of three men and three women was sawing equal lengths for the treads and screwing them onto the assembled frame. Stan was careful not to hover, allowing the volunteers to make mistakes and learn from them. He kept a close watch out of the corner of his eye, though, prepared to intervene when necessary to avoid ruining expensive tools and materials, and to correct poor workmanship.

Speaking of seeing things out of the corner of one's eye ... now that I knew a bit about the history of the house next door, I couldn't seem to keep from glancing over at it. The house had obviously been vacant for some time. But ... there was vacant, as in uninhabited, and then there was vacant, as in inhabited by those not of this time and space.

My ability to see and interact with ghosts had manifested itself not long ago out of the blue, and took me by surprise. At the time, my knowledge of all things ghostly had been shaped by popular fiction and cable television shows, neither of which offered much that proved useful. Since the ghosts gave no sign that they intended to leave me alone anytime soon, I thought it wise to learn more about them, and I signed up for Ghost Busting 101, a course offered by my ghost-hunting friend Olivier at his new ghost-hunting store. The very idea of taking "ghost-busting" lessons was embarrassing—I was an established business owner with a local reputation to maintain—but I was determined. So far, most of the spirits I'd encountered had been harmless or well intentioned. A few had been more threatening but incapable of inflicting serious harm. Still, I knew so little about ghosts and what they were capable of. The thought of going up against something malevolent while armed only with a courage born of stupidity and stubbornness seemed like a Very Bad Idea.

Fortunately, ghost-busting class met tomorrow night. I might just run a few specific questions by our intrepid instructor.

I noticed the blond fraternity volunteer, Jefferson, looking through the windows of the house again. What was with this guy? The place was vacant, but still. Did he go around peeping into everyone's windows?

Out in the car, Dog began barking frantically.

Could Jefferson be seeing something . . . more?

"Mel, check out the sorority," said Luz, distracting me from my thoughts. "Or, as I like to call them, Team Amoeba."

"Are they biology majors?"

She shook her head. "Watch them for a moment. They

won't move. They stand in the same spot, the whole gang crowded together, not reloading their paintbrushes or anything."

She was right. The girls were talking nonstop, but otherwise not accomplishing much as they flicked their paintbrushes over the rough stucco. The fact that they were using brushes instead of rollers was crazy. Done properly, brushes would access the divots in the stucco better than rollers, but that required a level of skill these young women did not have.

"Watch this," Luz said as she grabbed the girl on the left by the shoulders, and marched her down the wall ten feet. The other young women shuffled down to join her, and without losing a beat picked up the story about some boy's inability to commit emotionally.

"More paint on those brushes, girls," Luz said, and held up the bucket of paint. Again, without a pause in the story, each girl dipped her brush in the paint can and listlessly stroked the paint onto the wall.

Luz joined me at the tool blanket. "Team Amoeba: They change shape but ultimately come back together."

"That's brilliant," I said, laughing.

"I know."

I headed down the alley between the two houses, shimmying around both the ladder leaning against the side and the stacks of asphalt roofing tiles. I tried not to look, but . . . there it was again: a flash in my peripheral vision.

Monty rolled out onto the corner of the wrap-around porch.

"Hey, Mel, that's not the right shed," he said. "They're supposed to clean out the one at the back of the yard, not that one—"

There was a crash and I saw someone had managed to shove a length of new copper pipe through a basement window. *Better add a new pane of glass to the Home Depot shopping list.*

"Hey, Mel!" Monty called again. "They're cleaning out the wrong shed."

"What?"

From the backyard, I heard a scream.

Chapter Three

No one who works construction sites is a stranger to on-the-job injuries, whether painful blisters, bloody cuts, or broken bones. Without pausing to think, I grabbed a nearby first-aid kit and ran in the direction of the cry. Stephen was hot on my heels, a bright orange bottle of sunscreen in one hand and a box of Garfield Band-Aids in the other.

I knew it. I knew it, I thought to myself. Hangovers and tools were a dangerous combination. What had I been thinking?

"What's the story?" I demanded as I reached the frat boys, who were crowded around the ramshackle shed. "Who's hurt?"

"No one," Jefferson said, his face pale. It looked like his hangover was hanging on.

"So what was the screaming about?" I asked, angry. "Not cool, guys. You scared me."

Jefferson pointed to the shed. "It's in there."

"What is it?" I asked. "A rat?"

"It's not a rat," said Jefferson. "It's . . . Well, look for yourself." He placed one hand on the door and gave it a little shove, then stepped back.

Annoyed at this unnecessary drama, I peered in.

The first thing I saw were locks of hair. Long hair, from someone's head. Baffled, I searched for an explanation. One of the sorority girls? But their hair was long and silky, with the shine of expensive hair care products. The hair I was looking at was wild and frizzy, a dull mousy brown.

I glanced at Stephen, who was swallowing convulsively but who remained by my side, loyal pal that he is.

Only then did the horror wash over me. It was a person. A woman . . .

"Is she . . . ?" he asked, unwilling to complete the sentence.

"I think so," I said. "I don't know . . . but yes, I think so." I blew out a breath, crouched down, and switched on the tiny flashlight on my keychain. Its faint light did little to illuminate the shed's dark interior, but I could see that the woman's skin was a shade of gray that looked more like a Halloween dummy than a person. I guessed her age at around forty.

"Call your friend in the SFPD," Stephen suggested.

"I don't *have* a friend in the SFPD." Inspector Crawford wasn't a friend, not exactly, and I worried that she might grow suspicious of my tendency to stumble across dead bodies. Such a thing wasn't normal, I thought. What were the odds yet another body would turn up when I was around?

"Jefferson, you have a phone, right?" I asked, noting that the confident young man was looking a bit green.

"Call nine-one-one, please. Tell them we have a suspicious death."

"Yes, Captain," Jefferson said, and pulled out his iPhone.

"Everyone else, listen up," I said, hoping I sounded calmer than I felt. The buzz of excited chatter around me fell silent. "Do not go anywhere. The cops will want to take a statement from each of you. You haven't done anything wrong, so there's nothing to be nervous about. Just tell them what you saw."

"What if we didn't see anything?" a scared young woman asked.

"Then tell them that," I assured her.

"What can I do?" Stephen asked quietly.

"Take the phone and talk to the cops," I said. Jefferson was staring at his phone, not dialing. I realized he probably didn't know the street address or any pertinent details. "Will do," said Stephen.

"And then come back and stay with me? In case I go all girly and faint?"

In the past year I had been involved in several disturbing incidents, but most had involved immaterial ghosts, not all-too-material corpses. But as much as I wanted to flee, it seemed wrong somehow to leave the body alone. I turned back to the shed and crouched to examine her.

"Don't touch it!" Stephen said, pausing with the iPhone in his hand. "*Her.* I meant don't touch *her.* That's what I meant."

"You don't have to worry about that," I replied, switching the tiny flashlight back on. "I'm just looking. Call nine-one-one, please."

Stephen nodded and went to stand near the house.

I flicked the penlight over the woman's face and noticed specks of vomit on her collar. Her eyes appeared swollen and small, and red bumps dotted the back of her hands—hives? Had she died of a bee sting, perhaps?

"With those hives and swollen lips and stuff . . . maybe she had an allergic reaction?" suggested Jefferson from behind me.

"Do you know about that sort of thing?" I asked.

"I saw it one time with a frat brother of mine. He was totally, like, allergic to opioids, but he didn't know it. He had some pain pills when he broke his collarbone playing rugby, but he swole up like that, eyes and lips and hives. Looked terrible."

This poor woman looked terrible, too, no doubt about that.

I noticed a tattoo on her neck. It appeared to be a hand holding something. It was upside down from my perspective, and as I was angling my head to get a better view, I felt a hand on my shoulder and fell back onto my butt.

It was Luz.

"She's been dead for a while, Mel," she said, her voice gentle. "This has nothing to do with you."

"But . . . could this be . . . ?" My mind flashed on the Murder House next door. Had its evil seeped onto this property? Could Monty, to all appearances a decent guy in a wheelchair, have been killing women and stashing their bodies in his shed? Could there be a whole cache of bodies hidden in the home's crawl space?

Don't be ridiculous, I scolded myself. I was letting my imagination run away with me. Monty didn't have the mobility to get into the crawl space of his house even if he wanted to. Nor would he be able to transport a dead body here to the shed at the bottom of his sloped yard.

He told me he hadn't even been to the basement floor of his house since his accident. He couldn't even get out of his house unassisted, which was why we were building the ramp.

Luz's dark eyes scanned the area, checking out the neighbors' house.

"Could be anything," she said. "In fact, I heard those kids talking about drugs being dealt out of the vacant house next door. And the way this shed is situated, it looks like it straddles both properties. Look, there are access doors on both ends . . . are we even sure this is Monty's shed?"

I shook my head. "I guess . . . not. Monty's cottage used to be an outbuilding to the big house. Since there's no real fence . . . it's hard to tell where one property ends and the other begins."

"It's probably as simple as that, then," Luz said, wrapping an arm around me. "Probably someone bought some drugs, wandered down here for privacy . . . and that was the end of the story."

The end of her story, that was for sure. Poor woman.

"Cops are on their way," said Stephen as he joined us. He was as breathless as if he'd run a 5K. "I asked for Inspector Crawford since we already know her. I figured that way you wouldn't have to go through the whole 'why do you keep finding bodies' routine."

"You think her knowing me from other crime scenes makes my being here *less* suspicious?"

"I hadn't really thought of it that way," said Stephen, his hand flat on his chest, as though willing his heart to slow down. "My heart's pounding. Are your hearts pounding?"

"No," said Luz. "My heart's steady as a rock. Sounds

like a guilty conscience—you sure you didn't kill her, Stephen?"

Stephen ignored her. "I don't really think I should call back and cancel, though, do you? That would seem suspicious, wouldn't it?"

"You got that right," said Luz, glaring at him.

"This is ridiculous," I said. "I'll just call her myself to explain why we requested her." I had Inspector Annette Crawford's direct number stored on my phone as a result of our earlier interactions. Her number was *not*, however, on speed dial. That was something, I reassured myself.

Inspector Crawford said that she would send over a car immediately and we were not to touch anything. She repeated "don't touch anything" several times.

Now what? Luz planted herself in front of the shed, arms akimbo, prepared to ward off invading hordes. Stephen stood nearby for moral support, though he was still breathing hard and looked so ill at ease I half expected him to blurt out a spontaneous confession of homicide. The frat boys and a dozen others attracted by the commotion stood around them in a loose semicircle, whispering and trying without success to peer into the shed's dim interior.

I looked at the volunteers swarming over Monty's house and wondered, *Should I shut everything down?* It felt unseemly to worry about such prosaic issues at a time like this, but I hesitated to send everyone home. That might mean leaving the project half-finished, and if that happened I might have to pay my regular, nonvolunteer construction crew to come out here to complete the job.

I crossed over to Luz's tool cache, unearthed a small

brown paper bag, and brought it to Stephen, who was now—quite predictably—hyperventilating.

"Luz, do me a favor?"

"Sure. What do you need?"

"Stop me before I volunteer again."

I couldn't get folks to leave. Although the police had, as I had feared, ordered the renovations suspended pending the outcome of the investigation, most of the volunteers loitered out front, curious about the goings-on. I had thanked them, suggested they volunteer across the street at my dad's site tomorrow, and offered them the leftover food, but still they lingered.

It's odd how fascinated we humans seem to be with the demise of other humans, but, like the impulse to check out a car crash as we roll by, it seems to be pretty much universal. Unfortunately, I was learning this with experience.

At last, Inspector Annette Crawford arrived, took my statement, and began inspecting the scene for the third time.

I noticed Kobe standing by my car, petting Dog through the open window, watching the police, and nodding in a world-weary way.

"You know anything about this?" I handed him a bag full of bagels and cookies.

"I'm just sayin'." He shrugged, then nodded his thanks for the food. "They don't call this the Murder House for nothin'."

I followed his gaze to where paramedics were carrying a stretcher with the woman's remains. The black plastic body bag gleamed in the brilliant sunshine, an affront to her untimely death. We observed the sad procession in silence.

Suddenly, Inspector Crawford appeared.

With her typically imperious air, she looked at Kobe and said, "What did you call this place?"

"The house next door? They call that the Murder House," said Kobe. "Everybody knows that."

She looked at me. I shrugged.

"Okay, I'll bite," she addressed Kobe. "Why do they call it the Murder House?"

"A man killed his family there. Only one kid escaped. Maybe two. Depends on who you believe."

"Uh-huh," murmured Crawford. "When was this?"

"Long time ago. In the eighties, I think," he said, then added, "The *nineteen*-eighties."

As though we might be confused as to which century.

"That's twenty, thirty years ago," the inspector said. "Why are you bugging me about something that happened in the neighbor's house thirty years ago?"

"I'm just sayin', is all."

"How about recently? What do you know about this place?"

"Used as a drug drop sometimes, maybe. Only sometimes."

"You know that, or are you making it up?"

"I hear things."

"You have a name or description of these supposed drug runners?"

He shrugged.

"Got anything else for me?"

"Nuh-uh."

"Then go get me a cup of coffee with sugar, no cream."

To my surprise, Kobe shuffled off toward the refreshment table, where the big container of coffee still beckoned.

The inspector turned to me. "You and the college boy . . . Jefferson—you were the only ones who touched the shed door or the body?"

"As far as I know, yes. I asked the fraternity brothers to clean out the shed, though it seems we picked the wrong one. The homeowner meant the small metal garden shed, not the old wooden one. I'm not even sure that one's even on Monty's property."

"Okay. I want to talk to the students. You can tell everybody else to leave."

"I did. They didn't leave."

"Tell them again," the inspector said, looking surprised. I doubted she ever had to say anything twice, unlike me. "Looks like the body's been there for a few days, so I doubt any of you have anything to do with it."

"About the project . . ."

She fixed me with her patented don't-mess-with-my-crime-scene look. "The project is on hold until we figure out what happened."

"You think it was a homicide?"

"Too early to tell. It's a death under suspicious circumstances, that's for sure. There are a whole lot of people who will have to weigh in on this one, starting with the medical examiner. Until he makes his determination as to cause of death, we gather evidence. It's how we do it."

"Gotcha."

I glanced with regret toward the piles of donated food on the card tables, the hand-lettered signs directing the volunteers to the cleanup and first-aid and tool stations, the heaps of costly supplies, the stack of lumber for the handicap ramp, the proud Neighbors Together banner flapping in the wind.

No good deed goes unpunished.

Stan, Luz, Claire, and Stephen, as well as a handful of the volunteers—including Jefferson and a couple of other frat boys, who seemed to feel guilty about their late start—assured me they would return next weekend to help finish the renovations on Monty's house. If I could guilt—or, at last resort, pay—a couple of my employees into joining us, we would be able to complete the unfinished projects without much trouble.

Fortunately, the most weather-sensitive project, the roof, was nearly finished, and the projects that remained could be completed come rain or shine. The ramp was three quarters of the way done, and several of the rooms inside had been primed and prepped for painting. The yard and shed cleanup had been bonus projects to make use of the volunteer labor and to make things nice, but they weren't necessary for Monty's health or safety, especially since he wasn't able to access them anyway. Monty had said something about converting the aboveground basement into a rental studio, but that wasn't in the scope of our project. He could hire someone to do that if he so desired.

I should be able to finish up next week, I reassured myself once more, without too much trouble.

Unless, of course, I was embroiled in yet another murder investigation.

Which I wouldn't be, since the woman's death had nothing to do with me or my project.

Monty confirmed to the police that although he had

occasionally used the portion of the shed that faced his yard, it was actually on the neighbor's property. Which meant the crime scene was the neighbor's problem—yet another tragedy related to the Murder House.

Junkie or no, the poor woman's death was shocking, sad, and unsettling.

But what really bothered me were the faces I kept seeing in the windows of the hulking, vacant house next door. Did those ashen, flickering countenances belong to the long-ago murdered family?

And . . . did they have something to tell me?

Chapter Four

Sunday morning, I made a leisurely—some might say slothful—arrival at my dad's jobsite, the sweet little cottage belonging to Ms. Etta Lee.

The project was humming along smoothly, while mine was covered in DO NOT CROSS police tape.

I stood for a moment, staring at it glumly. I should be hiding in the Port o' Potty to get away from *my* volunteers, not helping my dad complete his project. Worse still, the suspension of the work meant I had lost our bet to see who would finish first and now faced an entire week of *NCIS* reruns.

As I viewed the scene from across the street, Monty's suggestion that his house was an outbuilding of the Art Nouveau house made sense. Monty's home had been built earlier than the others on the street, and though it didn't share the exquisite lines of the main house, neither did it have much in common with the stucco bungalows, which were typical of those built in the forties. These postwar homes typically opened onto a combination living room/dining room, which led to a kitchen and back door; a side hallway led to two small bedrooms with a bath in between. Compact yet cozy, the small bungalows were snug and neat, and when first built had been priced to sell to working-class families.

Monty's home, in comparison, was much more interesting than Mrs. Lee's, with multipaned windows and odd nooks and crannies indicative of a custom design. I wondered if it had originally served as the caretaker's home.

The Murder House must have been incredible when it was first built. I itched to take a peek inside. My eyes rested on the blue front door. A large, heavy-looking knocker hung on it. It was hard to make out from here, but it looked like knockers I had seen in Europe, with a hand holding a ball . . . I started over to take a closer look.

"Mel!" called my father. As he approached, I noted his distinctive Dad scent: the faint aroma of tobacco—he claimed he didn't smoke, but he wasn't fooling anyone—mixed with automotive grease and food. Today, it was onion from the omelet he had made this morning—the one I missed out on by choosing sleep over breakfast. "Glad to see you're still with us."

"Hey, the cops shut down my project, remember? I can sleep to a reasonable hour every once in a while." I winced at the defensive edge in my voice. Like it or not, I had inherited my father's early-to-rise work ethic. If I wasn't up at five in the morning getting ready for work, I felt like a slug.

"I gotta hand it to you, Mel. You do have a knack for being in places where people die. Kind of like—what's her name? Typhoid Mary."

"Gee, thanks, Dad," I said, annoyed. "I am *not* a Ty-phoid Mary. The police said the woman had been dead since before we arrived. It had nothing to do with me."

"Seems to me I hear that phrase a lot these days," said Dad. At the look on my face, he had the good grace to change the subject. "Did you get breakfast? We've got doughnuts."

"Thanks. I had a latte."

Dad rolled his eyes. He believed in the power of breakfast, even if it consisted only of fried dough drenched in icing and served in a pink cardboard box. A pragmatist, Dad had also arranged for a couple of boxes of Blue Bottle coffee and gallons of Jamba Juice for the jobsite. I felt myself relax just knowing that hot coffee was nearby if I needed it. Maybe he was right: I was be-coming a caffeine addict.

Dad and I love and cherish each other. We also drive each other crazy. Dad is former military, a tough guy who believes in hard work, beer, and football. Oh, and fire-arms. And because the fates like to mess with us mere humans, this man's man had fathered three daughters. He adored each of us, but he had taught us while were young to ride motorcycles and shoot guns. He also dragged us from one construction site to another, hoping to pass on the construction genes.

The daughter most like him turned out to be me, though we had fought a lot in my teenage years, and when it came to politics we remained in opposite camps. Still, I shared his love for old buildings and his talent for renovation. My sisters lived in brand-new housing devel-opments and refused to come anywhere near a compres-sor, much less a power saw. But Dad's gung-ho approach to life took a beating a few years ago when my mother passed away suddenly. Overnight, my tough-guy father just lost it. Somebody needed to take over Dad's construction business, and since I was at a crossroads in my own life, I had stepped in "for a few months." Three years later, here I was, still acting like the general.

I was a bit cranky about it.

"How soon can you finish up that project and move on to something that makes money?" he asked.

"The police need a few days. Monty's flexible, so there's no huge rush. Probably next weekend." I slewed my eyes toward him. "Say, any chance you're available next weekend?"

He stuck out his chin, which was peppered with white stubble. "I dunno. A job like this is hard on a man my age. Might need to spend next weekend relaxing and watching the game."

Behind us, Dad's project was buzzing along, alive with well-directed, skilled workers. In addition to his regular crew, several of my volunteers had shown up this morning as well.

"Doesn't look to me like you're working too hard," I pointed out, then realized how my words echoed Kobe's from yesterday. Speaking of whom . . . I wondered if the boy knew more about the poor woman in the shed than he had admitted. He seemed to know a lot about what went on in the neighborhood.

I heard Dad chuckle. "Course we'll come back. Turners aren't quitters, right, Caleb?"

He slapped my teenage stepson—my *ex*-stepson, actually—on the shoulder. Caleb wasn't technically a Turner, but he seemed pleased to be called one, and stood a little taller.

"That's right," Caleb said. Caleb was my ex-husband's

son by his first marriage, but I had raised him for years and thought of him as my own child. To my delight, my father had come around to the same conclusion, so much so that I was starting to think Dad considered Caleb the son he never had. Blood relative or no, Caleb was now a full-fledged member of Clan Turner.

I leaned over and ruffled his hair, then let my hand linger on the nape of his neck, where the dark hair met his smooth olive skin. Caleb squeezed his shoulder to his ear, as though to slough off my hand.

"You need a haircut, bud," I said, unable to stop myself. At some point I had switched from the cool stepmom who engaged in sword fights and made pirate costumes to the annoying stepmom who nagged about haircuts and homework. "Come by the house and I'll trim it for you if you want."

He shrugged. Caleb's hair was dark and wavy, curling at the neck. He wished it were straight, and boy, did I know that feeling. Since we weren't related by blood, Caleb hadn't inherited those genes from me, but I still felt vaguely guilty, as though associating with my curly-headed self had somehow rubbed off on him. Occasionally, Caleb would agree to let me cut it, though only because his father threatened to take him to a fancy place on Union Square, where they would charge a fortune to "style" his hair so that he would look, in his own damning words, "like someone running for class president."

"Bill, Ms. Lee's looking for you," said Caleb.

We turned to see the homeowner making her slow way down the front path toward us. Etta Lee was in her seventies, and though she walked with a cane, she had a look about her that indicated she was of hardy stock.

Lively, light brown eyes held an undeniable sparkle. She also looked as though she'd spent a day at the beauty parlor to look "put together" for the volunteers who had descended upon her house. Her gray hair had been carefully set and tightly curled around a pleasant face. She was the picture of graciousness, oohing and aahing over what the volunteers had accomplished.

Me, I got stuck with "Hey, Mel?" Monty.

Ms. Lee stepped carefully, the sort of tread that suggested she knew a fall might cause a hip fracture from which she would never recover. I felt a stab of regret, remembering the elderly woman from the last big Turner Construction project. She had not met with a good end, and the memory still haunted me. Figuratively speaking.

"Bill Turner," Ms. Lee declared, "you are a darling man. Has anyone told you that?"

"Not recently. In fact, I'd like to introduce you to my biggest critic, my daughter Melanie."

"I go by Mel," I said, offering my hand. "It's wonderful to officially meet you, Ms. Lee. I've heard so many lovely things."

"Please, call me Etta. And this is Dooley, my constant companion." Dooley was hands-down the ugliest cat I'd ever seen: a skinny three-legged tabby whose orange striped coat stuck up in random tufts. He meowed raucously until I leaned down and petted him.

"Mel is taking over the family business," said Dad. "My girl knows her stuff."

There was an unmistakable note of pride in his voice. That was my father for you—one moment I'd be ready to throttle the cranky old guy, and the next he'd do something sweet, like signing off on the phone with a gruff

"Love you, babe." He never used to say things like that before my mother passed away. Then he had been the distant, hardworking disciplinarian, the military man who seemed baffled that his three daughters didn't respond to his orders like a company of well-trained cadets. Having gone through a personal tragedy with the loss of his wife, Dad had become an odd mixture of Grumpy Old Man and sensitive New Age Dad.

I found it easier to deal with the Grumpy Old Man. It was more my comfort zone.

After a few more minutes of pleasantries, we settled in to work. Etta had hit the jackpot when my dad was assigned to her renovation project. A skilled crew was repouring a portion of the foundation, a major job that would clearly run beyond this weekend. Others were bolting and shear-walling in the basement, two methods of keeping a house from sliding off its foundation in the event of a major earthquake. Painting crews were at work in both bedrooms, and outside, an empty lot was being used as a staging area, though volunteers were cleaning it out to put in a vegetable garden. In the bathroom, the broken tile around the tub and the dry rot underneath had been removed, and now waterproof backing was going in to prepare it for new tile. And last but not least, Dad had somehow talked one of our regular suppliers into donating double-paned replacement windows for the weather-facing side of the house.

When Dad picked up a brush to help the painters, I pulled on my coveralls and joined the basement foundation crew. We had been working for several hours when we stopped for a lunch break, which today was pizza and salad provided by yet another group of volunteers. As I soaked up pizza and sunshine, I thought how amazing it was that people could get so much done when they worked together.

"Mel, you should check out the interior before you go back under," said Dad, as we finished up our slices. "It's small, but so well maintained. And you'll never guess what's in the sun porch."

I didn't have to be asked twice; I'd been working in the dark basement all morning and I love snooping around old houses. I stood at the front door and knocked. Even though it was a worksite, I didn't want to invade Ms. Lee's privacy any more than we already had. It's tough to live on a jobsite, even if it's only for a weekend.

"Oh, come in!" she said, greeting me at the door. "How polite of you to knock."

"I didn't want to startle you," I said.

Following her into the entryway, I saw Dad wasn't kidding. These old bungalows weren't fancy, but they boasted beautiful wood trim and panels in the Arts and Crafts tradition. I was betting there would be cross-sawn wood under that paint. Problem was, if I checked for it, I was obligating myself to strip the paint, as once it was scratched, there would be no fixing it. Was I willing to go down that road?

Neighbors Together, like most community groups, was underfunded and did the best it could with limited donations of time, materials, and money. House captains were encouraged to focus on health and safety issues first, such as fixing dry rot and installing handrails. There simply wasn't the time or the money to strip wood and bring a bungalow like this up to the standards of *This Old House*.

Still . . . it wouldn't take much to transform this place. It was small enough that the necessary work could be accomplished in a couple of weekends.

"I know I'm old-fashioned," Etta said. "But I used to harangue my students about common courtesy, things as simple as saying 'please' and 'thank you' or knocking before entering a room. Even when I visit a dear old friend, I always knock. It amazes me that people don't teach their children basic manners anymore. Of course, a lot of them are children themselves when they become parents. Children having children . . ." She trailed off, shaking her head and then chuckling self-consciously. "Well, would you listen to me? I'm sounding more and more like an old crank, aren't I?"

I smiled and shook my head. I am a sucker for public servants, especially teachers and librarians. The kind of people—usually women—who dedicated their lives to our children for low wages and crummy working conditions, and now even their pensions were in danger. Maybe I could talk my dad into coming back with me and stripping the woodwork. . . . I felt a plan coming on.

"Let me show you the best part," Etta said as she led me toward the back door.

At some point the former concrete patio had been enclosed, and judging by the quality of the construction, I was guessing Mr. Lee, or perhaps Etta herself, had done the work. Two-by-fours formed the skeleton, the roof was made of corrugated fiberglass, and the walls were thick plastic sheeting stapled to the wood frame. Raggedy plants and tattered wicker furniture sat around the perimeter, forming a circle around a huge model train set built on a plywood platform. Three adorable miniature towns were separated by tiny scale rivers, mountains, and forests. One town was hosting a carnival that appeared to have been there for some time—the revelers on the minuscule Ferris wheel were caked in dust.

Unfortunately, the enclosure smelled neither of the outdoors nor the interior, but of must and mildew. It really should be either demolished entirely or shored up properly.

"This is quite something," I said. "Are you the train enthusiast?"

"That was my husband. I haven't kept it up the way I should. I've got the arthritis, so I don't get around as well as I used to. Lord, I used to have such energy!"

"Does it still work?"

"The trains still run, but a lot of the smaller items don't work well anymore. The Ferris wheel is supposed to go around, that sort of thing."

"My dad's pretty good with electrical work," I said. "Maybe he can take a look at it."

"Oh, he's so busy I wouldn't want to ask. He's already doing so much."

"I bet he'd get a kick out of getting it to run properly."

Etta nodded, but looked distracted. "Listen, Mel ... I was wondering ... I heard about what happened at Monty's yesterday." She picked up a tiny truck and blew off some dust, then cleaned it with her hands before setting it back down on a tiny highway. "You poor thing. It must have been quite a shock. Do they know who it was?"

"I really don't know," I said.

"How sad. That place, all those lost souls ..." She trailed off with a sigh. "I swear, it must be haunted."

I studied her for a moment before realizing she was speaking metaphorically.

"Ms. Lee—"

"Oh, please, call me Etta. *Ms. Lee* is so formal. Makes me feel like I'm still a teacher."

"Etta, then. What grade did you teach?"

"Middle school at first, and then high school later."

"Wow. Teenagers. I'm impressed."

She smiled and brought a tiny bright yellow train engine over to a worktable. She studied it through a jeweler's glass, dabbed a minuscule brush in fresh paint, and then started painting the toy with surprisingly steady hands. Seeing Etta now, I realized she probably wasn't much older than my father, maybe five years at most.

"I love teenagers. I know, I know, I'm crazy. But there's something so . . . energetic about them. I love the way they throw themselves into things—feetfirst, all in, no doubts. Sometimes that impulsivity gets them in trouble, of course, or even puts them in danger. But there's something about that energy I just love."

"My stepson's sixteen. He seems to be stuck in the grunting, shrugging stage."

"My advice with teenagers? The more obnoxious they are, the more they're begging you to spend time with them, pay attention to them. They try their best to run you off, but they're really begging you to stay." She grinned, and it was clear to see that she had always been what one would call a handsome woman: tall, strong-looking, I was guessing Polish stock. Capable and, I imagined, unflappable in the face of whatever antics teens might dream up.

"I understand you've lived here a long time. You must know a lot about the history of the neighborhood."

She gave me a keen-eyed look. "By 'history' I assume you're curious about what happened over at the Lawrence house."

"Is that the house across the street, next to Monty's?"

She nodded. "The children call it the Murder House."

Once again, I told myself not to ask. The ghosts were

none of my affair. I was running a volunteer project, and a dead body entirely unrelated to me was found in a building entirely unrelated to my project. And even if the dead woman had been found on Monty's property, her death had nothing to do with the ghosts I had seen in the neighbor's windows, much less the foggy circles on the windowpanes, as though someone were breathing on the glass . . .

"It was the most interesting thing to happen around here in ages," Etta said as she stroked more paint onto the engine. She glanced up, wet brush held aloft. "That sounds terrible, doesn't it? I simply mean that tragedy is inherently interesting, far more interesting to outsiders than happiness. That's why all great literature is tragedy."

"I never thought of it that way."

"Of course, that pertains to fiction, not to life. When it comes to living a tragic life versus a happy one, I know what we'd all choose. Which is what makes what happened across the street all the more tragic. The Lawrences . . . They always seemed so happy."

"What happened, exactly?"

"Sidney Lawrence killed his oldest daughter, his wife, and then himself."

So Kobe and his gang exaggerated the details, but were otherwise on target.

"I met a few of the neighborhood children yesterday. Do you know Kobe?"

"Was he bothering you? I'd be happy to talk to him. I know his mother. No father in his life, unfortunately, which is what he really needs. So many of these kids just need their parents to be more involved in their lives, but a lot of their folks are juggling jobs, or addictions, or other problems. I know they can be bratty at times, but after years of working with them, I have concluded that without involved parents, they don't have much of a chance at life."

"Kobe was no bother at all. In fact, he and his friends pitched in on the cleanup at Monty's house."

She looked at me, askance. "What did they get in return?"

"Snacks and a T-shirt. But they were good-natured about it all. They told me a little about the, um, murders. And they mentioned one of the children escaped?"

"Two. The middle daughter apparently saw what was going on and helped her little brother to escape through a second-story window. Sidney killed himself instead of chasing after them; thank goodness for that. Can you imagine? Poor little babies. They ran over here, to our house." There was a catch in her voice, and she cleared her throat before resuming her story. "It was a little after nine on a cold spring night in— *Oh*, I just realized—this Friday will be the twenty-fifth anniversary."

The silver anniversary of a double murder-suicide. That isn't portentous at all, is it? I thought.

"That night, the doorbell rang over and over," Etta continued. "We thought it was some neighborhood children fooling around, so we debated whether to answer. The neighborhood was a little rough in those days, so we hesitated. But then Gerry looked out and saw . . . the poor little babies."

"Did you know them well?"

"Of course, I knew everyone then. Though as a teacher, I wasn't around much—spent most of the day at school. But the Lawrence family was very sweet, very steady. Or so it seemed." She set the yellow engine down and picked up a red caboose. "I'm sorry to say I was one of those neighbors you see on the TV, saying, 'Gee, they always seemed so nice. I never would have expected it.' But it was true."

"You never heard arguments, saw any sign of abuse?"

She shook her head. "But I'm not sure I would have noticed anything amiss. This is an urban neighborhood, closer than many, but we're working people and in and out so much it's not as though we exchange words every day. But . . . I suppose I could believe a man getting passionate enough to kill his wife—for infidelity, something that might push him over the edge—but to kill his baby girl? Sidney doted on those children. He was, according to everything I ever saw, a devoted father. That's why he was so upset with the goings-on at the house across the street from him."

"Which house?"

"The drug house."

Oh, boy. First a murder house, now a drug house.

"Which was the drug house?" Etta's house was right across the street. There were an empty lot to the right and another small bungalow to the left that didn't look much like what I would think of as a drug house.

"It's just an empty lot now."

"The one where all the equipment is? I noticed some of the volunteers were clearing it out."

"It's just been sitting there empty this whole time, so I thought I might as well spruce it up, put in some vegetables."

"What happened to the house that used to be there?"

She nodded. "It burned down and had to be demolished. Can't say any of the neighbors were too upset to see it go. That wasn't long before the Lawrence . . . incident."

She set the train down and sighed.

"This train set belonged to Gerry, my ex-husband. The neighborhood kids used to love coming here, watching the train go round and round. All the kids back then — Dave and Linda and the others — spent many a Sunday afternoon here, hands sticky from lemonade and cookies. I keep thinking if I get it back in shape, maybe I could resurrect the tradition now that I'm retired and have more time. What do you think? Do kids today still like model trains?"

Did they? Or were they so enmeshed in their electronic gizmos that the simple pleasure of a miniature world would no longer intrigue them?

"The Neighbors Together crew seems pretty interested," I said. "What does Kobe think?"

"Do you know, I don't believe he's ever seen it. After Gerry left, I stopped having the kids in. Just didn't have the heart, and then the set fell into disrepair, as you can see. If I get it cleaned up . . ."

"Maybe you should ask Kobe and his little gang to help you."

She looked up at me, alarmed. "Kobe's joined a gang?"

"Oh, no, not a real gang. But he seems to travel in a pack. They're too young for a real gang."

"Oh, believe me — they're not too young. You'd be surprised how the gangs pick up aimless kids, as young as nine or ten, and begin to indoctrinate them."

Something else occurred to me.

"You know, I was thinking about how we might help you fix up the rest of this place. The classic lines of this house, the woodwork and the built-ins, are amazing. I bet my dad could help with the train set, too. And he's great with kids."

Actually, Dad was gruff and demanding, but a lot of kids responded to that sort of treatment.

"Do you think so? I have to admit that as much as I like children, one of the reasons I stopped opening my home to them was that as a single woman, I felt a little nervous around the older teens. But if your father was here as well . . ."

"Couldn't hurt to ask."

"Would he have the time?"

"Oh, he's got all the time in the world."

"Mel?" Caleb called from the interior doorway. "Um . . . Sorry to interrupt."

"That's okay," I said. "What's up?"

"Bill's busy and I think"—he kept glancing nervously at Etta—"I think you should see this."

"Sure. Excuse me, Etta. I should probably get back to work."

"Oh, of course! It is so good of you all to do all this for me. I don't know how to thank you."

I smiled. "Sometimes charity is its own reward."

I stepped into the hallway and confronted Jefferson, the fraternity brother, who was holding a .38 Special.

Chapter Five

I froze.

"Jefferson . . . ?" I began, taking care to speak low and slow.

"Oh, hey, Cap'n. No worries," he said, flipping the gun around and handing it to me, the muzzle pointed toward the floor and the butt toward me, as was proper safety procedure. "I checked; it's not loaded."

Gingerly, I took the gun from him and double-checked. He was right; it was empty. I glanced at Caleb and three other college boys standing in a semicircle.

"Who brought a gun to the worksite?" I demanded.

"It's mine," said Etta from behind me. "Don't worry; I know how to use it—I go out to the shooting range at least once a month, up by San Quentin."

Dear Ms. Etta Lee, retired schoolteacher, was getting more interesting by the moment.

As I carefully handed the gun over to her, she explained: "It's for protection. I told you, this used to be a rough neighborhood. I'm a single woman now. And to tell you the truth, I enjoy the feel of it in my hands."

That clinched it: Etta and my father were perfect for each other.

By four o'clock, we were winding down. Dad was conducting a careful walk-through and checking items off the punch list, while the majority of the volunteers were busy with the final cleanup of the jobsite and the tools, which is no small thing. With our energy flagging, we were digging into the sugary snacks. I was helping myself to what I swore would be my last Krispy Kreme—for the day, at least—when I glanced across the street.

A shiny silver Lexus was pulling into Monty's driveway.

Great. Our house sponsor, Ray Buckley. I blew out an exhausted breath. I should have called to let him know about what had happened yesterday and that the project was on hold. Between the commotion and chatting with the police, it had completely slipped my mind.

It was common in the Bay Area, despite—or perhaps because of—its rampant entrepreneurialism, to deride successful capitalists for their greed. Then along came someone like Ray Buckley. Ray had donated a check for Monty's project that was so generous, the organization had allotted part of it for Ms. Lee's house. Without the contributions of businesses and businesspeople, Neighbors Together wouldn't have been able to accomplish half of what it did.

"Ray, how nice to see you," I said, hailing him from Etta's side of the street.

Ray must have been pushing seventy years old, but in his elegant suits, he still cut a fine figure. With his silver hair and upright posture, he looked like the sort of model you see on vitamins for older people that promise youthful vitality no matter one's age.

He gestured to the crime scene tape. "What happened? Was there an accident? Is everyone all right?"

"Sort of." I gave him a brief rundown of the previous day's events. "But it looks as though the shed is actually on the neighboring property, not Monty's, so it shouldn't be a problem in terms of the project, long-term."

"The woman was found in a shed? That's terrible. Who was it?"

"I have no idea. The police think it might have been someone looking for shelter—and there may have been drugs involved."

His eyes fixed on me.

"Did you see her?"

"Yes, I was there when they found the body. She was in her forties, maybe? Light brown, curly hair. She had a tattoo of a hand on her neck. . . ."

As I said it, I realized what the tattoo reminded me of: that knocker on the blue door of the haunted house, the hand holding a ball.

Ray turned white as a sheet. "Not . . . *Linda*?"

"Linda?"

"Linda Lawrence? The . . . the girl who escaped the Murder House?"

When a person goes into shock, there's nothing quite like fruit juice to set them aright. Or at least that's what my father always said, and he'd dealt with more shock than I had over the years. So Ray and I sat in the shade, and I urged him to down some Jamba Juice while we waited for Inspector Crawford. Dog, who I had let out of the car, was doing a much more effective job of comforting Ray than I was. Ray kept up a steady rhythm of petting Dog's silky brown coat while sipping his smoothie.

For my part, I had served myself yet another cup of Blue Bottle coffee, because that morning's earlier jolt of caffeine simply wasn't cutting it anymore.

"You told me you were familiar with this neighborhood, but I didn't realize you knew the Lawrence family," I said quietly.

"I did know them. Quite well."

I nodded, remaining silent while I tried to formulate my next question: *Did you know of the massacre? Could you tell me about it?* No matter how I phrased the query in my mind, it seemed rude, even ghoulish.

He looked at me out of the corner of his eye. "I'm going to assume from your silence that you've heard something about what . . . happened?"

"I heard a man killed his family."

"You heard right." He blew out a long breath. "That man was my best friend."

I looked over at him, shocked.

"I know what you're thinking. Sidney Lawrence must have been a madman, right? And how could a madman have friends?" He shook his head and ran a hand through thick salt-and-pepper hair. "I don't know what to say, except that what Sidney did that night . . . that wasn't Sidney."

"Then who was it?"

There was a long silence, and he took another swig of juice. The scent of the smoothie's strawberries and bananas wafted toward me, melding with the aromas of tilled earth and sawdust. Pleasant smells, comforting smells.

"Do you believe in demons, Mel?"

"I ... uh ..." I stammered. A year ago I wouldn't have admitted to believing in ghosts, but now I understood that our human energy lingered on long after the physical deaths of our bodies. But demons were a whole different ballgame. I didn't know much, and I didn't *want* to know more. Quite frankly, I didn't even want to consider the possibility that they might really exist. "I don't ..."

"I know, I know. . . . It sounds crazy. I don't know that I believe it myself, except that it's the only thing that could explain what happened that night. Some sort of demon possession. But maybe that's my Catholic upbringing talking. I guess in the modern world, we would refer to it as a psychotic break. Some kind of mental problem, where he snapped, became someone other than himself."

"Were there any signs? Odd behavior leading up to that night?"

He shrugged. "I guess ... I mean, we were both under enormous stress. We worked together and the business was facing a number of challenges—we were undercapitalized, and we had both sunk everything we had into it. I was okay; I had some other resources. But Sidney had a wife and three children to provide for. He was ... at his wit's end, I guess."

"Was he acting strangely at work?"

"There were allegations ... some unexplained financial activity, though I could never believe it of him. Even after ... It's funny—in a way, the idea that Sidney snapped and struck out in violence would be easier for me to believe than his cooking the books. He just wasn't that kind of guy. We were ... He was my best friend."

Another long moment of quiet passed. I imagined we were both pondering the sort of thing that could have driven a man to do such a horrific thing, to destroy his own family in a few moments of rage and betrayal and madness. Ray was right: It would be easier to believe—almost comforting that a demon had possessed your best friend than to accept that he could knowingly and willingly inflict such pain.

I felt my father's eyes on me and looked up to see him giving me the "What, are you gonna sit around on your fanny all day rather than help me get this job done?" look. He had no clue what Ray and I were talking about, which was best. Looking at my dear, cantankerous father, I tried to conceive of him turning on me. Inflicting mortal wounds. Impossible. I couldn't imagine the sense of betrayal, the disbelief Sidney's doomed daughter must have felt.

Relief washed over me when I spotted a beige sedan pull up in front of Monty's house: an unmarked police car. Inspector Crawford climbed out and crossed the street to join us. She was going to take Ray's statement and see whether he could provide a positive ID of the body.

After a brief greeting, Ray went with the inspector, and a few of us went back down into Etta's crawl space to finish up the foundation work.

After all, when all was said and done . . . there was no use in going over the family tragedy again and again. It was in the past, thirty years ago. Water under the bridge and all that. It had nothing to do with the body we had found.

Unless, of course, the walls of the Murder House had absorbed the spirits of those souls so unfairly slaughtered on that night — as well as the father who had done the evil deed. Unless those spirits were still there, searching for meaning, for understanding . . . or for victims.

After a day working with my dad and explaining to Monty why we couldn't continue construction on his place at the moment, I was about plumb worn out. So, after we had packed up the tools and dumped the last of the trash into the happily named Dumpster, Etta thanked the volunteers and took a picture with everyone lined up on her cement stoop. Everyone went off weary and slightly sunburned but proud of themselves.

It was a good project, successfully completed. Etta would now be able to live without worrying about falling through her rotting kitchen floor, the building was newly strong, and the paint was not only pretty but would protect the building from the elements. She even had a new vegetable garden planted. And the charity could not have been bestowed on a more grateful recipient.

Monty, however, was unhappy.

"Hey, Mel? How come you finished up old lady Lee's house, but not mine?" he demanded for the third time, wheeling his chair out onto his sagging wooden porch.

"I told you," I said. "We have to wait for the police to clear this place, and we'll come back and finish up. I promise. It's not like we'll leave it half done." I was such a stickler for finishing the jobs I started — that early-childhood training stuck with me — that I was always a bit shocked when people didn't trust me to fulfill my commitments.

"Hmmph," he said.

"Monty, could I ask you something . . . a little odd?"

"Shoot."

"You said earlier that the house next door was 'kind of' vacant. What did you mean by that?"

"I don't know exactly, but lights go on and off, even though supposedly no one lives there. I guess you've heard the stories by now, about what happened."

"I did, yes."

"Some people say it's haunted."

"Do you believe that?"

"I don't know. Maybe. Do you?"

"Um . . . maybe. I might have noticed something in the window. . . ." We stared at each other for a moment. "Anyway, I was just going to check something down in the yard real quick."

I knew it was stupid to snoop. But if the body really was Linda Lawrence, would that mean it was somehow related to the ghosts I had seen in the windows of the house? It seemed so tragic that she should survive that long-ago night only to die like she had.

I could hear Dog barking in my car.

Would her ghost be here, somewhere? Could she have been one of the faces I'd seen in the windows of the house next door? Was she now back with her family, and was it indeed just a sad suicide by pills?

I felt compelled to investigate, just a little, on the off chance any lingering spirits would talk to me or give me some clue. I wasn't committed enough to break into the main house—not to mention not brave enough—but the least I could do was look through the shed.

Bright yellow crime scene tape covered up the door of the shed. I thought about it for a moment, but I wasn't anti-establishment enough to just break through it. However . . . there was another entrance from the other side. On the lot of the Murder House.

I crept around the shed, squeezing through the gap between the fence and the shed. I gained a few slivers in my hands from the rough gray wood. I felt the slight sliminess of fresh green weeds underfoot, smelled the damp earth as I walked. I tried looking in the window, but it was caked in grime and even the beam from my mini-flashlight couldn't make it through the layers of dust to show anything more than some old shelves shoved up against the glass.

At least there was no sign of ghosts.

I continued around to the other opening of the shed, feeling guilty and looking over my shoulder. Slowly, I turned the old brass knob on the door. The air inside was chill and dank, and smelled vaguely of rodents. Slowly, I pushed the door in, trying to peer into the dim depths of the small building.

I heard whistling.

"Hello?" I said, and the whistling stopped.

I felt strong hands on my back, and before I could turn around, I was shoved headlong into the shed.

Chapter Six

The door slammed behind me. I rushed to it and tried the knob; it was locked from the outside. I banged and yelled for a long moment before thinking, *Is this ghostly behavior? Or some sort of joke?* I thought of Kobe's little group and what Etta—and Monty, for that matter—had told me about possible drug dealing around here. Could I have stumbled across some kind of drug deal?

I'm from Oakland, so I'm not particularly skittish around street thugs, but I do know one thing: You don't mess around with anything having to do with the drug trade. Young people in possession of guns but no future added up to people getting shot—a lot.

I stopped yelling. If I had unwittingly interrupted some sort of drug exchange, it was best to play along, hunker down in here until everyone had cleared out.

Of course, I hadn't seen a soul around other than Monty or heard anything next door while I was talking with him. But . . . if not that, who could have pushed me in here?

I heard it again—the whistling. Faint, off-key, the way my dad did when he used to work in his woodshop after hours.

It sounded like it came from inside the shed.

I stopped and listened for a moment, pondering my options. I had my phone with me, but it would be embarrassing to have to call Luz or Stephen to come let me out. And it was hardly high-security in this shack. If worse came to worst, I could always break the window to escape and replace it along with all the other outstanding work we still owed Monty. For that matter, given the state of these wooden walls, I could probably bash a hole in the siding without too much problem.

Or . . . I could just go out the other side, crime tape or no.

I started to make my way through the building, crawling over old chairs, past cans of old house paint and motor oil, around cracked storm windows, atop a large wooden crate with CALISTOGA MINERAL WATER written on the side. Everything was covered with spiderwebs and accumulated grime, as though it hadn't been touched for decades. Finally, I emerged at the other end of the outbuilding.

The place where Linda's body was found.

The floor held numerous footprints and scuff marks in the dust, and an evidence marker lay on its side. There was no sign of blood. The police must have bagged all the evidence after photographing the scene. I wondered what they had found, though I knew it wasn't my business. None of this was. Probably the death was the result of an accident, an overdose, or maybe the grim outcome of a hard life.

But perhaps, just perhaps, Linda would talk to me.

I peered back the way I'd come. It didn't seem like she had come in that side, as I'd had to clear a path to get through myself.

I heard something behind me. I swung around to face the closed door.

Someone started banging on the door with something heavy: *Bam bam bam . . . bam!*

There wasn't a knocker on either access door. Maybe they were pounding with a rock or a bar of some sort.

Bam bam bam . . . bam!

As I watched the door, little puffs of dust arose with each hammering. Orangey rays seeped in through the cracks surrounding the door, reminding me that while the afternoon was waning, there was still daylight out there. A lot of good that did me.

Then I realized that I didn't see a shadow cast through the cracks in the door.

The banging stopped. But then I heard whistling again . . . this time from the opposite end of the building.

"Hello?" I said. My voice came out as a low croak. I cleared my throat and tried again. "Are you trying to communicate with me?"

Two more bangs on the door. I wondered . . .

"Two bangs for yes, one for no."

I waited. Silence. So much for the Morse code approach to ghosts.

"Linda? Linda, if you're here, I'd like to help. Could you give me a sign, talk to me?"

Bam bam bam. Bam!

"Stop banging already," said a child's voice from outside. "I'm opening the door."

The door swung open.

It was Kobe, the other kids loitering behind him, trying to look around him into the shed. Kobe gave me a disgusted, patronizing look, as though I were the child and he the adult.

"You not supposed to be in here," he said. "Don't you know not to cross crime scene tape? Says right there, DO NOT CROSS."

"I didn't. I went in the other way," I said before I could stop myself. Why did I feel compelled to explain myself?

"Who you talking to, anyway?" he demanded.

This time I didn't answer.

"And what are you wearing?" he asked, looking at today's outfit, a bit worse for the day I'd had working on the foundation, plus the dust and grime of the shed. I pulled a twig out of my fringed hem and swiped at a smudge of grease on my arm.

"Never mind my dress. I'm a grown-up; I get to wear what I want. Did you push me in here?"

"What are you talking about?"

"Just a few minutes ago, someone pushed me in here. On the other side of the shed. Is this some kind of joke?"

"You crazy, lady," Kobe said, shaking his head and looking at me with disapproval. "We was just walking by and Monty told us someone was back here, banging on the shed door, and would we come see who it was fool enough to get their sorry selves stuck in the shed where they just found a body."

I glanced up to the top of the side alley and saw Monty on the porch, craning his neck around the corner. He raised a hand to me.

"Hey, Mel? You okay? What are you doing in there?"

"Yeah, thanks, fine," I called. Then I turned my attention back to the kids. "Thanks for letting me out."

"I'm tellin' ya, you shouldn't be here. Even if it wasn't the actual place she was killed, it's still creepy."

"What do you mean, 'not the actual place she was killed'?"

"I overheard the police talking. They couldn't find the pill vials or whatever and there was some throw-up that should have been on the floor or whatever. They think maybe she was moved."

"Why were you listening in on the cops?" I asked as we walked back up the alley between houses.

"Wasn't listening, exactly. 'Cept grown-ups think kids are like the furniture or whatever. Can I help it if they talk right in front of me? I got ears, don't I?"

"Yeah," said a couple of kids behind him in support. His very own Greek chorus. I wondered what Kobe would grow up to become: CEO of a global corporation, leader of a cult, bestselling author? No matter what, I was willing to bet this young fellow would lead a fascinating life.

"Anyway, we're outta here. Stay out of the shed, will ya?" said Kobe as he strolled down the street, followed by his entourage.

"Thanks again. Hey, we're going to be working here again next weekend, and the deal still stands: You come help with some cleanup, there's a good lunch in it for you."

"Um . . . maybe," was the only reply.

I joined Monty up on the porch.

"I think we should be all clear to resume the work next weekend, Monty, no problem. And if I get a chance, maybe I'll try to come with some help in the next day or two, to finish up the ramp at least."

"Oh, good. Thanks." He seemed distracted. "Did you, like, see anything in the shed? What were you doing in there? You see any evidence or anything?"

"Not really."

"I guess she was a junkie," said Monty.

I didn't want to spill the beans about the possibility it was Linda Lawrence . . . among other things, I really wasn't much of a gossip, and I didn't know anything certain yet.

"Why do you think that?"

"She was found with pills. You didn't hear that?"

I shook my head. How come everyone else knew so much? I was thinking of my father's refrain: *Nobody tells me anything.* Or maybe I hadn't been listening. . . . I remembered hearing a sort of roar in my ears for some time after finding the body, from exhaustion or shock.

"Did you hear maybe the body was moved?"

"Nah. I don't think so. I think she probably just went into the shed, and then that was it. At least it's not a bad way to go. One final trip." He made a sort of flapping gesture with his hands. "Floated away for good."

It felt unseemly, this sort of speculation over a soul lost. Junkie or no, it was a tragedy. She was once someone's baby. If she really was Linda Lawrence . . . now that I knew her story, that she had survived the murderous rampage of her father only to succumb to death in such an ugly way, it felt even more wretched.

"Anyway," I said to change the subject, "until we can get back in to finish up, I was going to offer to take down the plastic sheeting over your bookshelves."

The entire living room was full of bookshelves, all loaded with two rows of books, one in front of the other. It made it hard to see all the titles, but I did the same in my room at home. Too many books, not enough time. I remembered when I first met Monty, he told me, "One of the great things about being at home is I get to do my reading. It's hard to make the time when you're working and all." He made my heart break with how game he was being about his sad lot in life.

"I already took 'em down. I asked one of the volunteers to help me before they left."

"Oh, good. Anything else you need before I go?" I asked, feeling awkward.

Monty really seemed like he wanted to chat. I had to admit I found him a little annoying, even grasping, but I could only imagine how I would be if I were alone all day, unable to leave my house without help. I was tired and grimy, and a bit off my game after what had just taken place in the shed. But my friends had informed me that three years out of my ugly divorce was plenty of time to heal, and that I no longer received a pass for being in a bad mood. I was trying to be a nicer person.

"You really do have an impressive collection of books," I said. "Do you have a favorite author?"

"Too many to name. I read a lot of nonfiction, biographies and the like. Right now, I'm reading about the early industrialists, real jerks like Rockefeller and Carnegie. But then, you have to hand it to Carnegie—after making all that money off of exploiting workers and the like, he got afraid of what would happen after he died. He was afraid he'd go to hell."

"Really?"

He nodded eagerly, rolling over to one section of the shelves and pulling out a thick tome. He handed me the book. "That's why he started with his philanthropy."

"I know he funded libraries all over the country," I said. "You have to like that in a person."

"Libraries and so much more. A lot of his philanthropic funds are still active today. Whether the money got there through guilt or fear or rivalry, it was still good for society."

"Rivalry?"

"He and Rockefeller went after each other, each trying to outdo the other with the extent of their philanthropy, just as they'd tried to do in business."

"I'm guessing the competitive drive was strong in them both. But at least this way they gave away a lot of money, right?"

"Right."

As I put the book back on the shelf, I wondered how Monty accessed the volumes on the upper shelves. Then it occurred to me that someone with his physical challenges could benefit from recent technological advances. Stan loved using his e-book reader, since it was so lightweight and easy to slip in the pocket hanging from his chair. He never had to reach for a book.

"Monty, have you ever tried electronic books?"

"Nah. I'm old-school. I like to see them on my shelves," he answered. "Sitting there like old friends. I only keep the ones I love, give the rest away to Friends of the Library."

For some reason, Monty's love of books—a passion which I shared—made me feel even worse for entertaining, even momentarily, the horrid thought that he might have been hiding bodies in his crawl space. I really did have to stop watching TV with my dad. I had plenty of murder and mayhem to keep my imagination stoked in real life; no need to add in the greater culture's obsession with crime.

"I'm really sorry about the work delay, Monty. I know the officer in charge; I'll call tomorrow and try to get a definite date we can come back and at least finish up the ramp."

"Don't sweat it. What I'd really love is the rest of the interior painting and if we could finish putting up those extra bookshelves."

"I'm sure we can manage that much, at least. I don't think there would be any harm if I come by for a couple of evenings and finish up the interior stuff—I'll make a phone call, okay?"

"That would be great."

I escaped to my car, where Dog whapped his tail maniacally and crooned at me as if to let me know he thought I'd *never* come back. He did his best to crawl into my lap, which is something I usually discourage—Dog is not a lap-sized canine. But today, I wrapped my arms around the wiggling, hairy brown dog, reveling in one of the simple, normal pleasures in life.

But I couldn't stop wondering . . . what the heck just happened in that shed?

Chapter Seven

I lay in bed the next morning, hardly believing it was Monday.

After such an eventful weekend, it was hard to get back to work. The thing about construction is it's a juggling act: finishing up one job, starting a new one, writing contracts and pulling paperwork and job permits for the next project, and meeting with prospective clients and selling yourself for yet another. As long as all of these processes rolled along nicely, you kept your employees working and getting paid. When things backed up, though, it was easy to fall off track. And I feared we might be jumping the rails.

At the moment, Turner Construction was working steadily on a haunted bed-and-breakfast over in the Castro neighborhood, where we had partnered with another construction company, and it was coming along well. Also, we were finishing up *(oh please, oh please let us be finally finishing up)* on my friend Matt's place, which was the first building in which I'd knowingly seen a ghost.

But we needed other jobs in the pipeline, and though we had a few in the paperwork stage, I was starting to get nervous that we hadn't had much new work coming in. In large part, the high-end construction business is recession-proof: Our clients are generally well-off, and though I'm no economist, I'd noticed that no matter what, there were some damned wealthy people in this country. Moreover, they didn't seem to lose their money with the vagaries of the market, much less by losing their jobs. These people were the one percent. And since they were my bread and butter—especially those who had the re- sources and inclination to save beautiful old buildings—I was hardly in the position to come down on them for having more than the rest of us. And heck, a few of them even did good things with their money, giving to charity and setting up foundations and the like. Maybe not on the level of Carnegie and Rockefeller, but every bit counted.

But could the ongoing economic sluggishness finally be coming home to roost at Turner Construction? I cer- tainly hoped not, because besides supporting me and my dad and our friend Stan, we also employed a handful of full-time workers, as well as subcontracting in the trades. I liked to think of us as a small but important economic engine, but it couldn't run without the oil provided by people with enough money to say, "Yes. What the heck? Why don't we do it right and slap some real gold leaf on there?"

These were the thoughts I had while I lay sleepless in bed, waiting for it to be time to get up.

Finally I showered and pulled on a dress. I had a rather eccentric style, especially rare for those of us in the building trade. Stephen was a frustrated costume designer raised among showgirls in Vegas, and he kept me well supplied with somewhat low-cut dresses featuring spangles and fringe. I matched these with my steel-toed work boots and carried coveralls around in my car for crawling around in the muck and mire of jobsites.

Downstairs in the kitchen, I heard voices. Dad's was no surprise; he was always up before me, whipping up a hearty and nourishing breakfast that I was sure to decline as politely as possible. But the second voice didn't belong to Stan, that was for sure. It was a woman's voice

That was odd. Other than me, there were no females in this house. Dad, Stan, my frequently visiting stepson, even the dog . . . nothing but boy energy, day in, day out.

I proceeded downstairs, through the living room, past Turner Construction's home office off the hall, and rounded the corner to the kitchen.

"*Mel!*" a woman's voice squealed, and my sister Charlotte flung her slender, sweet-smelling arms around my neck. I returned her hug, stunned.

"What are you doing here?"

"Oh! That's a fine way to greet your elders! Does a girl need a reason to visit her daddy and favorite sister?" She flashed our father a smile worthy of a prime-time toothpaste commercial.

"I'm not your favorite sister," I said.

"Oh, pshaw!" she replied with a giggle.

The usually grumpy "daddy" was bustling about the kitchen with a broad smile on his face, the one he habitually wore when Charlotte—his golden child, though he denied it—was around.

Stan met my eyes, chuckled, and shook his head, then sipped his coffee.

I like my sister. I do. I love her like, well, a sister. But we had nothing in common. Nothing but our parents and youngest sister, Daphne.

For instance, Charlotte went by the nickname "Cookie." On purpose. She wasn't even being ironic.

Right there, I thought. Right there was where our problems started. Cookie was perky, long-legged, and naturally slender yet curvy. And a blonde. Though we had grown up on a series of construction sites, she had not only managed not to learn her way around the business end of a hammer, but had done so without encountering our father's wrath. Instead, Dad found Cookie's ineptness "cute." I assumed Cookie had mastered the fine art of flirtation about the same time she had graduated from diapers to pull-ups. Unlike me, my sister had been born with that rare, mystical feminine quality of getting pretty much any man in her vicinity to do pretty much anything she wanted.

Why learn how to swing a hammer when you can talk anyone with a Y chromosome into doing it for you?

After graduating from high school (in her senior year, she was voted homecoming queen, "most popular," and "prettiest eyes"; in my senior year, I was accidentally left out of the yearbook entirely), Cookie enrolled at San Francisco State with vague plans of becoming a teacher or an interior decorator. She left without a degree but with a husband, Kyle, who was the nicest guy in the world. Kyle Dopkin was patient where Cookie was impulsive, reserved where she was outgoing, and responsible where she was flighty. I could not imagine what the accomplished IT professional was drawn to in my sister—other than the obvious—but he seemed convinced he had won the marital lottery, so I was happy for them. They had two beautiful children and a long-haired cat, and every December sent out holiday cards featuring photos of the entire well-coiffed family posed in front of their marble fireplace in what Cookie referred to as "The Condo in Redondo."

In this instance, she *was* being ironic—she and Kyle actually owned a gorgeous seaside home in Manhattan Beach. Since I'm not familiar with the LA area, I wasn't clear on why this joke was funny, but Cookie assured me it was.

"So . . ." I continued, filling my favorite to-go cup with strong coffee and noting the matched set of designer luggage sitting near the back door. More bags than one person would need for an overnight visit. Then again, Cookie never traveled light. "To what do we owe this unannounced visit?"

"Why, Mel, it's almost as if you weren't happy to see me!" Cookie gushed as she rooted through her Gucci handbag for her smartphone. "Oh, hey, Daddy, look at these pictures!"

She held up the device and started flipping through images.

I peered over my father's shoulder, expecting to see photos of my adorable towheaded niece and nephew.

Instead, it was a major appliance of some kind.

"What is it?" I asked.

"My new wine refrigerator, silly!" Cookie said, as though it should have been perfectly obvious. "Kyle wanted a different model, but I insisted on stainless steel and glass, which I think is *just* the thing, don't you? It keeps our wine at the *perfect* temperature, not too cold, not too warm. Our dinner guests *love* it!"

"We've got a wine refrigerator, too," I grumbled. "It's called the basement."

Stan barked out a laugh, and my dad chuckled. Cookie left me in the dust in the good-looks and perfect-life categories. But I was not without charm.

Cookie wrinkled her nose and immediately recaptured the limelight.

"Daddy, you know what I would *love*? Would you make me some of your super-duper waffles? I *dream* about those waffles."

Stan made a sound between a chuckle and a cough and hid his grin behind the newspaper.

"Waffles, eh? What do you think I am, a short-order cook?" Dad groused happily as he crouched and began rooting around in the cupboard under the stove for the ancient waffle iron. "I haven't made waffles in ages. Your sister Mel doesn't deign to eat my breakfast."

"It's not *your* breakfast I refuse to eat, Dad, it's *any* breakfast," I pointed out for the millionth time.

Cookie shook her golden head and frowned adorably, laying her hand on my shoulder. "Mel, I worry about you. You need to take care of yourself, and breakfast is the most important meal of the day. Now, tell me, are you seeing anyone lately? You're not still bitter over the divorce from Daniel, are you?" Before I could answer, she continued. "You know what you need to do? You need to—"

"*Boy*, will you *look* at the time!" I topped off my travel mug and screwed on the sippy top. "Love to sit here and chat but I have *got* to run. You'll be here for a while, though, right? I want to hear all about Kyle and the kids. We can have a nice visit when I get home."

"Of course! We'll spend some quality girl time together. Oh, I know! How about a mani-pedi? My treat?"

"Um, yeah, maybe. Soon as I have a free day. Busy, busy, busy this time of the year; you know how it is. Bye, Dad, Stan."

I darted out the back door, hurried down the flagstone path to my car, jumped in, and gunned the engine. After a not-so-great weekend, I was looking forward to getting back to my work routine. Since the police hadn't called, I was hoping the body in the shed had been a drug overdose. Heartbreaking, but it would have nothing to do with me or my volunteers' jobsite.

But as I neared the approach to the Bay Bridge, I started to wonder what my sister's sudden arrival meant. I was guessing trouble in paradise.

Cookie had left Kyle before, but she had always brought the kids with her, and the crises had blown over as soon as Kyle caved in to whatever it was she wanted. This time, though, she had come alone. Did this mean the problem was more serious? But if so, why would she leave the kids? Cookie had a lot of faults—I had a mental list of them that I had started when I was eight years old and updated occasionally—but she was a loving mother. Then again, for all I knew, she was in town for a few days to make sure a new couch was upholstered in the perfect raw silk or to buy a trousseau for the renewal of her wedding vows. Or something innocuous like that.

It was hard for me to fathom Cookie's world, to imagine what she did with her days. Like many of the well-to-do women I worked for, Cookie was too intelligent and energetic to just sit around looking pretty, but with a gardener and a maid and a nanny to do the household chores, and no job outside the home, she had lots of empty hours to fill. Kyle was gone all day and the kids were now in school. That much free time could be a burden, and was likely to lead to trouble or to depression.

As I zoomed through the tollbooth and started across the bridge, I realized that just as I had no idea what Cookie thought or did all day, neither did she understand who I was or how I passed the time.

For example, one thing I did *not* do was mani-pedis. I work with my hands, so fingernail polish was immediately ruined, and in any event my nails needed to be kept short. Pedicures were even more useless, since my feet were almost always clad in steel-toed boots. Also, thanks to Cookie, I had learned to hate that kind of girlish fussiness. Four years my senior, Cookie had treated me like a human doll when we were children, dressing me up in ribbons and bows and makeup, and staging elaborate tea parties when all I wanted was to put on my OshKosh B'gosh overalls and play in the yard with my Hot Wheels. Even now I wasn't very girly, despite my tendency to wear sparkles and feathers. Come to think of it, maybe those years as Cookie's fashion mannequin were why I dressed so absurdly now. Certainly, she no longer dressed this way. Cookie's love of bows and ruffles and gewgaws had long since given way to cool linen and elegant silks in simple, classical designs. Cookie always looked fabulous. I glanced at what I was wearing today—yup, unsuited for my profession as usual—and pondered. Was I only now going through an adolescent phase of fashion experimentation? If so, could I blame it on my sister?

Speaking of awkward adolescence and fashion

choices, I was reminded of Kobe's remarks upon my dress when I emerged from the shed last night.

I still hadn't been able to come up with any rational explanation for why someone would have pushed me in. And who would have done so? Had the banging on the door been a sign from the spirits, or were Kobe and his gang having fun with the crazy construction lady? Or could it have been a local drug gang, as I'd first thought, or ...? I suppose it could have been the spirits themselves, somehow, desperate to communicate with me?

I wondered who owned the vacant Murder House. The yard was maintained—more or less—and the lights appeared to be on timers, and even the heater was working...so someone must be in charge of the place. I imagined the police had already been in touch with the owner, asking the pertinent questions. And as I'd told myself repeatedly since Saturday's discovery, the situation didn't have anything to do with me or mine.

Still, after checking on Matt's project, I had to head to the city offices to expedite some building permits.... While I was there, what could it hurt to look up the owner of the house? I was pretty sure Inspector Crawford already knew who it was, but despite our newly cozy-ish relationship, I didn't feel comfortable asking her, especially since I could find out for myself easily enough. Most folks don't realize just how accessible property ownership information was. In fact, if I'd thought of it at home I could easily have looked it up on a public website.

I was just curious. No harm in that, right? And I was proclaiming a moratorium on snooping around the crime scene. So this was just ... information.

I drove past San Francisco's City Hall, a domed Beaux

Arts building so large and ornate that when I was a little girl, I thought it housed the President of the United States. It was built in 1915 by architect Arthur Brown, Jr., to replace the building toppled by the 1906 earthquake; Brown was so fastidious that he specified which door-knobs to use, as well as the typeface for signage. City Hall's dome was the fifth largest in the world, bigger than that of the U.S. capitol. Inside the central rotunda, a sweep of marble stairs led to catwalks that overlooked the courtyards. It was beautiful, a crown perfect for a world-class city like San Francisco.

In contrast, the city's permit office was located in an uninspired building on Mission. I stopped by to look up the Murder House, otherwise known as 2906 Greenbrier Street. A quick look through records in the musty administrative offices revealed this information:

Built in 1911 by Cicorelli Brothers Construction, for the Jeffress family.

It changed hands in 1929, 1942, and 1978, the price increasing steadily but not crazily over the years. Sidney and Jean Lawrence were the buyers in 1978.

In 1983, the house was transferred to a bank-operated trust.

Hubert Lawrence took ownership in 1991.

I did a double take. I supposed it could be a coincidence . . . but though Lawrence was a reasonably common name, Hubert was not. I remembered the fellow under Monty's sink on Saturday, telling me he had to leave early. "Hubert, but I go by Hugh," he'd said.

Interesting.

I finished up my other paperwork and left, but before getting back in the car I bought a cup of coffee from a small stand, then wandered through a tiny micro-park, through rows of espaliered trees, pondering and sipping my drink.

Then I called Luz.

"Do you remember someone named Hubert Lawrence at Monty's house on Saturday?"

"You mean the poet laureate?"

"The what?"

"Hubert Lawrence. He's the California poet laureate."

"Um . . . no, I meant the guy who showed up to work at Monty's on Saturday. He was a little odd, but did a decent job with the dry rot under the kitchen sink."

"Yeah, that was Hubert Lawrence. He's the poet laureate. Don't you read?"

"Of course I read," I said. And I do. Just not, apparently, Hubert Lawrence. "I'm not what you'd call 'up' on our state's best poets, though, I'll admit."

"You really are a Philistine, aren't you?"

"If I knew what that was, I'd probably be offended."

Luz laughed. "He was there with his wife, Simone— tall woman, long dark hair? She was very protective of him, and when I recognized his name, she made it clear he didn't want anyone to know."

"Do poet laureates get mobbed like rock stars?" I asked, as I recalled a tall woman with long, silky dark hair. She was in her forties and had been working on the dry rot with two men.

"Only in their dreams," continued Luz. "Other than by lit geeks like me, it's a safe bet the poet laureate is not often recognized. He wrote 'Hugh' on his nametag, and I only realized who he was when I saw his full name on the release form. But then I had him sign my arm, which totally rocks."

"You groupie, you."

"Does that make me delightfully eccentric or just sad?"

"You'll always be eccentric to me, Luz."

"You do realize that, coming from you, that's a bit unsettling?"

I laughed. "So you're telling me a famous poet spent his weekend fixing a stranger's dry rot?"

"'Famous poet' is sort of an oxymoron. Sadly, it's been that way ever since the era of Yeats passed. I suppose you could make an argument for Ginsberg and Kerouac, but people don't really read poetry anymore, much less make the scribes into celebrities—unless their words are set to a beat, of course. But in general, an interest in poetry has been replaced by a fascination with the antics of half-literate Jersey housewives."

"That's depressing."

"Tell me about it."

"Do he and his wife live in the city?"

"He mentioned he was local, but wasn't more specific."

"Any chance he owns the house next to Monty's?"

"The place the kids call Murder House? They told me all about the gruesome tale. What makes you ask that?"

"His last name is Lawrence—the same as the family who owned the house."

"You know, I remember reading something about his having lost his parents at an early age, a personal tragedy that informed his poems. His early work was obsessed with themes of violence and loss. So I suppose there could be a connection. Then again, Lawrence isn't exactly an unusual last name."

"That's true. And if he was connected to the murdered family, why would he want to hold on to a house where the tragedy had unfolded?"

"Could be lots of reasons. One horrible event might not outweigh years of happier memories. Plus, the place isn't inhabited, is it? Houses where murders have occurred are often hard to sell—they're stigmatized. I think you can understand why."

I thought about that. How would I feel about my family home, had similar events taken place there? I quickly gave up; I couldn't even imagine such a thing.

"So, have you washed your arm yet?"

"No way. Permanent marker, too. I'm gonna take some pics, tweet about it. All the poetry nerds will swoon. What's the story on Monty's place? Will we be able to finish up this weekend?"

"I think so. I'll let you know for sure as soon as I hear."

"Anything on the woman in the shed?"

"Nothing definite. It might well have been an overdose. It's possible it was Linda Lawrence; I guess she's Hubert's sister?"

"And his savior. In one of his most famous poems, he talks about the older sister who helped him escape out a window. He writes about her, describes her as lost."

"Lost? As in missing?"

"I think it was more lost, as in to drugs and alcohol. I can't remember exactly."

"They escaped that night, and now she's found dead in a shed on the property . . . ? This is rapidly developing into one of the saddest stories I've ever heard."

"Perfect fodder for poetry. Or, you know, suicide."

We both mulled that one over for a moment. It never ceased to amaze me how some people seemed to have more than their fair share of tragedy, while others of us were, by and large, so lucky. My life held a lot of annoyances and some sadness, but no tragedy on this level. Another reminder to count my blessings.

"Oh, hey," I said in a bid to change the subject. "Guess who's back in town? Cookie."

"You mean back for a visit, or *back* back?" Over the years, Luz had heard a great deal about my sister and our relationship.

"I'm not sure. We haven't exactly talked."

"How long did you last this time?"

"Ten minutes, easy. So I'm improving."

"What was the trigger?"

"She started giving me advice."

"*I'll* give you some free advice: Keep her away from Graham. When does he get back?"

"Day after tomorrow. But what do you mean, keep him away from Cookie?"

"If she's left Kyle again, she'll be looking to compensate. You think your handsome hunk of man will be off-limits?"

"Cookie wouldn't go for Graham."

"Are you sure?"

"I'm pretty sure Graham wouldn't go for my sister."

"Oh, of course not. Men don't go for flirtatious, stacked, leggy blondes who tell them what they want to hear. I forgot. They would never fall for such an oh-so-obvious act."

Okay, so after an especially unpleasant breakup, Luz had become a little bitter on the subject of men. I wasn't in any position to throw stones, since I'd been a card-carrying member of the Bitter Club since things went south between me and my former husband. But . . . Graham would never go for someone like Cookie, would he? I mean . . . he had free will and self-control, didn't he? And if a man liked *me*, surely Cookie wouldn't exactly be his type. Would she?

On the other hand, there was that whole "flirtatious, stacked, leggy blonde" thing. Over the years, I had witnessed man after man—otherwise intelligent, caring men—whose jaws would go slack and eyes go soft as Cookie turned on the charm.

I was toast.

I blew out an exasperated breath as a wave of self-consciousness came over me. I was wearing my typical odd ensemble, my hair was pulled back in a simple pony-tail, and I didn't have on a hint of makeup. Not even my usual lazy effort at a little eyeliner and mascara. I had intended to go upstairs to primp a bit before leaving the house, but instead ran out into the still, dark morning.

Anyway, it didn't matter. Graham and I had been dat-ing, and it had been great . . . until I started freaking out. I liked kissing him a *lot*. But he wanted to be with me, as in *be* with me. I had lots to do, and I wasn't in the habit of checking in with anybody. I already had my dad to deal with, and Caleb was around all the time, and the business, and Dog . . . I decided I had no room in my life for a steady boyfriend.

"Maybe he and Cookie would be good for each other," I heard myself saying. "He likes kids, and she comes with a ready-made family."

"Are you still trying to set him up with all the women you know?" she asked. "You know, far be it from me to tell you how to interact with men, but I don't think you're supposed to be foisting your boyfriend off on other women."

"I'm not foisting. I rarely foist."

"You tried to get him to go to the movies with me the other night, remember?"

"You two share a fondness for the current James Bond that I simply can't get behind. It's Sean Connery or nothing, as far as I'm concerned. And anyway, he's not my boyfriend."

"Right. And you're moving to Paris any minute now."

"This is different from the Paris thing. I can't have a boyfriend. I don't like men enough."

"You adore men. You live with them and work with them, and have great respect for them."

"Okay, let me amend my previous statement: I like men as people. But not as romantic partners."

Luz snorted.

"Plus," I continued, ignoring her. "I don't live a normal life. Every time I turn around I find a body, not to mention I'm plagued by ghosts. I wouldn't wish that on any man."

"What's this about being plagued by ghosts?" Luz had a knack for zeroing in on what was important and ignoring my bluster. "Did you see something at Monty's place?"

I paused for a fraction of a second before telling her. Knowing Luz, she'd get it out of me sooner or later anyway.

"No, next door. The big house."

"The Murder House?"

"That's the one. But really, they have nothing to do with me, I swear. Not this time."

I heard Luz blow out a long breath.

"Okay, *chica*, one more piece of free advice, and then I've got to run to a faculty meeting: Finish up the work at Monty's, and get the hell out of Dodge before the next-door-neighbor ghosts, I dunno, decide to come a-knocking, wanting to borrow a cup of sugar."

"I was thinking along those very same lines."

Chapter Eight

I got back to work. Today, that involved going by the job-site for a bed-and-breakfast in the Castro district. A *haunted* bed-and-breakfast, to be more precise. I had managed to spend the night in the place, and broker a deal with the ghosts, and catch me a murderer—sort of—several months ago, so Turner Construction won the bid on the project.

This was not what one might call an "industry standard" for how to go about winning renovation bids ... but whatever it took.

Unlike the typical San Francisco Victorian, the Bernini B&B, as it was now called, was a Greek Revival with Italianate flourishes. We were painting the entire exterior in several different shades of cream, in keeping with the traditional monochromatic palette. Inside, it was fabulous: the new owners were committed to restoring the house and converting it into a charming inn without updating it cavalierly so as to strip it of its historic charm.

We were modernizing things inside the walls: central vacuum, internet wiring, modern piping, heating, insulation, and electricity. And we were revamping some of the historic methods that still worked well and were, in fact, "green," such as passive ventilation and the natural insulating effects of series of chambers that could be closed off from one another.

But the real show was in the interior details. We had removed all the ancient plumbing fixtures and hardware, cleaned them up, fixed them, and brought them up to code. For those items that were missing, I scoured junk shops and salvage yards—and occasionally found things on the internet—from the same era. We had removed broken tiles and had them reproduced by an Arts and Crafts Revival tile factory. Warped oak floors were patched and repaired where possible, or replaced where necessary. Original lamps and sconces were removed and taken to an old man who worked out of his garage and could fix anything made before 1950.

I knew if we worked hard enough, we had a shot at the AIA award for historic renovation. But, more important, I could feel the house coming back to life, blossoming under our care and attention.

Long before I was introduced to the concept of ghosts, I had come to believe that historic homes—some much more than others—held whispers from the past, tiny wisps of energy from all the souls who had passed through their doors. I used to think I was just being silly, superstitious. Now that I knew about spirits . . . I still felt superstitious. And I was even more confused. Was it the houses that whispered to me, or the ghosts within?

Not that it really mattered. Once I had accepted that I am, for better or worse, some sort of ghost talker, I was trying my best to roll with it. That was one factor that led to my signing up for my friend Olivier's ghost-busting class. I felt like a fool, but I was learning a whole heck of a lot about things like electromagnetic waves and, believe it or not, theoretical physics.

"Mel, good to see you. How'd that project go this weekend?" asked Raul, our lead foreman.

Raul had volunteered to work with me on the community service project, but I wouldn't let him. He and his wife were already busy with helping to run a food pantry and afterschool tutoring activities through their church. He worked too hard as it was, and I needed him on site. A good foreman could make or break a project, and his presence on a job as complex as the Bernini B&B meant I didn't have to be here every second myself. He felt so guilty about not helping out, however, that he and his wife had brought over tamales for the volunteers.

"It . . ." I trailed off. One of these days I was going to have to figure out a way to respond to people's simple queries after I'd been involved in the discovery of yet another dead body. "It's not quite finished yet."

His eyes searched my face.

"No?" He knew how I was about finishing what I started. And Raul didn't let a lot get past him. "You need my help after all? I'm happy to do it."

"I know you are, Raul. No, there was a . . . We found a . . ." I blew out a breath. "The police shut down the project for a few days. A woman was found on the property— sort of. Actually, it might officially be the neighbor's property. Anyway, that doesn't really matter, does it?" I said to myself much more than to Raul. "What I mean to say is that we found a body."

Raul was a quiet man, the sort who spoke only when he had something relevant to say. He nodded, still holding my eyes.

"You okay?"

"Yes, thank you. She had been deceased for a bit. I really didn't have anything to do with it. It wasn't like what happened here."

He nodded thoughtfully. "That's good."

Raul and I hadn't talked openly and explicitly about the whole ghost thing. When he started with this B and B project, I let him know there might be a few unexplained events in the house, and he accepted that in his usual calm manner.

"Hey, before you go, you should check out the friezes in the bedrooms. You were right about those antique borders."

One of my favorite local architectural supply stores, Victoriana, had somehow unearthed a stash of original, hand-tinted wallpaper borders. They cost a fortune, but it was almost unheard-of to find original paper pieces rather than reproductions.

I peeked into the master bedroom, where the wallpaper hangers were just finishing up. Raul was right—the borders were perfect. They replaced a hand-painted frieze that had been irreparably damaged from a water leak.

The spaces above the moldings were perfect for such a decorative pattern. Looking at the moldings, I was reminded of the lovely interior design of Etta's small house. Her simple wood moldings boxed off sections of the wall so they could frame separate portions of color or paper. I would check with the hangers to see if there might be enough leftovers to run the perimeter of Etta's

front room. Though her house was nowhere near as fine
as the Bernini B&B, the wallpaper would suit it just as
well.

After meeting with the clients and taking down a few
more items for the punch list, I ran around town checking on our other current projects, including a personal
favorite in the turret apartment of an old Victorian. It
was tiny, but so lush and detailed it reminded me of a
jewel box.

I grabbed a late lunch from a taco truck, and was on
my way to the lumberyard to order supplies when my
phone rang. The readout said Turner Construction. That
was odd.

My phone rang incessantly: Calls about supply problems, worksite issues, permit glitches. Meetings set up
and canceled. Disgruntled neighbors. It was one thing
after another.

Stan knew this, so he almost never called me during
the day. Instead, we would usually reconvene in Turner
Construction's home office at the end of the day, while
my father prepared dinner.

"Everything okay?" I asked him.

"Oh yeah, sure. No big thing, but . . . we got an inquiry
about a new job."

"Oh . . . great." I was surprised, but Stan knew I was a
little worried lately about not having enough jobs in the
pipeline, so maybe he wanted to cheer me up. "Who is it,
and what's the job?"

"That's why I called. He was a little elusive on the
phone, but he said it was urgent that he speak with you
directly rather than give me any details. He says he met
you the other day at the Neighbors Together site, and he
wants to hire you to renovate his house. He, um . . . he

also mentioned that his house is full of ghosts. His name is Hubert Lawrence."

Call me overly curious, but within half an hour I was zooming up to a modern apartment building not far from North Beach.

"You're here," Hubert Lawrence said as I stepped off the elevator. He stood in his wide-open door at the end of the hall.

"I am, yes," I said. I checked the clock on my phone. "We said two-thirty, right?"

"Yes, I believe we did." Hugh stared at the taupe hallway carpet as though it would give him some further detail about the situation. "That's exactly what we said."

In the hustle and bustle of Monty's worksite, I had barely noticed Hubert, and now I understood why. He seemed vague, barely there. Ghostlike, in fact. He had sandy hair and eyebrows that were an almost exact match with his fair skin, and his irises were so pale, they seemed to fade into the whites. He stood so still, he seemed almost ethereal.

It was kind of disturbing, to tell the truth. For a moment, my mind flashed on the possibility that he might be a spirit, but then I realized everyone else on the jobsite saw him, too. But I supposed that the life of the mind might make a person seem like he was living on a different plane.

"It's nice to meet you again," I said, holding out my hand to shake. "I'm sorry we didn't have more time to talk on Saturday. I get so busy on jobsites, and it was a little overwhelming with all those volunteers. I didn't get the opportunity to speak with everyone one-on-one."

He nodded in acknowledgment but gazed down at my

hand as if he wasn't sure how to respond. Back when I was an anthropologist, I learned to be careful about approaching people from different cultures. It was easy to offend someone entirely by accident by pressing one's customs upon them. But Hubert looked at me as though I were presenting him with a fistful of fermented fish heads.

Which actually happened to me once. But even then I wasn't as rude as he.

After a moment, I let my hand fall. We were still standing awkwardly in the doorway.

"Could I come in and sit down?" I suggested. "You wanted to talk about redoing your house?"

"Yes, yes, I did." He turned around and wandered into the apartment. "I couldn't believe when Simone told me *you*, the house captain for the Neighbors Together project right next door to my house, were named 'California's most promising up-and-coming ghost buster.' She read it in *Haunted Home Quarterly*."

I closed the door and trailed him down a book-lined hall and around the corner, which opened onto a room that served as an office. The place reminded me of an upscale version of Monty's front room, everything lined with bookshelves, though these were neatly arranged and only a single book deep. Nice to know there were still booklovers in the world.

In the center of what must have officially been the living room sat a utilitarian beige office desk paired with a standard-issue desk chair. And on the desk sat a pad of heavy stock paper—the expensive kind—and half a dozen new, sharpened number-two pencils. A black mesh wastepaper basket sat by the desk, and a series of framed photographs sat on the table in an arc. What looked like a vintage eight-millimeter camera sat on a tripod in one corner. A huge fresh floral arrangement sat in a crystal vase on a marble-topped display table.

That was it. No computer. No stacks of papers. No Post-it notes, crumpled papers, or pencil holder in which half the pens were dried up, like on my crammed desk in Turner Construction's home office. And no dust. Anywhere. On the contrary, it smelled of lemon polish and scented candles and lilies.

It was a shrine to poetry.

Hubert took a seat behind the desk, placed his hands palm-down on the laminate wood top, and stared at me.

I haven't known a lot of poets in my time. Nothing beyond the high school boys who thought their words were deep and mournful, rather than just simplistic rhymes. I still didn't really *get* poetry. What made one set of sentences great, while others were just silly or self-indulgent?

But this guy was a poet laureate. That counted for something. That counted for a *lot*.

Also, he had lived through the events at the Murder House, so my heart went out to him.

And far too late, I wondered whether Ray had been right—was the woman we found in fact Linda, Hubert's sister? And if so, had her brother been informed?

"Hubert, I—"

"Please, call me Hugh. Everyone does."

"Great. Hugh. And call me Mel—I never use my full name, either."

He continued to stare. So much for bonding over nicknames. It was a weak attempt, I knew, but I wasn't sure we had much else in common.

"How are you?"

He looked at me for a long time, in what I was coming to know as his patented stare.

"How am I . . . ," he repeated, not in question form. His affect remained as flat as the hands still on the desk in front of him. He turned his head to look out the window, which displayed a view of the building across the street. "How are any of us?"

I had no response to that. I was beginning to think that, poet laureate or no, this guy was a little bit off his rocker. Or perhaps a certain detachment from reality was what it took to be a great artist. If I were talking to Vincent van Gogh under similar circumstances, I imagined the conversation might be a bit stilted as well.

Suddenly, Hugh looked at me straight on, intensity in his eyes.

"I want to talk to you about renovating the house. You know the house?"

"Um, the place next to Monty's, right? That's the one you're talking about?"

"You know what happened in that house?"

"I've heard a little bit," I said, thinking that I wasn't sure I wanted to know much more.

"I was lucky enough to have slept through most of it. It was my sis—" His voice choked up for a moment. He held a fist up to his mouth, swallowed loudly, then resumed his story. "My sister Linda was the one who looked down and saw my father at the foot of the stairs. My father, who used to take us fishing. Who taught me to ride a bike, to play ball . . . Did you hear about Linda?"

"I, um . . ."

"She passed. A couple of days ago, but I didn't even know. Amazing to think that someone so important in my life could pass, and I didn't feel it. I didn't feel a thing.

Had no idea until Ray called me last night. Then the police came. We talked for a long time."

"I'm so very sorry, Hugh. Is there anything I can do?"

"Do you know our story?"

"I've heard a couple of versions. . . ."

"On that night, I remember the smell of dinner cooking. I think it was chicken casserole. My favorite. There was someone at the door, and my oldest sister Bridget went down to answer it, but I guess Mom got there first . . . There was the sound of a tussle, and Linda was headed downstairs to check it out when she saw my father at the foot of the stairs, plain as day in the entryway, a gun in his hand, pointed at our mother. Linda was about to say something when . . ."

He held his hand out and pointed as though it were a gun, then pulled the trigger, his eyes taking on that now familiar faraway look.

"Boom. *Boom.* Two shots. One in the back"—he reached behind himself and patted a spot behind his left shoulder, then tapped the side of his neck—"one in the neck. The neck. Carotid artery. No chance."

There was a long pause. *In for a penny, in for a pound.*

"And your sister, Bridget?"

"Blunt force trauma. He used a big log for the fire. Up against the side of the head."

"But you escaped."

"Linda saved me. She came into my room and barricaded the door behind her, then made me go out the window with her. I fought her; I didn't understand what was going on. I didn't want to go."

"How old were you?"

"Linda was fourteen, I was ten. Almost eleven. My parents had agreed to have my birthday at the beach that weekend. It was his last promise to me. Broken, of course, when he killed half my family, then himself."

"I'm so sorry, Hugh. It's . . ." *Unimaginable* was what I was going to say, but this man had not only imagined it but lived through it. "It's awful. No one should have to go through something like that."

"It was my fault, really. Please"—he held up a pale hand—"don't say it wasn't. I've heard it from one therapist after another, but the truth is that if I hadn't gotten sick, Mom would have taken us all to the beach house. I suppose my father still would have killed himself, but at the very least Mom and Bridget would have been spared. But I've always been the sickly sort. . . ."

He pulled out a drawer of the file cabinet and brought out a big box of photos. He grabbed a handful and shuffled through them, picking and choosing some to show to me.

"Here's my father and mother on their wedding day." He gazed at the photo for a long moment before handing it over. The photo was faded; they were both dashing in sixties-era clothing, she in a simple white shift and small veil, he in a dark suit. They were laughing and pushing wedding cake into each other's mouths. I looked up to see Hugh's sad, distracted eyes fixed on me. "Hard to imagine what he would do to her later, isn't it?"

There were no words. He passed more photos to me: babies, little children on the beach, his father holding a boy about two years old in strong arms.

"Is this you?" I asked.

He nodded.

"You look a lot like your father," I said, before realizing perhaps I shouldn't underscore his resemblance to a killer.

He smiled faintly.

"Yes, I took after his side of the family. There was a strong family resemblance between him and my grandfather, as well. I used to think I would grow up to be just like him, and I was proud. Of course, now that I look like him . . . well, it's a dubious honor."

"It doesn't mean you're anything like him."

"It's funny—the last time Linda and I were in the house, just a few days ago, she saw me at the bottom of the stairs, and she thought she was seeing our father's ghost. But it was just me. But I thought to myself, that's a poem: '*I am my father's ghost.*'"

He paused for a long moment, then picked up a pencil and a piece of paper and scribbled something.

Again, I felt at a loss for words. I wondered whether everyone who spoke to Hugh wound up feeling like a reluctant psychiatrist. I wished I could channel Luz, to know what to say or do. But then, I guessed this was why Luz didn't pursue a career in therapy, preferring instead to teach. She said she didn't like hearing people's problems. Luckily, she made an exception for her best friend.

"Anyway . . . ," Hugh said at long last, putting down his pen and turning back to the pile of snapshots. He gave me another handful, a series of photos taken on a fishing trip, he and his father and Ray standing together, wearing matching plaid hunting jackets. "The reason I asked to talk with you is that I understand you do specialized renovations?"

"I do, yes. That's my business, Turner Construction. We do historic restoration, that sort of thing."

"I've kept the house preserved, just as it was when we lived there. When . . . it happened. At first, of course, I was just a kid; the house was kept in a trust for me and

Linda. We didn't need the money—between life insurance and my uncle, Linda and I were fine. And then . . . Linda was slipping away, and in a way, the house seemed like our last concrete connection. She signed over her power of attorney to me and didn't seem to care what I did with the place, but I wanted to keep it. I'm not sure why. . . . A part of me thought I could keep it enshrined and perhaps work out what happened. If I could only mature enough, learn enough, understand the world enough, I might be able to figure it out. Figure it all out."

There was that far-off look again.

"And have you?" I asked at last, after it seemed he wasn't talking anymore.

He shook his head. "But no matter how many times I go through there, no matter how I cast my mind back, it makes no sense. My father had taken a large life insurance policy out on himself and my mother not long before, but . . . his didn't pay out, of course. Suicide isn't compensated. Luckily for Linda and me, being *murdered* is covered, so we collected on our mother's policy. It's possible he meant to kill her in order to collect, and took the same policy out on himself to avert suspicion, but things got out of hand. Maybe killing his own daughter pushed him over the edge, so he wound up killing himself." Hugh shrugged. "He shot himself in the chest before killing himself with a shot to the head. Maybe he meant to graze himself, make it look like he'd been injured in the attack as well, but the muzzle slipped. Maybe . . ."

It seemed Hugh had thought everything through. Probably at three in the morning, when he was supposed to be sleeping. I wasn't surprised—it was hard for *me* to stop thinking about any of the deaths I had encountered recently, and I was only tangentially involved with any of the victims. I could only imagine that if it happened to your family, especially as a child, you would roll it over in your mind persistently, doggedly, unconsciously, like a tongue worrying a sore tooth. Perhaps you would ponder the senselessness of something like this until quite literally losing your senses.

Could that be what had happened with Linda? Hugh may be a poet laureate, but he was obviously fragile. It didn't seem like it would take much to push the poor man over the brink into entirely losing touch with reality.

"Oh, here's something else you should see." He went to a bookshelf and pulled down a white screen. Then he crossed to the opposite corner and turned on the movie camera I had noticed when I first walked in.

Bluish images flickered on the screen. I recognized young Hugh and Linda, playing with their father in the surf on Ocean Beach. I recognized the locale by the distinctive Seal Rock and the Cliff House restaurant in the background, jutting out into the Pacific.

"Old home movies?"

He nodded, eyes fixed on the playful images. "Wait a moment; the next sequence was filmed inside the house. You can get a sense for it by watching carefully."

As promised, moments later the scene shifted. It was a holiday of some sort, a large dinner on the table, a nicely dressed group gathered around the table.

"Would you be willing to give me a bid on redoing the house?"

"But, Hugh, I don't understand why you would want to have anything to do with it, after . . . after what happened."

"Don't you see? I have no choice. That house defined me, made me what I am today."

"But . . ." It wasn't my place to make this observation—I barely knew the man. And I knew that uninvited advice was just about the most exasperating thing to experience. But I couldn't help myself. "Wouldn't it be better to not let it define you anymore? You're a brilliant success as a poet; couldn't you just enjoy that about yourself?"

Hugh didn't seem offended by my unsolicited advice. He just shook his head.

"I have to put the house back in order. Just as it was."

"Didn't you say you left it just as it was?"

"There have been some changes, the unavoidable effects of time." He rifled through the box and pulled out another album, this one strewn with yellow sticky tabs. He flipped to one of them to show a picture of a young girl and her mom, presumably one of Hugh's sisters and his mother, in a kitchen very much of the period. "But I have pictures here, and I want you to restore it so it's just the way it was then. Same wallpaper, appliances, everything. A lot of it is still there, but it's shabby, mildewy after all these years."

"I just don't . . ." I began, wondering whether this was some sort of brilliant scheme or just a sign of mental illness. I wished Luz were present to form a professional opinion. I should have called her when I heard that Hubert wanted to meet with me.

On the screen, the images spoke, but there was no sound other than the clicking and whirring of the camera. The film had faded, so the colors were washed out to shades of blue and yellow. I tried to ignore it, but I noticed the images out of the corner of my eye, the way I often saw ghosts. It felt almost nightmarish to witness such remnants of happy memories, before tragedy struck.

I was about to come up with an excuse to leave when I heard the sound of keys in the front door. Simone walked in, a canvas tote full of groceries in each hand. She dropped them in the hall and hurried toward us.

"What are you doing?" she demanded, switching off the camera. "I've told you, you can't watch these films alone. Hugh, I asked you what you were doing."

Her hair was swept up in a simple bun, and she wore a fashionable wool coat over a simple but chic red dress, matching lipstick, and fine gold jewelry. A few steps up from the stained sweatshirt and jeans she'd worn to Monty's the other day.

Hugh gave a far-off look and shook his head. Simone looked as though she'd been through this routine before; when her husband had no response for her, she swung around and fixed her gaze on me.

"This is about that house, isn't it?"

"Yes. Hugh asked me to come over so we could talk about it."

"How soon can we get back in there, do you know?" She flicked a switch to rewind the movie. "The police haven't been in touch."

Her words surprised me. I had expected Simone to be protective of her husband, to say he shouldn't be going back there, that it wasn't good for him.

"I don't really . . ."

"Have you asked her about taking the job?" she said, addressing her husband.

"I did ask," he replied. "But she has yet to answer."

Nothing got past this guy.

"I, um . . ."

"Isn't this the sort of thing you do?" Simone demanded as she removed the reel from the camera, then unlocked a box sitting on a bookshelf and placed it inside. Then she started gathering the snapshots that Hugh had scattered atop the desk. I thought of the theory that opposites attract; Simone seemed to have all the energy and focus that her husband lacked.

"Renovating old places," she continued. "Bringing them back to their glory days . . . ? And if possible, talking to the ghosts? I read all about you in *Haunted Home Quarterly*."

"So, you believe the house is haunted?" I asked her. "The neighbors mention lights going on and off."

She waved a hand. "I had the place wired as a 'smart house' so we could turn lights on and off from afar, that sort of thing. That's not the haunted part. It's the thoughts, the memories that plague Hugh. Those are the real ghosts."

Despite myself, my curiosity was stoked. Why were Hugh and Simone so intent on having the place put back to the way it was?

Though it seemed macabre, it would be interesting to do a walk-through of the Murder House with Hugh.

I had to admit that, as with so many historic homes, something about the house at 2906 Greenbrier called to me. And not just the faces I had seen in the windows. For some time now, I'd had the feeling that my unique talent might be to seek out and find homes filled with pain and strife, and maybe, by renovating them and communicating with their ghosts, bringing them back to life. My mother used to find homes that felt warm and inviting, and she and my father made a pretty penny over the years bringing those homes back to high standards and reselling them. So maybe I'd inherited her talent but added my own unique, rather dark twist.

"Why don't we do a walk-through together?" I heard myself saying. "You could tell me what you're envisioning, and we could go from there."

"Excellent," said Simone, and I could swear there seemed to be avarice in her eyes. "I'll check in with the police, just to be sure it's okay with them if we go inside and look around. I don't suppose there will be a problem; it's our house, after all, and Linda was found outside in the shed."

There was a slight whimper in response to her last words. Hugh had brought his fist to his mouth again, as though to stifle tears.

I stood to leave. "I'm so sorry, Hugh, for your loss."

"The police seem to think she killed herself," Hugh said. "Do you think that's true?"

"Of course she did," Simone answered. "She's been unstable ever since . . . ever since the incident. It's only gotten worse with age."

The Incident . . . Sounded like a title for a terrible movie: *Incident at Murder House.*

"Or . . ." Hugh said in his quiet, thoughtful way, looking at dust motes dancing in the light of the window. "Perhaps they finished the job."

" 'They' . . . ?" I asked.

"Whatever evil is in that house . . . my father became a monster that night. Maybe . . . maybe he won't stop until he's killed us all."

Chapter Nine

I limped home, feeling beat-up. It wasn't my usual end-of-the-day fatigue. I could handle that. I was used to long days on jobsites and meeting with clients, accustomed to at least ten things going wrong every day that for some reason only I could put aright. What I wasn't familiar with was the depth of sadness I had felt in Hugh's presence. There was a level of pathos there that left me feeling ... I don't know, maybe compelled to write some poetry of my own?

That impulse departed as quickly as it arrived—luckily for all of us—but it dawned on me that art or literature provided an outlet for feelings that can't be expressed any other way. The only thing I did that was close to being artistic—besides building, which was arguably an aesthetic labor of love—was putting together the scrapbooks I made for our clients. For each job, I gathered bits and pieces of construction-related ephemera like old wallpaper and purchase orders, took before-and-after pictures as well as progress shots, and included comments and funny stories from the crew. Homeowners loved the scrapbooks, and I kept floor copies to show prospective clients, like a very personal portfolio. It always gave me a nice feeling of satisfaction to see how everything turned out. Maybe I should do some scrapbooking tonight.

I pulled up to the old farmhouse I shared with Dad and Stan—and, most recently, Cookie—in Oakland's Fruitvale section. The silhouette of Dog's head popped up in the living room window, and I could hear him barking to welcome me home as I skirted the house to the back door.

Dad was standing in front of the old Wedgewood stove, wooden spoon in hand. A huge soup pot sent billows of steam toward the ceiling, and the air carried the delicious aroma of tomatoes, garlic, and oregano.

"Hi, babe. Spaghetti night," he announced happily as I walked in.

"Smells great."

"Stan's still in the office. About half an hour to dinner. You want regular spaghetti or one of your fancy kinds?"

Dad was a fan of spaghetti, though he occasionally ventured into linguine territory. He considered my interest in other shapes of pasta to be exotic, even erudite.

"Chef's choice. Thanks, Dad."

As I started down the hall to the office, I noticed the lights were on in the dining room. The dining room rarely saw much use, as we all preferred the homey informality of the pine table in the alcove off the kitchen.

"What's going on?" I asked.

My sister was seated at the dining room table, surrounded by the papers and photos I'd been collecting to make a scrapbook for the Bernini B&B. Scattered across the table were colored pencils and pens; several glitter glues; a pile of cutesy labels; a pair of scissors that made a scrolly design instead of a straight edge; ink pads and stamps; a stack of patterned paper; and something that looked a lot like cotton candy. Somebody had had a very good time in the local arts and crafts superstore.

"Hi," I said. "What's going on?"

"Guess!"

"I'm not very good at guessing, so why don't you just tell me?"

"Oh, don't be a spoilsport! Guess!"

I felt like snapping at her. Cookie's cheerfulness inevitably had this effect on my grumpy self. I swallowed my irritation and guessed.

"Is it . . . somebody's birthday?"

"Nope! Try again!"

"Um . . . One of the kids' school projects?"

Cookie looked shocked. "Don't be silly! You *know* I'm not one of those parents who does their kids' projects for them! Really, Mel. Give me some credit."

"I give up."

Cookie pouted. "You didn't really try."

"I really did."

Cookie sighed. "Well, Dad keeps saying how hard you work, so I thought I'd help out. You know I've always had a knack for crafty things."

I nodded. Cookie and Daphne had inherited from our clever mother a full complement of crafty genes. Daphne knitted and sewed and crocheted. Cookie had a huge loom that took up the entire garage, forcing Kyle to rent space in a nearby parking structure for their matching Lexus SUVs.

I, on the other hand, didn't have a flair for crafts of any kind, other than building houses. I was good at that.

Still, even though I wasn't particularly inventive or clever with the scrapbooks I created for Turner Construction's clients, I had modeled them on the ones my mother used to make. They weren't as good as hers but were reasonably well put-together. I had been rather proud of them, given that I was usually so lame at such things.

But now, Cookie was taking scrapbooking to a whole new level: layering different textures and patterns in a way that somehow worked.

"Doesn't this look great?"

I had to admit it did. The glitter glue and use of lots of pink and lavender shades wouldn't have been my choice, yet the proprietor of the Bernini B&B was a Doris Day lookalike who wore a strand of pearls even when cleaning the bathrooms. She was going to *love* the glitter.

"It really does," I said, thumbing through the pages. No globs of glue, no ragged edges. She was right—she was better at this than I was. I imagined it sitting on a credenza in the front hall of the B and B, the guests turning the pages, imagining the history of the place as well as visualizing its transformation into the graceful inn it had become. "Um, thanks for doing that. I'm sure they'll really like it."

"No prob! Do you have another one you want me to do?"

"I thought I'd put together something for last weekend's client, Monty. But I don't have nearly as much stuff—the Bernini B&B was a huge renovation, and we've been working there a long time."

"Well, hand it over and let's see what we can do!"

Speaking of Monty's house, I meant to check in with Luz about getting copies of the photos she took on Saturday. And that reminded me to call the Neighbors Together office again. I'd tried twice but had received no callback. I could only imagine that once the big push for the Work Weekend was behind them, the staff took a few well-deserved days off. Still, I needed to speak with the director and let her know what had happened and that I was continuing the project this coming weekend. I hoped. I couldn't imagine why we couldn't, but as Inspector Crawford often reminded me, I don't think like a cop.

I left the scrapbooking to Cookie and met with Stan in our home office. I returned a few phone calls, tried the Neighbors Together number and got the machine again, and then Stan and I went over some paperwork issues that had come up during the day.

"Mel, not to change the subject, but have you noticed anything . . . odd about Monty?" Stan asked.

"Odd like what?"

He stuck out his chin and inclined his head. Stan hailed from Oklahoma and had a calm, folksy way about him that charmed everyone around him. He was a quiet sort who rarely had a bad word to say about anyone.

"I just wondered . . . you say he's a T-three paraplegic?"

"I think that's what he said. I don't remember the details of his injury, though. He's been in the chair for a few years."

He nodded thoughtfully.

"What is it?" I asked, my curiosity piqued.

"Does he have a motorized chair, do you know?"

"I've only seen him in the manual one. Why?"

"It's unusual for someone with that level of injury not

to have a motorized chair. It's also unusual for someone who uses only a manual chair not to have developed more muscle in his chest and arms—that's why I'm so well built." He added the last with a smile.

"Huh. I guess I never thought about it."

"Probably his motorized chair is in the shop. Those things cost an arm and a leg—no pun intended—so probably he's using his manual one in the interim."

"Probably. Now tell me the rest."

"The rest?"

"Come on, Stan, I know when you're holding back."

He shrugged again. "It's nothing, really. It's just . . . you know how when you get together with builders, y'all talk shop? It's natural. Well, when I'm with others in chairs, sooner or later we start comparing our chairs, or sharing notes on new products or methods, or recounting our physical ailments. There was none of that with Monty. He didn't even seem to want to talk about the ramp very much—and let me tell you, when you're in a chair, a ramp is a very big deal."

"Are you saying he's making this up?"

"Nah. Not really. He's a bit of a character; maybe we just didn't mesh for some reason. Personality conflict and all that."

The phone rang, and Stan answered with his practiced "Turner Construction. Stan speaking." Before he had finished his conversation, Dad yelled that dinner was served.

"Hey, I got a bone to pick with you," said Dad as he, Stan, Cookie, and I sat down to spaghetti, salad, garlic bread, and cheap Chianti—everything, with the exception of the wine, liberally dosed with garlic. We would all be reeking tonight. "Etta said something about you volunteering me to be ... what? A neighborhood big brother?"

"Something like that. It'll be fun."

"I don't have time for that sort of thing."

"Look, volunteerism isn't something you can do once a year and that's it," I said as Dog landed heavily on my feet, taking up his position under the table in case any food fell. We hadn't had to sweep in the kitchen since he'd arrived in our lives. "You have to commit yourself. And this will be fun—you know you can whip that model train set into shape, and you're good with kids. Besides, you yourself said you'd like to see some further work done on that house. And Etta's a sweetheart."

"She's a nice little old lady, true."

"She's not much older than you are, Dad."

Cookie snickered and passed on the buttery garlic bread, citing her diet. I took her portion.

"Anyway," I continued, "I don't see why we can't do some work over there, strip that woodwork, and fix up the front entry and living room, while you spend a little time working on the railroad." I laughed. "Get it? Working on the railroad, all the live long daaay ..."

Cookie and Dad both grimaced—even Dog barked. Only Stan appreciated my musical stylings, and since he was a devoted fan of some truly wretched backwoods Oklahoma bands, I should probably consider the source.

The next morning, my phone rang way too early. Afraid it was a construction emergency, I answered. Unfortunately, the voice on the other end of the line was one I had been hoping not to hear for a while.

"Sorry to bother you so early," said Inspector Crawford in a tone that indicated she wasn't all that sorry when it came right down to it. "I remember you told me you were an early bird. I was hoping you could meet me somewhere before work. I'll buy you a cup of coffee."

"You want to buy me a cup of coffee?" I croaked.

Annette and I weren't exactly coffee buddies. We were more along the lines of ... She thought it was weird that I showed up at crime scenes and talked about ghosts but she wasn't ready to throw me in the slammer yet and occasionally I was actually able to resolve the situation and even though it seemed suspicious to her she couldn't pin anything on me. Like that.

"Or tea. Choose your poison." There was a note of false humor in her voice. What was up with her?

"Um ... okay," I said, ignoring the little voice saying *noooo.* I really didn't want to get up and showered and dressed to be interrogated once again about something that—really, this time—I had nothing to do with.

But one of the reasons I got involved with volunteer projects, had the dog currently curled up on the little rug next to my bed, and was living at my father's house and running Turner Construction was that I had a very hard time saying no. *That* should have been my New Year's resolution: Grow a backbone.

I agreed to meet Annette at Stephen's workplace, Caffe Trieste, off Columbus Avenue. Because if you're going to be roused from your bed by a homicide inspector, the very least you can ask for is some decent coffee and a friend at your back.

After showering and dressing, I tried to sail through the kitchen, hoping my father was too busy cooking for my sister that he wouldn't notice I wasn't going to eat or even bother with coffee. But Cookie wasn't in the kitchen yet. Sleeping in, no doubt. What with her busy schedule of scrapbooking and all.

"Take your sister with you today," Dad said, drawing me aside and speaking in a loud whisper.

"What? Why?"

"Just do it, please. She has nothing to do all day but sit around moping."

"She could answer her husband's phone calls," I suggested. "That would be something to do. What's going on with them, anyway?"

Dad shrugged and started breaking eggs one-handed, skillfully letting only the whites fall into the mixing bowl.

"Nobody tells me anything around here. Maybe you can figure it out."

I had the sense that he knew more than he was letting on. One thing I can say for my father: He's the soul of discretion when he feels something isn't his business.

"All I know is that the kids are at Disneyworld with Kyle's parents," said Dad.

"So she hasn't mentioned how long she'll be in town?"

He shook his head. "Just take her around with you; show her the ropes. She was saying last night she might like to get involved, go into the family business."

I froze.

"You have *got* to be kidding me."

"It might not be such a bad idea. You're always talking about moving to Paris. Think about it. If your sister stepped in to take over for a while, you'd be off the hook."

Cookie in charge of project schedules, client relations, and construction workers? The mind reeled. The dust level alone on the typical jobsite would give the woman palpitations.

"Dad, I really don't think—"

"Sometimes you don't give your sister enough credit. She's a good girl, and she's smarter than people think."

This battle was not worth fighting. I didn't want to disparage my own sister, and Dad was defensive of her. Whether he really couldn't see it or was simply living in a state of denial didn't much matter. The results were the same.

I had one more possible out today, though.

"I'm not just working construction today, though, remember? I've got ghost class tonight. I won't be home for dinner."

He rolled his eyes. "For cryin' out loud, when are you going to stop with that ghost stuff?"

"You told me yourself I needed to take ghost busting seriously if I was going to keep doing it. So this is me taking it seriously. There's a lot to learn, not the least of which is how to run things like an actual business and get paid for my services. There are forms and licenses to consider."

He snorted and started chopping onions.

"Making omelets?" I asked, trying to change the subject. Dad wasn't buying.

"Just do what I tell you and take your sister."

I saluted. "Yes*sir*, Commander, sir."

I had lost this round, but at least I made him smile.

The morning air was crisp and cold. I started up the car and put on the defrost, then climbed out to wipe the dew from the windows and mirrors. Dog immediately jumped into the passenger's seat, happy and ready to go. No matter that he got carsick, he always leapt into the car, excited to be going somewhere, apparently failing to connect the sick feeling to the vehicle. As much as I loved him, I had to admit that Dog was a profoundly dim bulb.

Cookie came out of the house wearing fashionable boots and a pink wool pea coat, looking like a perky Lands' End model, even at this early hour. She stomped her feet and wrapped her arms around herself.

"*Brrrr*. It's so coooold."

"Tell that to people in Montana. This would be downright temperate for them."

"In LA, the weather's always perfect: not too hot, not too cold. Every day's the same."

I managed not to express my next snide thought: *Sounds boring.*

"Does the doggy have to come?"

"We're trying to help him get over his carsickness," I explained. My father and Stan had taken Dog to a holistic veterinarian in Berkeley. None of us could get behind the suggestion that the poor canine go vegan, but we were giving the suggested exposure therapy a shot. "He's supposed to ride around with me at least three or four times a week."

"Why can't he go tomorrow?"

"He's already in and ready. Let's just go."

"He's in my seat."

Dog's big brown head lolled over in our direction, tongue hanging out the side of his muzzle, chocolate eyes huge and patient and benign.

"He likes to ride shotgun," I said. "Would you mind riding in back?"

Cookie made an outraged gasp, her mouth hung open, and she gaped at me.

"Just kidding." I chuckled at her reaction. Okay, it wasn't much for humor this early in the morning, but it made me smile. "In the back, Dog," I said with an exaggerated gesture, pointing toward the rear seat.

Why I did this was anyone's guess; Dog had never once responded to my verbal command. Finally, I put a hand under his butt and urged him on until he finally jumped awkwardly into the back.

"There you are," I said to Cookie. "Let's go. I'm already running late."

"There's hair all over the seat! It'll get on my coat."

I blew out a breath and tried to draw upon my shallow reserve of patience.

"We're *working* today, Cookie. That involves dusty, muddy jobsites. If you were wearing something appropriate to construction, you wouldn't be worrying about a little dog hair."

"Look who's talking. How come you get to wear party dresses to jobsites?"

She had me there. I tossed her a clean towel from a supply I kept in the back. She arranged it over the seat, tucking the ends in carefully, and finally climbed in.

"Now, isn't this nice?" said Cookie as I headed for the freeway. "The Turner sisters, out for a day on the town!"

"We're working," I reminded her.

"Oh, I *know*. Two career girls, out for a day on the town! Where should we go to lunch?"

Chapter Ten

Caffe Trieste is on a corner just off the famous strip of the Italian part of town. At this hour on a Tuesday, the hordes of tourists that crowd the streets looking for really great lasagna and music and strip shows were still sleeping off last night's fun, so I found a parking spot within a couple of blocks.

"Mel!" said Stephen, and we hugged over the counter. "How are you? What a surprise! You hardly ever come in, you—" His eyes flicked over to where Inspector Crawford sat at a small table toward the back, already nursing a latte and making notes in her ever-present notebook. "Oh. Are you here for . . . ?" He gave an exaggerated gesture with his head in the inspector's direction, in a move that was much less subtle than if he had merely said her name aloud.

I nodded. "Stephen, this is my sister, Cookie. Cookie, Stephen."

"I'm sorry; you want a cookie?" asked Stephen as he shook her hand.

"No, *I'm* the Cookie!" she said with a delighted laugh. "I get that all the time."

"Oh . . . nice to meet you. I like your outfit."

"Thank you! How sweet of you to say," she said, casting a significant glance my way.

"How about me?" I demanded. "You designed this dress."

"Yes, but . . . to tell you the truth, it's looking a little out-of-date at this point. It still looks great on you, of course, but—I don't know—maybe the spangles are a little early two thousands, if you know what I mean."

He stood back, cocked his head, and assessed me. Cookie followed suit.

"I think she might benefit from a slightly different style given her . . . curves," suggested Cookie. "I'm not so sure the bugle beads are doing her any favors."

Stephen nodded and stroked his whiskerless chin. "Yes, I see what you mean. I think a plainer fabric might be just the ticket."

"Could I get a double cappuccino, please? Full fat." I'd be damned if I ordered my usual skim milk after a comment like that. "Come on, Cookie, I'll set you up over here."

I chose a table for Cookie near the entrance, out of hearing range of Inspector Crawford. I set up my laptop, on which I'd bookmarked several home renovation sites, as well as an industry glossary and a builders' chat room.

"Study these sites so you have a sense of what's going on with the business. I'm going to chat with someone for a few minutes. You stay here and be good," I told her, as though she were a child.

As I approached Inspector Crawford at long last, she looked over at Stephen and Cookie, then raised her eyebrow at me.

"What? You felt a need for backup? This isn't an official inquiry. I merely asked you to coffee."

"Well, you know me. I like to travel with an entourage. And there's no way you 'merely asked me to coffee.'"

An imperious lift of an eyebrow was her only response.

I shrugged. "Plus, I get a little nervous around cops."

"I've noticed. Why is that? You don't have a police record."

"You investigated me?"

"In the course of two murder investigations, yes, I have had occasion to type your name into the computer. I'm a cop; I like to do that sort of thing. Check into suspects' backgrounds."

"Are you saying I'm suspect?"

"Not this time."

"Mmm," I mumbled. I guess it made sense the authorities would look into the backgrounds of all the key players. And I had, after all, been at more murder scenes than the average innocent person. But it still felt unsettling to think that someone was snooping around my life.

"Don't worry; the background check didn't turn up anything interesting."

"Oh, good. Or should I be insulted?"

She shrugged. "Why so nervous around cops?"

"My father tells me I have an inborn problem with authority figures."

"You and a million others in this city."

"So. To what do I owe this pleasure?" I asked, as though having coffee with a homicide inspector were an everyday occurrence. Whether or not this was an "official inquiry," I was braced for some sort of grilling as well as the suggestion—implied, never stated—that I knew more than I was admitting. It was our usual MO. Still, the café smelled of dark-roasted coffee, an intense aroma that I loved, and my body was having a Pavlovian response to the promise of caffeine. I glanced around to see how soon Stephen would deliver my cappuccino.

"I can't believe I'm asking you this," the inspector said as her eyes scanned the room, as though to make sure that the caffeine-deprived ranks at the café this early in the morning on a Tuesday weren't going to blow her cover. "But . . . I'd like your help."

"*My* help? What kind of help?"

She cleared her throat and brushed an invisible something from the mosaic tabletop.

Finally, still not meeting my eyes, she spoke quickly, as though afraid to allow the words to linger on her lips: "Ghost help."

Well, knock me over with a feather.

"Beg pardon?"

"You heard me."

True, I had heard her. But Inspector Annette Crawford of the San Francisco Police Department—doubting, cynical, imperious Inspector Crawford—was looking chagrined, and I found myself enjoying it. It was the flip side of my discomfort with authority.

"Ghosts, you say?" I queried in an oh-so-innocent voice. "Surely not. An esteemed policewoman of my acquaintance informed me on more than one occasion that there's no such thing as ghosts."

More clearing of the throat, more obsession with invisible dust motes. Finally she blew out a long breath and met my eyes.

"Hubert Lawrence says there are ghosts in his house."

"The Murder House?"

"I wish everyone would stop calling it that. But yes. That house."

Newsflash, Inspector, I thought; there *were* ghosts in that house. But before I could say anything, Stephen brought my coffee, and after taking a sip, I decided that, discretion being the better half of valor, I should concentrate on my drink.

My eyes wandered over to Cookie, who appeared to have encountered some technical difficulties that required the assistance of three men. They hovered over her table and the computer, discussing their options, chuckling at Cookie's comments. I couldn't make out the words, but I got the gist.

I turned my attention back to the homicide inspector.

"I feel as though we're switching roles here," I said, "so I guess it's my turn to ask: What do ghosts in the house next door have to do with your crime scene?"

"The victim's name was Linda Lawrence. She was Hubert's older sister."

" 'Victim'? It's not a suicide? Hugh said she had tried to kill herself before."

"Mmm," the inspector said. Or maybe she was just enjoying the latte. "Linda Lawrence appears to have been troubled for some time. Problems with substance abuse, mostly pills and alcohol."

"But you don't think she purposefully killed herself? Could it have been an accidental overdose?"

"I don't know what to think. But the whole thing seems . . . fishy to me."

"Enough to make you believe in ghosts?" That must be quite a fish.

"I didn't say I believed in ghosts," she replied, a touch defensively. "I'm checking out possibilities, that's all," she said.

"Like a good cop should," I said solemnly.

"Like a good cop should," she agreed, and relaxed a bit. "Here's the thing: Hubert Lawrence really believes what he's saying. He and Linda had visited the house last Friday, and Linda thought she saw something."

"Something being a ghost?"

She nodded.

"Hugh mentioned that she thought she saw the ghost of her father at the bottom of the stairs. Turned out it was Hugh. He looks a lot like his father."

"When did you speak to Hubert Lawrence?" she asked me.

"Yesterday. He called and asked to meet with me about renovating the house for him. And . . . I think he wants me to communicate with the ghosts as well."

"Really?" We were back to the relationship I was more familiar with: the one where she thought I was snooping around in her homicide investigation.

"*He* called *me*," I said. "Not the other way around. There's no law against meeting with a potential client, is there?"

"Huh," she grunted. "Anyway, after the walk-through of the house, Linda never made it back to the halfway house. The medical examiner puts her time of death as later that night."

"Okay . . . ," I said, wondering where this was heading. If Linda had seen ghosts at her old home, had she turned to pills for solace, misjudged the amount she was taking, and overdosed? Why did it seem Annette thought there was something more to it?

"The thing is, there are indications that the body was moved, postmortem."

I sipped my drink. "Moving corpses around would be unusual behavior in a ghost."

Annette gave me a scathing, don't-even-*think*-of-messing-with-me look, and I shut up.

"I'm not suggesting a ghost moved the body, Ms. Turner. But if Hugh Lawrence believes there are ghosts in that house, and Linda did as well . . . I want to know how he reacts if we go in there and—I don't know—talk to them. To the ghosts."

Something in the inspector's manner struck me as odd, and I decided to go for it. "There's more to it than that, isn't there?"

"I may have . . . that is, I thought . . . Well, there are some strange things going on at that house."

"Strange how?"

"I'm not sure how to characterize it," the inspector said, dodging my question. "Tell me: Have you seen anything?"

"Enough that I'd like to take a closer look. Listen, Hugh Lawrence asked me to walk through the house with him and his wife. He wants to hire Turner Construction to redo the place, but here's the interesting thing: He doesn't want to renovate the house. He wants it restored, exactly as it was when the murders occurred."

"As if to recapture a moment in time?"

"Exactly."

The inspector frowned. "So Hugh Lawrence learns his sister is dead and her body was found in the shed behind their family home—and the first thing he does is hire a construction crew to make the house look exactly as it did on the worst night of his life?"

"I know it sounds odd, and you would know better than I if Hugh has something to hide. But I have to say, I didn't take it that way. You've met him. He's a bit . . . I don't know. A little . . . off."

She widened her eyes as if to say, *You can say that again*.

"Also, he seems to believe that the house is the key to helping him overcome the trauma of the crime."

"Yes, that's what he says about Linda. That's what they were doing on Friday—just walking around and helping her re-create that night in her head. Poor woman. I don't think anyone meant any harm, and I'm not a psychotherapist, but it seems to me that sort of thing should be done under the direction of a mental health professional."

She looked out through the front window of the café, shaking her head, and when she spoke, her sadness and frustration were palpable.

"I'll never understand this sort of thing. Beautiful family, lovely home, the whole enchilada . . . and then, the kind of craziness that makes someone destroy it all. What is it with some people? You want to kill yourself? Fine—slink off into the woods and shoot yourself. Have done with it. Why take your family with you?"

This was easily the most personal thing I'd ever heard Inspector Crawford say. The last thing I expected was to be this hardened cop's confidante. Then I reminded myself: She was dealing with the possibility of ghosts. That pushed people out of their comfort zone and often resulted in saying and doing things you thought you'd never do. I should know.

A peal of girlish laughter indicated that Cookie found something hilarious. No doubt in response to one of the males in her orbit.

"Friend of yours?" asked Annette, checking out Cookie.

"My sister."

"No kidding? You don't look much alike."

"Yes, I'm aware of that."

"She's a piece of work, huh?"

I blew out a sigh. Happily, Crawford wasn't expecting a response to her query.

"You said there is something strange at the house," I said. "Have you . . . seen something?"

The pause was too long not to be eloquent.

"You have, haven't you?"

"I've been a homicide inspector for a long time, Ms. Turner. And before that, I was a beat cop. Suffice it to say, in all those years I've seen a lot that I couldn't make sense of. I've learned not to jump to conclusions and not to make assumptions. And when I see evidence of something . . . no matter how crazy it might seem, I follow it up."

"That's very commendable," I said, meaning it. Those whose jobs decide the fate of others should be especially conscientious.

"I know—but I'm telling you all this for a reason. I want you to go into that house with me." I hadn't expected *that*. My feelings must have registered on my face because the inspector smiled. "Surprised?"

"You could say that. Why do you want me to accompany you through the Murder House?"

"If there are ghosts in the house, maybe you could. . . . That is, you might. . . . Actually, now that I'm saying it out loud, I don't quite know what I'm expecting you to do."

"How about I try to communicate with them?" I suggested. "It's possible they could tell me something helpful, about that night or about Linda's recent death."

Her eyes met mine. I had respected Annette Crawford since I met her. Liked her, even, as much as one can like someone whom one does not really know. I found her thoughtful, almost preternatural calm appealing. I identified with how she seemed vaguely pissed off much of the time, and wondered if she was always like that or if it was the murder scenes that put her in a bad mood.

"When should we do this?"

"You have plans right now?"

"It . . . takes a little preparation. There's some equipment I should take with us, for example."

"What kind of equipment?" The inspector's customary skepticism had returned, replacing her open, almost vulnerable facade of a moment ago.

"Just your average, everyday ghost-hunting equipment," I said. "Listen, I know it sounds odd. Believe me, I do. But dealing with ghosts is a lot more complicated than people realize, which is why I'm taking a class in it."

"A class. Huh."

Ooh, boy. Now she was raising one eyebrow.

"Look, you can't have it both ways, Inspector: Either ghosts don't exist, in which case you don't need my help, or ghosts *do* exist, in which case it's wise to learn as much as you can about them before seeking them out."

She nodded, conceding my point.

"The equipment I have in mind measures energy frequencies, which helps to determine the possible presence of a ghost."

"How does that work?"

"All of us on this plane of reality vibrate at a particular frequency, which we can see or feel. But there are other frequencies, like those whistles that dogs can hear but humans can't detect."

"So ghosts are like dog whistles?"

"Something like that. Ghosts exist on a frequency only a few people can sense. Like me. Special equipment, if properly calibrated, can also identify a spirit, 'see' a ghost, in effect. A recorder picks up sounds we hear only when we go back over the recording and amplify them. A camera can reveal movements too fast for the human eye to register. The electromagnetic field, or EMF, detector perceives energy we can't feel."

"Uh-huh."

"That being said, I don't usually use equipment, at least not properly." My ghostly encounters so far had been the result of the ghosts' reaching out to me, not mine to them. "I could go in cold. But we should wait until dark, when spirits are stronger. The quiet makes it easier for them to manifest."

Another raised eyebrow. Not long ago, I would have had the same reaction. Sometimes I couldn't believe what I heard myself saying these days. Nothing like a few ghostly encounters to alter one's world view.

Nowadays, instead of rolling my eyes at the idea of ghosts, I was considering becoming a Catholic so I could have a rosary to clutch and recite. None of the ghosts I had met had actually harmed me, but they did scare the stuffing out of me.

"Here's a thought: After my ghost-busting class tonight I'm doing the walk-through with Hugh and Simone. How about we make it a foursome? It might help to have Hugh there."

"Tonight, then," she said, standing and leaving a sizable tip on the table. "I'll call and square it with the Lawrences. And, Mel? Thank you."

"Anytime, Inspector."

After Annette left, I hung around for a while chatting with Stephen, but the café started hopping with the before-work crowd, so we left. My mind was on murder and ghosts, so I had to ask Cookie to repeat what she'd just said.

"I'm sorry?"

"I *saaaiiid*, mind if we stop at Sephora?" asked Cookie.

"What's a For-a?"

"Sephora. *Hello*? The cosmetic store?"

"We're not going shopping for makeup, Cookie. It's a workday."

"They do full makeovers, Mel," she said, her eyes wide. "I'm just saying it wouldn't hurt ... Dad tells me you're having trouble nailing down this Graham fellow."

"Things are perfectly fine with Graham. Exactly as I want them to be. And if they weren't, overpriced makeup wouldn't be the solution."

Cookie looked at me sympathetically. "A little rejuvenation wouldn't hurt, would it? Every girl likes to look her best for her man."

"He's not my man," I said through gritted teeth.

"So there *is* something wrong."

"Besides, the store's not even open at this hour, is it?" I said, trying to ignore an annoying stab of insecurity. "And even if it is, I'm working. Running Turner Construction isn't some hobby, Cookie. It's work, *real* work, that pays the bills and keeps a roof over our heads."

"Oh, don't be silly, Mel," Cooke said, making a pretty little twist of her carefully colored lips as we approached my Scion and climbed in. "Dad paid off the mortgage years ago. You can afford to take a spa day."

"Spa days are for people with more dollars than sense,

not for people who work for a living," I said, wondering where this working-class-hero stuff was coming from. I didn't normally talk like this.

"You sound just like Dad." Cookie sighed.

"And I most certainly could 'nail Graham down' if I wanted to, though I have no intention of doing so. What a terrible metaphor. It just so happens he wants me to be his girlfriend."

How old was I, twelve? Why did I regress so quickly when my sister was around?

"Mm-hmmm," she said with a half shrug, all innocence. "And where might Graham-the-perfect-boyfriend be these days?"

"Out of town. He'll be back tomorrow," I said, before realizing she would want to meet him. That must not happen.

"Oh, super! Let's all have dinner, shall we? Or did he have a romantic tête-à-tête planned for just the two of you? I wouldn't want to get in the path of true love."

"I'll have to get back to you on—oh, rats, the phone's ringing," I said, and grabbed for it as a drowning person grabs for a lifeline. "Excuse me, gotta take that."

For once I was glad to have a call interrupt my day.

Chapter Eleven

I spent the rest of the day dragging Charlotte "Cookie" Dopkin, née Turner, from jobsite to jobsite, alternating between thinking I should find something to interest her and hoping to find something that would appall her. What was supposed to be a quick meeting with a client in Union Square turned into a lengthy delay when Cookie disappeared into the bowels of Williams-Sonoma and refused to leave until she had found just the right French café press pot to bring home, because all Dad had was an old-fashioned Mr. Coffee drip machine. One might think that I'd find common ground with a fellow coffee snob, but Cookie's forty-five-minute discussion of the comparative merits of German versus French press pots drove me smack out of my mind. It was only when I threatened to buy a domestic press pot and smash her over the head with it that she agreed to leave.

"Well, that was fun, wasn't it?" she asked as I stomped

out of the store. "Hungry? Methinks *somebody's* feeling the effects of low blood sugar."

"We could grab some tacos at the taco truck if you'd like."

"You know, I'm afraid I gained a few pounds over the holidays that I'm *still* trying to lose. I don't have to tell you how hard that can be! How about a salad?"

"No time for yet another sit-down meal." I had given in and let her take me to a fancy café earlier for lunch. "I don't want to be late for my class."

"I see the perfect solution—pull in there!" Cookie said, pointing to a strip mall. Ten minutes later, we were sitting at the juice bar of an organic food store drinking wheatgrass shots.

"Isn't this the *best*?" Cookie chirped. "*Mens sana in corpore sano!* A healthy mind in a healthy body!"

"You bet," I said, using a toothpick to Roto-Rooter the wheat germ that was clogging my straw so I could finish the yogurt-mango smoothie. "Who needs carne asada and fresh salsa when you've got . . . whatever this sludge is?"

"Oh, you goofball!" Cookie said. "You can't kid me; you've always liked yogurt."

"I've always hated yogurt. Daphne, our other sister, likes yogurt."

"Really? I could have sworn . . . Well, a little yogurt never hurt anybody."

By the time we arrived at Olivier Galopin's haunted supply store, I was more in need of a stiff drink than of a lecture on how the metal in household locks, doorknobs, hinges, and the like can retain energy from beyond.

As we approached the brick building in Jackson Square, one of the oldest neighborhoods of San Francisco, Cookie reared back.

"A 'ghost hunting and spiritual supply shoppe'?" she read from the painted sign, hanging like a pub medallion over the door. "How come you refused to go shopping all day and now we're at your friend's shoppy?"

"The *e* in *shoppe* is silent."

She glared at me. "I was making a joke. How come no one ever gets my jokes?"

"Sorry." I forced myself to smile. Cookie was right; I'd been a Grumpy Gus all day long, while she'd been relentlessly cheerful. I suspected the two were connected. "Anyway, we're not here to shop. Like I told you, I'm taking a class in ghost busting."

"Oooh, creepy."

"No need to be scared," said a short, pudgy man as he rushed up the stone steps to open the black-painted shop door. "There's nothing to be afraid of. Spirits operate in other dimensions, but they have no intention of hurting us."

Cookie favored him with a brilliant smile and swept into the spiritual shoppy. Pudgy followed her in, allowing the door to swing shut in my face. Just inside the door was a bulletin board bristling with notices and announcements, many hand-printed and hand-illustrated. Although Olivier's shop had only been open a few months, it had already become a hub of activity, both spirit-hunting and personal, for the "open-minded" folk, as they liked to call themselves. Covering the bulletin board were flyers for ghost walks, the kind the tourists take in Chinatown or the Haight, or on Olivier's own Pacific Heights tour. There were also signs touting the services of spiritual cleansers to rid homes of haunting, advertisements for the services of those who liked to document hauntings, and information for those in search of meditation classes, spells for protection and hexes against neighbors, and séances. It was one-stop shopping for spiritual needs of all kinds. I found it fascinating.

While I was scanning the board, a long arm reached around me and yanked down a bright pink flyer advertising hexes.

I watched Olivier Galopin crumple the paper in one large hand.

"Not a fan of curses?" I asked.

"I don't believe in such things, nor do I associate with those who do."

"Good policy."

Olivier took down a few outdated notices from the bulletin board. "You are looking lovely today, Mel, as always."

"Thank you," I said, though I didn't put much stock in his flattery. Olivier was French, and he knew his way around women. I could only imagine what he'd say when he saw my sister. "You're not looking bad, yourself."

Olivier liked to dress for the occasion and often wore a formal jacket that appeared to be straight from the Victorian era. The effect was rather dashing and suitably un-twenty-first-century. Olivier's dramatic streak—and the fact that he led the touristy Pacific Heights ghost tour—was one of the reasons I had been slow to trust him. But he'd turned out to be much more helpful, and far less larcenous, than I had at first expected.

"Oh, hey, I'm sort of babysitting my sister tonight. I hope you don't mind; I was thinking perhaps she could audit the class? She'll be quiet."

"You do not think the subject matter will frighten her unduly?"

"I don't think so. . . ."

"Then she is most welcome to join us this evening. Where is the little darling?"

"Talking to Dingo, over at the counter."

Upon spying her, he raised his eyebrows. "I thought you were talking about a little girl, but your sister—she is a beautiful woman, no?"

"Yup."

Cookie was pawing at trays of Celtic jewelry while chatting nonstop with the odd fellow named Dingo, who was clad in a tie-dyed Grateful Dead T-shirt and who ran the register. The two were getting along famously, and I overheard Cookie recommending a cream rinse of avocado, salt, and olive oil to tame the flyaway gray hair that stood out sideways from Dingo's head.

And here I'd thought that in this setting, at least, Cookie's easy charm would fail her and *I'd* be the one smoothing the way. But I had underestimated my sister, and not for the first time.

Olivier led me over to meet our guest lecturer for this evening's class.

"Mel, I'd like to introduce you to Rosie Parker. Rosie, Mel is one of my star students, a gifted medium, though she still doesn't like to admit it."

"I'm happy to admit it," I said. "The problem is, I still have no idea what I'm doing. Nice to meet you."

"Same here." Rosie was probably many years younger and a few inches shorter than I, with dark hair and hazel eyes. Around her neck she wore a rusted piece of metal on a hand-forged copper chain.

"I love your necklace—it's so unusual."

"It is, isn't it? It's an old key, actually. From the fourteenth century."

"Are you kidding? I've never seen anything like it."

It wasn't shaped like any modern or antique key I'd ever seen. Instead, it was a bar that had a slim sheet of metal wrapped around it, rather like the bacon-wrapped asparagus my sister and I had enjoyed for lunch at the chic bistro on Chestnut Street that Cookie had insisted on. My stomach growled at the memory. I had to admit it was a darned good lunch, much better than that yogurt fiasco we'd had for dinner.

"Rosie is an expert in locks, hardware, doorknobs, that sort of thing," said Olivier.

"I didn't realize a person could specialize in that."

"Oh, sure," said Rosie. "I used to teach university classes on it, believe it or not. Just the standard architectural and technical history, though, not the more . . . interesting aspects of antique metal pieces."

That reminded me. "Could I ask you something?"

"Sure; fire away."

"Would a door knocker be a particularly sensitive item—I mean, in the paranormal sense?"

"You will see," interrupted Olivier with a smile, "that my friend Mel always comes here full of questions. She has a curious mind."

I wondered whether he meant curious as in *curious* or as in *strange*.

Rosie laughed. "A door knocker could definitely be a paranormal conduit. I mean, all metal conducts energy really well, which is why antique jewelry and watches and the like often conserve a bit of the person who wore them."

"I didn't know that, but I guess it makes sense."

"But a door knocker, in addition to being made of metal, is also symbolic of the point of entry. A door, of course, is the entry to a home, and the symbol of a door can be the symbol of a point of entry to something else."

"So a banging door knocker might symbolize . . . ?"

"Somebody—or some*thing*—seeking permission to enter."

"Enter what?"

"A physical place, of course, but also a spiritual place."

"You mean . . . like a person?"

Rosie paused. "Potentially."

But the residents of the Murder House, I realized, were trapped *inside*. Who would be seeking entrance?

"If I heard knocking when no one was at the door . . . could it be residual? Left over from a traumatic incident? Could the knocking be attached to that, somehow?"

"An echo across time," said Olivier.

Rosie nodded thoughtfully. "It would make sense. As I'm sure you know, paranormal activity, by definition, isn't hard science; it's all open to interpretation. Is it possible the knocking could be trying to tell you something? A message of some kind?"

"It might well be. If only I had a clue. That's why I'm taking Olivier's class. So, how did you get interested in the history of locks?"

"I learned early about locksmithing. Sort of a family business, you might say."

"Have you ever heard of Neighbors Together?" At the shake of her head, I explained the program.

"It sounds like a great organization. I should get involved next year."

"Your locksmith skills would come in handy in some of these old houses."

She blushed. "I'm not what you'd call a certified lock-smith—"

"The Key Master's work is much more interesting than that," interjected Olivier.

"Thanks so much, Ghost Boy. I was telling it my way," Rosie teased, and Olivier laughed. "What our French friend means to say is that I am not a conventional lock-smith. I was trained in safecracking. It's a very long story and one I am happy to share with discerning individuals, though at a time and place of my choosing. Which usually involves dirty martinis."

I smiled. "I have found the inclusion of dirty martinis enhances many a discussion."

"This sounds like a lovely evening! Am I invited?" asked Olivier.

"No," Rosie and I said in unison, then shared a smile. I felt a friendship coming on.

"Maybe another time," I added.

Olivier sighed theatrically. "I understand. The girls' night out is a highly respected tradition in this country, no?"

"You betcha," Rosie said, and she handed me her business card. "Call me, Mel, and we'll have those marti-nis."

"And now, dear ladies, I believe it is time for class to begin. If everyone will please have a seat?"

After her lecture on antique metals—which was much more fascinating than I'd anticipated—Rosie departed, and Olivier devoted the rest of the class to the protocol for ghost hunting. As far as I was concerned, the protocol was to avoid being scared to death, but Olivier and the other five people in the class were focused on recording and documenting incidents of haunting. They hoped to find evidence that could be used to prove to a skeptical world that spirits indeed existed.

We then watched portions of a popular TV show about ghost busting. Olivier led the class in analyzing the show, breaking it down into what was done correctly and what was done incorrectly. From what I gathered, the biggest problems occurred when the crews didn't document fully—noting not only the noises and sights they were seeing right there, but also the ambient noises, so there would be proof later. The discussion was interesting but not all that pertinent to me. I might be jumping on the ghost-busting bandwagon, but I wasn't driven by the need to prove to the world that I wasn't crazy. I was more about getting the darned renovation done.

Although I supposed I had a new motivation: Inspector Annette Crawford had asked me to lead her on a ghost tour through the Murder House.

Never thought I'd live to see *that* day. Mel Turner: SFPD ghost consultant.

When Olivier started going over the benefits and limitations of infrared camcorders, my mind wandered again. Why was I so fixated on that door knocker? For one thing, the banging I heard while I was in the shed had sounded like the smart rapping of a metal knocker, but there was no such thing on the plain wood doors. And when I looked at the knocker on the front door . . . I could still hear that sound, reverberating through my head. What could it mean, if anything? Had death come knocking that terrible night? Linda had a picture of the distinctive hand-holding-a-ball knocker tattooed on her neck; it *must* mean something. *I should ask Hugh about it,* I thought. *Speaking of Hugh, maybe I should read some of his poetry.* Luz—and whoever named the poet laureates—seemed to think it was worthwhile, and maybe there were some clues in it.

I noticed that Cookie, who at first claimed to be fascinated by everything spiritual, was now passing notes back and forth with an attractive man in his thirties. It was high school study hall all over again. I gave her a little kick under the table, but I couldn't really blame her. If I hadn't experienced ghost sightings personally, I would probably be much ruder than Cookie while listening to such things.

I wondered . . . did Annette now believe in ghosts? She hadn't been specific, but clearly she'd seen something in the Murder House that had shocked her enough to call me in. Did she really think Linda's death had something to do with ghosts? But if so, had Linda been killed in the Murder House? Then how had the body been moved to the shed? I had seen ghosts move lightweight objects such as papers and cause candles to flicker by creating a disturbance in the atmosphere. But no atmospheric disturbance—short of a tornado—was capable of relocating a corpse. That suggested human intervention. But who? Did the inspector suspect Hugh was involved? Or was she merely trying to set her own doubts to rest? As I knew only too well, the first encounter with a spirit can be traumatic.

A babble of voices and the scraping of metal chairs signaled the class was over, and I came out of my reverie.

"Listen, I'm going to take another look at that jewelry," said Cookie. "I know I shouldn't, but there are a few things I just *can't* resist. Do you mind?"

"Take your time," I said. I caught Olivier's eye as he was saying good night to another student.

"You rang, madam?" he asked.

"What's involved in holding a séance?"

"Why do you ask?"

I gave him the abbreviated story of what had happened at 2906 Greenbrier.

"So you don't believe it was suicide?"

"I don't know. She was clearly troubled, and drugs and alcohol don't usually lead to sound thinking. But the inspector on the case is suspicious, and I trust her professional opinion."

"And?" Olivier prompted.

"And what?"

"I am getting to know you, my friend. Something more is troubling you. What is it?"

"Even if it was suicide, I'm afraid there's something going on in that house." As I spoke, my previously unformed thoughts coalesced. "I'm worried that if Hugh moves back in, he might lose his own grasp on reality. It's one thing to confront the demons of one's past. It's quite another thing to be savaged by them."

Olivier nodded. "What is it you wish to accomplish in this séance?"

"To speak with the spirits—figure out who they are and what they want. And, you know, maybe solve a murder."

"You have never done such a thing, I take it?"

"No. Can you help?"

"If you are to do this, it must be done right. You would agree with me, no?"

"Can it be done this weekend? Friday is the twenty-fifth anniversary of the murders."

His eyebrows rose. "Well, in that case, yes indeed. We should take advantage of the timing."

"I'll have to check with the interested parties and see

what they want to do. I'm supposed to do a walk-through tonight, so I'll let you know what happens then. Maybe there will be no need for a séance after all."

"Or perhaps there will be more need than ever."

"So how would the séance work, exactly?" I asked. "How many people do we need, and can we summon the ghosts in some sort of controlled fashion? What if the spirit of the father is violent? Would we be putting people at risk?"

"Excellent questions all. I am a ghost hunter, not a medium. I believe we need an expert to make contact with the ghosts. You are a medium, of course, but you are still untrained and unsure. It's best to have someone experienced to conduct the séance so as to control the situation better."

"By all means, let's call in someone experienced. Believe me when I say I have absolutely no ego attached to being the one who talks to ghosts."

"I will make some phone calls to see if it is possible to set it up for this Friday. Presuming, that is, you still want to after your walk-through tonight."

I nodded.

"Mel, I want you to know I am very proud of you," said Olivier. "When I met you just a few months ago, you were afraid to go into the building by yourself. But this time you have not even asked me to accompany you on your walk-through."

"Thanks. I guess I'm getting a little more accustomed to the idea. It helps to have a sense of what to expect." I didn't think I would ever become blasé about ghosts—it was just too weird an experience—but there was no denying that repeated exposure to the beyond had led to a certain amount of desensitization.

Downstairs in the shop, Dingo was finishing up a makeover on Cookie. She was covered in chain jewelry and bedecked like an adolescent Goth. All she needed was heavy black eye makeup and black lipstick, and she would be the perfect Queen of the Dead.

"Remember that look for next year's Halloween Party," I said as I stripped her of the jewelry. "Ready?"

We bid farewell to Olivier and Dingo and headed out to my car.

"So listen," I said, glancing over at Cookie from the corner of my eye. "I have to go and do a thing this evening, so I'm going to drop you off at BART."

BART, or Bay Area Rapid Transit, is our local subway system. By and large, it is fast, efficient, and environmentally friendly. I would take it into the city more often if I could, but since I was usually running from one worksite to the next, it simply wasn't practical. Still, it was a great train service.

"*BART*?" Cookie gaped at me, as though I'd suggested she ride a water buffalo while wearing her favorite Jimmy Choo shoes.

"Sure. Dad can pick you up from the Fruitvale station."

"*I* don't take BART. I have *never* taken BART. I don't even know how to go about taking BART. Do I need a ticket?"

"Of course you need a ticket. It's not free."

"I don't know how to buy a ticket."

"Then this will be a whole day of firsts for you. Hanging out on jobsites, going to a ghost supply shoppy, buying a ticket for BART. Where will the adventure end?"

"Getting mugged and murdered on BART?"

"You're not going to get mugged *or* murdered. Good heavens."

"How do you know?"

"Because BART's safe. I take it all the time."

"Not at midnight, you don't."

"Actually, I do take it at midnight. And anyway, it's nowhere near midnight."

"It's dark."

She had me there. "BART's perfectly safe."

"Where are *you* going?"

"I have something to take care of." Carting my sister around jobsites was one thing, but of this I was sure: I did *not* want Cookie tagging along on my ghost walk.

In the end, I had to park the car and go into the station to physically assist Cookie in buying a ticket from the machine, since BART really did suck at customer service. Once you knew what you were doing, it was a simple enough system, but it was far from intuitive; the uninitiated usually took a while to figure it out or were forced to rely upon the kindness of strangers. I had lost count of how many times I had helped some hapless tourist buy a ticket from the machines, get through the turnstiles, and figure out which train to take.

Of course, Cookie probably would have fared just fine with any one of the men who would likely have flocked to help her, but she got stuck with her sister instead. It worked out, though, so she could complain to me the whole time and try to wheedle me into driving her home.

"Just remember you're going toward the East Bay, and take either the Fremont train or the Pleasanton."

"I don't want to go to Fremont!"

"*No* one really wants to go to Fremont. But that's the direction the train goes. There will be an announcement, and it also comes up on the overhead board. And then you just hop off the train at the Fruitvale station."

"I honestly don't see why you can't just drive me across the bridge. It isn't that far."

"Think of the environment you're leaving for your children. How are they, by the way?"

"Fine," she said glumly, and I realized, once again, that I needed to be a better sister. We had spent the whole day together, and I still didn't know what was going on with her and Kyle. But how could I get her to tell me?

"Listen, Cookie . . ." I checked the clock on my phone. I could squeeze in a quick chat over a cup of coffee. "Why don't we take a few minutes and grab something to drink? You can tell me what's going on and what you're really doing here."

That was enough to compel her to head for the train. She fumbled while putting the ticket in the slot of the turnstile, and a man in a BART uniform rushed over to help. Not once, in all my years of living in the Bay Area, have I seen a BART employee help anyone with the ticket machine or the turnstile, or provide any sort of information. Or anything, for that matter. I was always unclear on what they *did* do, exactly. Perhaps they were all mechanics or engineers who kept things humming behind the scenes, but they *never* put tickets into the turnstile.

Safely on the other side, Cookie turned and gave me a tragic smile, then headed down the stairs for the train platform.

Feeling mildly guilty, I assured myself Cookie would throw herself on the mercy of her fellow BART riders and make it home to Oakland without too much trauma.

Just to be sure, I called Dad and told him to expect Cookie's summons from the Fruitvale station.

"You put Cookie on *BART*?"

"Why is everyone so shocked by this concept? I've been negotiating BART since I was in middle school."

"You're a different person from your sister."

Yes. I'd noticed.

Chapter Twelve

Annette had already arrived at Murder House, and was standing by a royal blue sports car.

"Nice car," I said.

"Thanks. It was my present to myself when I turned fifty. Pretty sure it's a middle-aged crisis, but I look so good in it I don't mind the stereotype."

"You're fifty?" I had wondered. Her skin was smooth and unwrinkled, but I could never quite tell; she had an ageless look.

"Fifty-five, actually. It took a few more years to save up. Anyway, you have all your equipment for this walk-through?"

"Yep." I pulled a sports bag out of the back seat of my Scion—which looked decidedly cheap next to her lovely waxed fantasy. "Are Hugh and Simone here already?"

"I called to make sure my presence tonight was all right with Hugh, and Simone said we should get started without them. Given her tone of voice, I'm not one hundred percent sure they'll be showing up at all." She shook her head. "Lord knows I wouldn't want to step foot in a place where I'd seen such horrors."

"I know what you mean. That part seems hard for me to conceive of as well."

I heard the distinctive sound of wheels rolling along a wooden porch.

"Whaddaya doin' at the Murder House?" Monty asked, coming to rest at the end of the porch nearest us.

"Must everyone insist on calling it that?" Annette snapped.

"What else would I call it?" he asked.

"How about 2906? That's the address," Annette responded.

"But there was a man there killed his family," he began. "He—"

"Yes, thank you. I know the story. Why are there lights on?"

"They go on and off all the time. All over the house," said Monty. "I even heard the heater come on from time to time and the sprinklers go off. A person might wonder why. A person might think maybe ghosts were still keeping house."

Inspector Crawford's carefully maintained professional attitude seemed as though it were fraying at the edges. This kind of talk was clearly out of her comfort zone, and though a part of me was still enjoying her discomfiture, the bigger part of me felt compelled to step in.

"A person might *also* think that maybe all those things can be set on timers," I said. "Just a thought."

"So you don't believe in the ghosts? I thought you said—"

"Just because there was a murder doesn't mean there are ghosts necessarily," I said, cutting him off before he could mention what I'd foolishly told him, that I thought I'd seen a face in the window. In fact, I was trying to ignore what I thought I'd seen flickering in the windows, along with the quick little quiver at the front drapes and the fog on the pane as though someone were leaning too close and breathing on the glass.

I was hoping to go in fresh.

Still, given what had happened in that house, there were bound to be some decidedly unhappy, tormented spirits within these walls. And at least one murderous one—not exactly the Dearly Departed Dad of the Year. I hoped Olivier was right—that the ghost of a violent murderer could not kill anyone anymore. He could scare the hell out of you, but he couldn't physically attack.

All this speculation and fearmongering was foolish; I knew that. The only way to deal with ghosts was to be firm in one's resolve and to understand that they can't actually hurt you. Being in their presence is spooky and makes you feel off-kilter, but it's not deadly. At least, I hoped so.

I paused on the front stoop of the Murder House, Inspector Crawford by my side.

"Hugh gave me the key," she whispered, and held it out to me.

"No need to whisper," I whispered in return.

"Then why are *you* whispering?"

I shrugged. "Peer pressure."

On the blue door, surrounded by peeling paint, was the knocker that had caught my attention earlier: a hand holding a ball. I stared at it, thinking of what Rosie had said. I loved these things, but . . . something about it seemed sinister, just resting there up against the door, holding that ball.

"Hey," I said to distract myself. "Now that we're ghost-hunting buddies, may I call you Annette?"

She gave me a snide look but inclined her head slightly. "Sure; why not? But I think we should take it easy on the whole 'ghost-hunting buddy' thing. I'm still a skeptic."

"And yet you're here with me, and we've got a bag of ghost-busting equipment," I wasn't above rubbing it in a little.

"Fine. Whatever. But if you ever breathe a word of this to anyone, I will make you very sorry. Now, I'll hold the EMF dealie. It's cool-looking."

"How do you even know about the EMF dealie?"

"I've been boning up. Watched a marathon of *Ghoul Getters*. Very informative."

"I'll bet."

I unlocked the front door and pushed it in, allowing it to swing wide. It opened with a little puff of air, like a sepulcher. The slight creak of the door didn't help any—it seemed to echo in the abandoned house, site of those long-ago murders.

It smelled rank. Musty, with the still, funereal air common to unopened and unloved homes.

Annette was rattled. So was I, but that wasn't news for me. For this tough homicide inspector, however, it was something rather new.

But, as was my wont, I was immediately distracted by my other profession. In addition to being a ghost buster, I was a general contractor. The architecture immediately grabbed my attention. The lines of the house were beautiful: graceful, asymmetrical, and elongated in the Art Nouveau style. In home building, Art Nouveau was a subset of the Arts and Crafts movement, which was a reaction to the stiff, dark woods and overwrought decorations of the Victorian era. The Arts and Crafts movement ushered in an era of cleaner, more natural lines and, in the case of Art Nouveau, curving lines stylized from recurring motifs taken from the natural world, like lilies, irises, and reeds.

Unfortunately, the interior decoration wasn't Art Nouveau in the least. It was as though we were stepping onto the set of an early-eighties television sitcom, one in which the cast had gone home for the evening, leaving stacks of newspapers and magazines spread out on the low brass-and-glass coffee table. I spied a *People* magazine circa February 1984. Silk ivy and ferns hung from butterfly hooks in the ceiling. Walls were painted ash mauve and dove gray and hunter green. They were colors from the early eighties, and I imagined that had Jean Lawrence not been gunned down by her husband, she might have redecorated soon to keep up with the times.

As Hugh had told me, it was a place frozen in time. Untouched, I presumed, since the murders. In fact, at the bottom of the stairs a patch of tile had been taken up, leaving only the subfloor, rough with chalky gray remnants of mortar. Crime scene cleaners often took out portions of floors or sections of walls that couldn't be cleaned of blood. It looked as though someone couldn't stand to see the results of violence that had seeped into the grout—and who could blame them?

"I can't decide whether I feel more foolish or afraid." Annette interrupted my little trip down architectural lane, and I realized I was supposed to be contemplating long-ago murders and contemporary ghosts, not architectural history.

"Welcome to my world," I said, setting one steel-toed boot-clad foot inside, treading heavily on the inlaid mosaic tiles of the entryway.

Lights were on in the foyer, in the kitchen, and at the landing at the top of the stairs.

Straight ahead of us was a central stairway, there was a hallway to the right, and to either side were openings leading to a parlor in one direction and a dining room in the other. The dining room had a built-in hutch. Light sifted in through the tall windows from a streetlamp, just barely illuminating the room in a gray light.

Annette kept looking over at me, as though expecting me to go into a trance or roll my eyes or some other equally impressive movement that indicated I was in touch with another dimension.

"I can't promise I'll feel or see anything," I said, rubbing the plain gold wedding ring that hung, solid and warm, on a chain around my neck. The ring was a present from my mother, who had inherited it from her own mother. It was the closest thing I had to a rosary. It made me feel connected to my mother, as she had worn it for years before giving it to me, saying it would connect the generations of Turner women.

I concentrated on it, took a deep breath, and tried to send out signals of welcoming and beckoning. Which was a bit of a joke, because the ghosts always appeared to me unbidden, but it was worth a try.

"You can't . . . call them, or something?"

I shook my head. "Hate to disappoint, but I'm not really that kind of medium."

"I thought maybe you were rubbing that ring for a reason."

"You mean, like a genie's bottle?" I teased. "It's not Aladdin's lamp."

"Look," said Annette, compulsively looking behind her. "Once I stepped through the looking glass, I'm open to just about anything."

Annette really was beyond her comfort zone. I reminded myself of just how hard this all was for me—still was—but especially the first couple of times it had happened. And I had the proof of what I was seeing, while this homicide-hardened cop had to take my word for it all.

"The thing is . . . I don't really know what I'm doing. I just sort of hang around and . . . I don't know; it's like the ghosts can sense there's someone who might be able to see or hear them so . . . sometimes things—"

Bam bam bam . . . bam!

Annette and I practically leaped into each other's arms. When the banging stopped, we looked at each other, chagrined, and pulled back in embarrassment.

Before I could say anything, Annette strode to the door, peeked out the eyehole, and then cautiously opened the door while standing to the side.

No one was there.

Annette closed the door and met my eyes. I thought it best not to mention that I had been pushed into the shed, and someone banged on the door four times in exactly that pattern.

"Probably the neighborhood kids," I said. "I met a few of them the other day, when we were working at Monty's house. Actually, you met Kobe, the leader of the baby hoodlums. They're morbidly fascinated with this place, and the tales of yore."

"Little ghouls."

"We were all ghouls at that age, don't you think?" I said as I started to look around the living room. The couches, the piano, a cupboard that held Lenox china figurines. Other than the dust, it could be anyone's home that hadn't kept up with the times. Like the stereotypical Grandma's house. "In fact, the song they were singing was set to the tune of *'Lizzie Borden took an axe. . . .'*"

Annette was doing that one-eyebrow lift thing she did.

"You have a terrible singing voice; you know that?"

"That's not the point. I'm just saying, there's a reason kids like horror movies. I know some people never grow out of it, but a lot of times I think kids like to be scared because they don't really believe bad things can happen. When they grow up and realize just how bad the world can be, the fascination tends to fall away."

"Or sometimes they live out their twisted fantasies, and then people like me have to step in and clean things up."

That was a depressing thought. She was right, I supposed, but *sheesh*. What a hard way to make a living.

Beyond the odd furnishings and the reminders of the tragedy within these walls, the artistic lines of the house called out to me. The entries were a series of arches using flowing Art Nouveau lines, all distinct from one another. The railing on the stair was metal, twisted and free-form in a stylized pattern of flowers and leaves. Everything from the crown molding to the baseboards was just a little different from the norm.

My father would go nuts over this place. In fact, if you stripped out the furniture and wall-to-wall carpet—

which I was certain covered up beautiful floors with, most likely, an inlaid wood design—and redecorated with the relatively simple furniture from the era, this house would be a showcase, a rare example of well-preserved Art Nouveau in a city that favored the Victorian.

The fireplace was perfect. It rose from floor to ceiling, its carved surface a mellow beige marble, asymmetrical and stylized. On the right was a trio of young, long-haired mermaids with graceful, elongated tails. They looked up and to one side, where a young man writhed among the reeds near shore. In the distance was a ship, as though the sailor had been lost. Or had he been found? The wind and rain were indicated by the swirling lines of the carving, everything smooth and curvy.

"The oldest daughter, Bridget, age seventeen, was found right there in front of the fireplace. Bludgeoned with a piece of firewood."

Annette's grim words shook me from my artistic reverie.

"The mother was there, blunt force trauma as well, then shot."

Annette strode back across the front hall and stopped short of the stairs.

"According to the deposition, Linda saw her father standing here, at the bottom of the stairs."

We both stepped back as though afraid of standing on the same spot where he had stood.

I started feeling the sensation of my own breathing, hearing the harsh sound. The beating of my heart seemed to fill the space. I couldn't tell whether it was, indeed, the presence of something else making me feel this way, or if it was my imagination.

I took a step toward the parlor, but Annette was headed for the dining room.

I looked over at her and noticed she was clearly uncomfortable but had a determined set to her face.

Slowly, she turned and flashed her beam toward the kitchen, the light illuminating harvest gold linoleum tiles with a floral design on them. I pointed my beam that way as well, then stood staring.

"You see something?" she asked.

I did. I saw wallpaper that was identical to the paper I had helped my mother put up in one of the houses they renovated, the first one I remember trying to take part in, when I was just a child. A pattern popular in the early eighties. A blue background with little geese on it in bonnets, ribbons around their necks.

"That wallpaper . . . I remember that pattern."

Annette rolled her eyes, thinking I was joking or at the very least focusing on unimportant details. But for some reason, the sight of that and the sudden memory of spending time with my mother sent my mind reeling.

And then I glanced into the reflection on the window and saw a woman.

The image was bluish and faded, like the home movies Hugh had shown me.

It was the mother of the family, Jean Lawrence. On the floor, pushing herself up on one arm, the other reaching up to me . . .

"*Sidney . . . ,*" came the fierce whisper, before it rose to a scream: "No . . . Sidney!"

I whirled around to look at the floor directly. Nothing. Annette watched me with hawk eyes.

My heart pounded; my head pounded. I blew out a breath, shook my head, and then nodded.

"The mother, Jean, was killed here, right?"

She nodded.

Something moved past the passage in the corner of my eye. Great. The first time I'd seen a ghost, I could see it only in my peripheral vision, or occasionally in a mirror or other reflective surface. It drove me nuts. As though seeing spirits weren't crazy enough already, a person had to see them and yet *not* see them, constantly wondering whether there was really anything there.

But my last spectral encounter was different—I saw the ghost as if she were as real as Annette. I had thought maybe my abilities were getting stronger, but Olivier had suggested that in that instance, the spirit's visibility had more to do with the ghost's wanting to be seen or having the power to manifest, rather than with my talents.

I paused and tried to get a handle on myself. Being resolute and centered was among the most important aspects of encountering spirits. They are people, just as we are, and might be confused or scared, angry or threatening, just as they might have been when they were alive, but even more so now that they were in limbo. Having a calm, serene countenance and reaction helped calm them down as well, making the entire interaction much more pleasant.

"You see something?" Annette asked, a slight frown on her otherwise smooth forehead, but at least she was sparing me the raised eyebrow. "The EMF reader is going crazy."

"Maybe," I said, hesitating. Not only did I not want to freak her out, I didn't want to muck up whatever I saw with preconceived notions. I wanted to remain open to whatever came. Like the position and mode of death. It made more sense for me to see, first, and check notes later to see how close I was.

Carefully skirting the area where I had seen the specter, I started up the stairs. An old runner, dirty and matted in spots, was plush mauve with a forest green edging. The fifth stair up squeaked loudly in protest as I stepped on it.

Annette practically jumped out of her skin.

"Just a squeaky tread," I said. "I can fix that, no problem."

"We're not here to renovate the place, but to find . . . ghosts. Or insight into the recent murder, at least."

"I know that," I said with a shrug, "Just saying."

She was still looking over her shoulder, staying as close behind me as decency would allow. She held the EMF reader out like a gun in her left hand, and I noticed her right hovering over the butt of the gun in her waistband.

"Hate to tell you, Inspector, but guns don't do much against ghosts."

"I'm not quite sure what I'm afraid of yet. Ghosts or people. And in my experience, guns do pretty well against people."

She had me there.

Upstairs, we peeked into the bedrooms, each more heartbreaking than the next. A teenage girl's room with a grass green printed bedcover, wallpaper, stuffed animals, trophies, and school albums. A boy's room all in shades of blue, a border of sailboats just under the crown molding. A large casement window led out of a dormer and onto the roof.

Was this the window Linda had led Hugh through on that night? I looked out and imagined what it must have been like to crawl out, escaping one's father in the middle of the night.

I saw occasional flickers and flashes, but not like what I'd seen below with Jean.

To make conversation, I asked Annette about what the children—and others—had insinuated: this empty house was sometimes used as a stage for nefarious activity.

"So you've said that empty houses like this, even in a nice neighborhood, might be used for drug drops? How does that work?" I asked.

"They just need a safe place to stash stuff temporarily, where it won't be found or disturbed. Happens all over the place."

"This isn't exactly a fancy neighborhood, but I'm surprised."

"Don't be. The foreclosure crisis has created a whole new crop of drop locations, even in the suburbs. The other day a friend of mine found a grow house in Blackhawk, of all places."

"Seriously?" Blackhawk was a wildly self-conscious, expensive, elite gated community on the other side of the East Bay Hills. "Blackhawk. Huh. Who knew?"

"You should hear some of my stories. They'd melt your mind."

I stopped my inspection of the bathroom and studied her.

"What?"

"Your vision of the world must be a little . . . twisted."

She appeared to ponder that for a moment, sticking her chin out slightly. "I guess I'll take that. What about *you*? You keep trying to fix up houses and end up finding corpses instead. That's got to do wonders for your worldview."

"I never really thought about it that way."

"I'm just saying, that can't add a lot to your mental health."

"Touché."

Bam bam bam . . . bam!

We both straightened, and our eyes met.

"Hugh would just walk in, right? We didn't lock it, did we?"

I shook my head.

"Let's . . . ignore it for now," continued Annette. "Probably those kids you were talking about."

"Okay. But I think we should go back down, anyway, since that's where the murders occurred."

The very moment I turned to go down the stairs, the overhead light went out.

An apparition appeared at the bottom of the stairs.

Was that Sidney himself? Holding out a gun?

But no, it wasn't a gun, but a flashlight. Simone came up to join him and I realized it wasn't Sidney at all; it was Hugh. Alive and breathing.

"What is it?" he said. "Do you see something?"

"Sorry," I said, shaking it off as we descended the stairs. "For a second, I thought I was looking at your father's ghost."

He nodded gravely.

"He gets that a lot," said Simone. "Linda thought the same thing when she was here that last . . . well, the last time we were here." She sighed and explained: "Hugh sent Linda to one of the best rehab clinics in California, but her counselor said her addiction was her way of trying to deal with past trauma. We were getting her therapy, trying to address the root cause, but not surprisingly, she didn't want to think about that night. We were hoping being in the house would help Linda to face the past, but when she saw Hugh standing here like this, she thought it was that night all over again. It was like PTSD. She panicked."

"Do you think that's what happened?" Hugh asked, looking into his wife's face so intensely, it was as though he knew the truth was there somewhere, if only he could find it.

"I think Linda was a disturbed woman," Simone said, placing her hand on his shoulder and returning his gaze. "You did everything you could for her, Hugh. You and Ray both. No one could have done more. This is all because of your father's actions, no one else's. Remember what the therapist said?"

Hugh nodded and took a deep breath, as though gathering his thoughts.

It was oddly fascinating to watch these two. Simone seemed to play the role of mother as much as mate, but they certainly seemed to care deeply for each other in a relationship that appeared beyond the norm. I supposed someone like Hugh would require a special kind of love. In fact, it was hard to imagine him romancing anyone, taking the time to court or even respond to another person's advances.

But then, as was pointed out to me so often, I was no expert in the field of romance.

Our foursome continued on the tour of the house, and Simone and Hugh suggested upgrades and renovations they'd like to see. By and large, the ghosts were still. I caught glimpses of movement in my peripheral vision, a sense of yearning, but no one spoke to me. Not that I really expected them to. In my experience, ghosts were pretty fickle about when they decided to make contact. Usually, they waited until particularly inopportune times.

Or maybe there were simply too many people here. If I was truly brave, I thought, I would come back all alone.

Nope. Not that brave.

Simone kept pulling swatches and samples out of her bag; I had no idea where she had managed to dig up such relics. There was a lot of blue with ducks, little diamonds, mauve and green and ferns. When she wasn't doing that, she was fiddling with the control panels in each room and synching them with her handheld electronic devices.

"Uh-huh, looking good . . ." She had a habit of talking to herself that I personally would find very difficult to live with. I talked to myself from time to time, sure, but usually I was actually talking to ghosts that no one else could see, so that didn't really count. But then I noticed her husband whispering something under his breath while stroking dusty curtains. I guess I cut him more slack because I assumed he was writing award-winning poetry in his mind, whereas for all I knew, he was crafting his grocery list.

Bam bam bam . . . Bam!

Then came more noises. And a thumping.

Annette swore under her breath. "Dammit, those kids are getting on my nerves."

"At least they knock," said Hugh. "Kids these days just walk in. A person's house is his castle; people should knock. Don't you think?"

He gazed at me for a long moment, until I realized that this wasn't a rhetorical question.

"Sure I do," I said. "I'm all for knocking."

"Wait," said Annette. "Do y'all hear that?"

Hugh looked vague and distracted, as per usual. Simone shrugged and shook her head. Clearly, this wasn't something she'd dealt with before.

Faint voices, as though whispering. Another thump. And . . . the smell of smoke.

Okay . . . this just got interesting.

As we turned down the little hallway behind the kitchen, we realized the sounds and the smells were emanating from the basement.

Carefully, we crept down the small staircase off the kitchen to the lower level: me first, then Annette, with Hugh and Simone bringing up the rear. As in Monty's house, the lower floor wasn't a basement per se, in that it was above ground at the lower backyard level.

At the bottom of the stairs was a closed door. There was light showing through the cracks. And then more noises . . . was that *chanting*?

Annette glanced at me as though I had a clue. Unfortunately, though she was a smart woman, she was off base in this one.

I made an exaggerated "no idea" shrug, hands palm-up.

She looked impatient, and I wondered whether she was considering turning me in for a more useful ghost buster on her next otherworldly case.

Annette held her gun up and at the ready. She put her back against the wall on one side of the door, and I mimicked her on the other, feeling like I was enacting every cop show I'd ever seen on TV.

Behind us, Simone and Hugh clutched each other. She was as tall as he, and held his head to her shoulder, patting him as though comforting a child.

Annette looked at me and telegraphed her intent, mouthing "on three" and holding up three fingers. She counted down: *One, two . . . three.*

Then she flung the door open.

Chapter Thirteen

At least ten teenagers sat in a circle on the floor. Dressed to a one in black, with heavy pale makeup and black eyeliner. There were candles everywhere, and a pentagram had been drawn in chalk in the center of a circle of salt. A Ouija board sat in front of them.

For a couple of seconds everyone froze, and you could hear a pin drop.

A bunch of teenagers were a lot less scary than encountering Sidney Lawrence's murderous ghost. Especially with an SFPD inspector at my side, with firepower.

"Seriously?" I said. "A Ouija board?"

But then Annette holstered her gun. As soon as she did, the kids bolted, scattering like rats on a sinking ship.

"Stop! Police!" ordered Annette, to no effect. They tore out the basement door, and one or two jumped through an open window.

One young woman, with hair dyed a sooty black, was shoved to the floor by one of her less-than-gentlemanly companions in his quest for escape. Before she could get back up, I put my boot-clad foot, gently but firmly, right between her shoulder blades. Meanwhile, Annette ran outside after the little miscreants.

"I hate it when my criminal cronies leave me behind for the police while they run away, don't you?" I asked my prisoner.

The young woman under my boot wriggled and swore a blue streak. I was unfazed. When it came to grumpy teens, like cantankerous old men, I wasn't easily moved.

Simone and Hugh lingered in the doorway, eyes wide and mouths agape. Annette came back a few moments later, winded and empty-handed.

"I caught one," I said proudly. "She's a wriggler."

Annette locked eyes with me, apparently questioning my methods of prisoner detainment. I shrugged and lifted my foot.

The girl stood, dusting dirt from her black lace top and ripped black skirt. Black boots and leather cuffs completed the look. I couldn't see the point in making sure the black was dust free, though; given the overall gestalt of the outfit, I thought the dirt fit in rather well. I told her so.

Her response was "Screw you."

"What is all this?" I asked. "What were you kids doing here? Don't you know breaking and entering is against the law?"

"I thought *I* would be the one to ask the questions," Annette interrupted, though her tone was decidedly amused. "What with me having the police badge and all."

"Be my guest." I stood back and made a sweeping gesture, like I was being gracious, allowing her to ask the questions of the nonghosts.

"Name," demanded Annette.

"Raven."

Of course, I thought.

"*Real* name."

The girl was cowed by Annette's laser cop eyes.

"Rhonda. Rhonda Andersen."

"ID?"

She shook her head.

"Address."

The girl gave her an address not far from there.

"What do you know about this place?"

"Some guy murdered his family here a long time ago."

I glanced over at Hugh, but his expression was as flat as always.

"And?"

"And, like, the anniversary's totally coming up and . . . they say the ghosts will be here, and we could, like, make contact with them."

"And did you?"

The girl looked at Annette, clearly stunned that this cop wasn't challenging the idea of talking to ghosts.

"Um . . . no."

"You're sure?"

I wondered about mixing the Ouija board with adolescent hormones. Olivier had once told me it was a recipe for poltergeist activity. But what I'd seen earlier was no poltergeist.

"Have you been here before?"

She shrugged. "A coupla times. We don't really hurt anything . . ."

Except for leaving trash, and the knowledge that people were conducting creepy séances in your basement, I thought. Then again, I was considering holding a creepy séance that Friday.

"The owners might have a thing or two to say about that." I looked back, but Hugh and Simone were nowhere to be seen.

"It's abandoned," said Raven. "There are no owners. Just the . . . ghosts."

"Have you ever seen this person?"

Annette brought out a photo of Linda Lawrence, clearly taken in better days.

Rhonda-Raven nodded. "She was here a few days ago."

"She was? Did you talk with her?"

"She chased us out, just like you. She was kind of, like, weird."

"In what way?"

"It was sort of, like, at first we thought she was a ghost, but then we realized that she couldn't even like, walk through walls? But then she started throwing things at us and telling us that her family had died here and that it was a shrine, not, like, a trailer park." I heard a gasp from Hugh from behind us, but we all ignored it.

Raven continued. "I'm not sure where the trailer park thing came in. Was she calling us trailer trash?"

Annette shrugged. "Then what happened?"

"Nothing, really. We all ran away, just like tonight. Except that time, no one totally *stood* on me." She cast a glare in my direction.

"If I had *stood* on you, you wouldn't be breathing right now." I had at least fifty pounds on the girl. "I showed a great deal of restraint."

Raven twisted her mouth and shrugged.

"So that was it?" Annette clarified. "You didn't see anyone else, and Linda didn't say anything else?"

"Nah. But I guess she was the lucky one, right? She was the girl who jumped out the window."

Yes. Linda was the lucky one.

"You want to tell me what the hell that was all about?" demanded Annette as we settled into a booth at a nearby café that served wine and beer—I had wine, she had beer.

Annette had taken Raven home and talked to her parents while I waited outside. I could only imagine the rousing "come to Jesus" speech Annette delivered with the intent to intimidate and ensure cooperation.

"I don't think they meant any real harm. Kids today—well, I think they're dealing with a level of alienation and—"

"Yes, thank you, Oprah. I wasn't looking for a bleeding-heart liberal explanation of why teenagers are little creeps."

"Okaaaay," I said, thinking that Inspector Crawford might need a vacation. Even considering her normally high-handed disposition, she seemed a little lacking in patience lately. "Then what were you asking?"

"I'm sorry. I apologize. Believe it or not, I actually *like* kids. But . . . I'm feeling a little on edge." She leaned closer to me, her elbows on the table. "The truth is, I'm feeling a lot of pressure to close this case. The medical examiner is saying overdose, that there's no sign of homicide. So it really should be open-and-shut. But my gut . . ." She shook her head and sipped her beer.

"There's something about this scenario," I said with a nod. "It's all so wrenching. That Linda should have saved herself and her brother, but then die like this . . ."

Annette nodded. "Exactly. So okay, that's exactly what I'm thinking: I can't get past the thought that this death has to do with the double murder suicide, even though that crime was forever ago. So that's what I want to know: What did you see in that house tonight?"

"It's a little hard to explain. It's not like I'm seeing something coherent and clear, at least not usually." I thought back on a little girl ghost I had met who had seemed just as real as Annette sitting across the table. But in my limited experience, that little girl ghost was an anomaly. "I get images, flickers of things happening, a lot of time in reflective surfaces like mirrors or windows."

"And at the Lawrence house? Did you see anything?"

I nodded. "I thought I saw the mother at the bottom of the stairs. Reaching up, as though begging for her life. Saying, 'Please, Sidney.' "

"Anything else?"

I shook my head. "That was about the extent of it. I felt the presence of spirits but didn't see or hear anything concrete."

We sat in silence for a moment, both of us nursing our drinks and lost in our thoughts.

"But there was the banging," I said. "I don't think it was the kids. There's something about the knocker on the front door, something that really bothers me."

"The knocker?"

I shrugged. "Maybe it's just symbolic of something. But . . . there's something I should tell you. The day after we found Linda, I snooped a little."

"Well, I'm flabbergasted. You? Snooping?"

"Funny. As I was saying, I felt compelled to look around a little in the shed where we found her."

"And did you see something there?"

"Not really. I thought I felt something, though, and I heard whistling. And then I was shoved from behind and locked in, and the banging started, just like when you and I were in the house. *Bam, bam, bam . . . bam.* Always the same pattern."

"Did you see who shoved you?"

I shook my head.

"Can ghosts shove?" asked Annette.

"I don't think so. I was assuming someone real pushed me in and locked the door, but maybe the ghosts were trying to tell me something."

"But we have no idea what."

I shook my head. We sat for a long moment in silence, nursing our drinks and pondering the situation.

"I like you, Mel. But as far as this ghost whisperer thing goes? You're a little lacking."

"Tell me about it."

On Wednesday, I was supposed to pick up Graham from the San Francisco airport at eleven a.m.

I woke up early, as usual, but under the watchful, curious eyes of Dog, I donned and then abandoned one outfit after another. One of the things I liked about my style was that usually I didn't have to think much. I just pulled on the next dress in the closet.

Usually. But *usual* did not apply today, because of a *boy*. As was often the case when it came to romance, I immediately regressed to about age fourteen.

Graham was tall and handsome and inexplicably patient with me and my moods. He was also a darned good "green" contractor who was making something of a name for himself among the rich and environmentally aware. This meant he worked in Marin County a lot, the local haven for liberal folks who drove hybrids and ate organic and spent the equivalent of a small nation's gross national product on making their homes as environmentally and technically advanced as possible.

My father loved Graham. Stan loved Graham. Caleb loved Graham. Graham was good to my dog and nice to old people. There wasn't a darned thing wrong with him, which made me very nervous. I mean, really, this was San Francisco. You didn't run across unmarried, un-gay, un-crazy men very often. One who was also attractive and employed?

A man like Graham was so rare Luz referred to him as my "San Francisco unicorn."

There must be something seriously wrong with him. I just hadn't figured it out yet.

And now Cookie was in town. And I had to figure out how to dress so I looked alluring but not like I got dressed up for him, which would give him the wrong impression. Didn't want to look like I was trying too hard.

Speaking of trying too hard: If I parked and met him inside at security, it would seem overeager. But pulling up to the curb meant going up against the ever-vigilant airport curbside parking Nazis, who seemed to imagine anyone slowing to more than a rolling stop was trying to blow the place up. So if he wasn't there when I drove by, I'd have to circle, which meant he'd come out and I wouldn't be there, and then what would he think?

These were the thoughts that had kept me up half the night. I was pretty sure I was sublimating, fretting over details like these because I was actually worried about my relationship with Graham. Not that there *was* a relationship. Not really.

I finally decided on a short peacock blue shift with

waves of spangles, but I drew a plain, thigh-length cream-colored sweater on over it. I did my regular makeup routine, but more carefully than usual, and took extra time putting up my hair in a carefully casual chignon.

Down in the kitchen, Cookie was chatting with Dad and Stan. All the years she lived here, she slept in until all hours. Now she was an early bird. I used to think it was because Dad and I were in construction that we awoke so early, but maybe it ran in the genes.

"Hey there, babe," said Dad as he handed me a cup of coffee, eyes flicking over my outfit but saying nothing, as was his wont. He didn't get my style, but he let it pass because I had threatened to walk away from the business if he didn't stop making comments.

"Mornin', gorgeous," said Stan.

"Well, don't you look pretty?" Cookie said. "You know, I like how you wear what you want, no matter that you carry a few extra pounds. I really admire that."

My sister, queen of the backhanded compliment.

"I see you made it home from scary BART in one piece," I said in a snide sibling voice. I really *was* fourteen.

"It turns out the BART train is lovely," said Cookie. "And the sweetest young fellow helped me find my stop."

"Isn't Graham flying in today?" asked Dad.

I coughed on a swallow of coffee. Hacking over the sink, I nonetheless saw Cookie and Dad exchange a significant look.

"*What?*" I demanded.

"Nothing," said Cookie, wide-eyed.

I looked at Stan, who just shrugged.

"Is he coming to dinner?"

"Maybe. I'm not sure. I'll let you know," I said, filling my commuter mug. "Dad, I'm going to leave Dog home with you today."

"How come you insisted on taking him yesterday, when I was in the car with you?" Cookie whined.

"All right, all right, I'll take him." On second thought, I could use his distraction when I picked up Graham. "Come on, Dog."

I spent the rest of the morning working with a single-mindedness born of nervousness, then headed to SFO. I decided to play my luck with the curbside pickup, and lo and behold, Graham was walking out of the double doors right as I was pulling up. Like we'd planned it.

Graham had the tall, athletic build of a man who knew his way around a construction site. He had dark hair, deep, searching eyes, and enough ruggedness and scars to speak to an interesting life.

He threw his small bag in the back, then climbed into the passenger seat. I inhaled deeply. Graham also managed to smell really, really good . . . even when stepping off an airplane from the East Coast.

I started to pull back into traffic, but he stopped me with a hand on my arm and a smile so warm it lit up the car.

"*Hey*. How about a welcome-home kiss?"

I glanced out the window, where the cop was walking toward us.

"The cops want us to go."

"They understand a welcoming kiss. Trust me."

I leaned over, intending to give him a quick peck. Predictably, it turned into something much more, much deeper. I forgot myself for a moment, reveling in the feel and scent of him, as I tended to do whenever we kissed.

Graham was the first one to pull back. He smiled at me and let out a loud sigh.

"Guess you're right; we'd better go before things get out of hand. The cops might not be *that* understanding."

I pulled away from the curb, concentrating on negotiating the congested airport arrivals area.

"So, have you thought about what we were talking about before I left?" asked Graham. This was the real question I had dreaded. I was hoping he might have forgotten somehow. This was the reason, I was pretty sure, why I kept obsessing about my wardrobe and whether to park or do curb pickup. I'm pretty good at self-deflection.

"Um . . . I've been really busy."

I stared straight ahead, but I could feel the heat of his intense gaze on my profile.

"Ghosts?" he asked.

What was I, a billboard? First Raul, now Graham. How did everyone know just by looking at me?

Finally, I shrugged. "It seems to be what I do."

"I thought you did home renovation."

"The ghosts seem to have other ideas."

"Is this why you've been avoiding my calls?"

"I wouldn't say *avoiding*, exactly . . ." He was right; I had been avoiding them. Maybe Cookie and I shared more than I'd like to admit.

"*Please* tell me there's been no body count this time."

I didn't answer as I maneuvered the tricky series of shifting lanes and ramps that led back toward the freeway.

Graham blew out an exasperated breath.

"It had nothing to do with me this time, nothing at all. Also, I'm getting a little sick of having to explain myself all the time. *I* don't know why this keeps happening to me. Maybe I'm like a death magnet or something. It's not like I have much control over the situation."

"I don't suppose you would consider leaving this to the police?"

"For your information, this time the police *asked* for my help. Inspector Annette Crawford, remember her?"

Now it was Graham's turn to be silent. He looked out the window onto the nothingness of this stretch of freeway, a sea of strip malls and identical-looking houses marching up the hills of Daly City and South San Francisco. Tourists are sometimes fooled into thinking SFO is located in San Francisco, but in fact it lies many miles to the south, in Burlingame. The ride to the city from the airport can take half an hour, or much more, depending on traffic. And the worst is that from this angle, San Francisco sneaks up on you rather than rising up like a world-class city. This would explain, I imagined, why so many movies show people arriving in San Francisco over the gloriously filmable Golden Gate Bridge, which in fact heads north, to Marin County.

"How was your trip?" I asked to change the subject. "Did you learn all sorts of new green techniques with which to torture me and my crew?"

Graham's latest client was a mysterious, reclusive, extraordinarily wealthy fellow who was planning on reconstructing an entire small monastery he was shipping over from Scotland piece by piece. He had sent Graham to a green convention in Boston to learn new techniques to adapt the historic building to modern life.

"Yes, because my life is all about torturing you. Like, for instance, I'd like to know what's going on with you and the ghosts and the body."

"It's a little complicated—"

"As usual."

"Yes, as usual. So, I was doing my community project last weekend, as you know—speaking of which, this is actually great timing, because I have to go back this weekend and finish up. Would you be willing to come with me? I sure could use some skilled labor on the site."

"Of course I will. In fact, I'm not sure I'll let you out of my sight for a while, and certainly not around ghosts and bodies."

"Only one body."

"So far."

"Anyway, a volunteer found a body in an outbuilding. She had been dead for a while before we arrived, so we weren't implicated in any way."

"And the ghosts?"

"They're in the neighboring house." And possibly the shed. But I was going to let that one slide.

"What do the neighbors' ghosts have to do with anything?"

"The outbuilding may have been on their land, officially. And the deceased, Linda Lawrence, grew up in the house, and when she was just a kid, she witnessed her father kill her mother there."

Graham swore under his breath. "I'm still not getting why you're involved."

"I told you, I was officially asked by a member of SFPD to investigate. A little."

"You mean you weren't planning on looking into it yourself?"

"Not really." Again, I thought about going into the shed. And the fact that I met with Hugh, and couldn't seem to leave the story alone. "Okay, maybe I would have. Probably I would have eventually given in to curiosity and looked through the house. Those ghosts are calling me, Graham. I think they need something from me."

"And you're going to respond, even if it means putting yourself in danger?"

"Like I said, I'm getting tired of explaining myself."

Twenty minutes of clipped, overly polite conversation later, I dropped Graham off at his place. He didn't invite me in.

Chapter Fourteen

I wasn't far from Monty's house. I figured I might as well stop by and see if it would be convenient for him if I came to finish up the ramp tomorrow afternoon, assuming my schedule stayed clear.

Also, given that Stan had shared some misgivings about my Neighbors Together client, I wanted the chance to talk to him with those things in mind. There were a few things Monty had said or done over the last few weeks that seemed off to me, too. It was worth a visit without the pressure of construction around us.

Monty answered my knock on the door, as he most often did, with a book in his lap. He invited me in, and we chatted for a moment about the unfinished work on his house. Then he changed the subject.

"Have you ever read any of Hubert Lawrence's poetry?" Monty held up a small green volume.

Twisted Memories: A Life Forged from Fire.

"I thought you were more of a nonfiction guy."

"I'm trying to branch out. And after everything that's happened ... I dunno. I guess that whole family's on my mind. I read this a long time ago, when I first moved in. Etta gave it to me."

"Do you like it?"

He shrugged. "It's a little ... raw. Especially when you know it comes from real life. Especially when you live right next to the freakin' Murder House."

I nodded.

"You know," Monty continued, "Etta told me the whole story when I moved in a coupla years ago, and how Hugh Lawrence was this famous poet. She said he wrote about what had happened, that his heart was still broken from it, but that it made good literature. Doesn't that seem like kind of a weird thing to say?"

"A little. She probably didn't mean anything by it."

"I wish I'd known he was actually going to be working on my house! I would have loved for him to have signed it."

"I have the sense he'll be around more. I'm sure you haven't missed your chance for an autograph."

"I guess that's true. I've seen him once or twice in front of the Murder House."

"What does he do when he comes here, do you know?"

"Just looks around, I guess. That's how I met Ray—he was with him one time. His wife, Simone, comes a lot."

"Simone comes a lot without Hugh?"

"Not 'a lot', exactly. But she's come through a few times with a Realtor, looking it over."

"Are they planning on selling it?"

"I guess. I mean, if you were Hugh's wife, wouldn't you want to get rid of the place? I don't even understand . . . why would anyone who had gone through something like that want to be in that house again?"

"I think he's using it as a sort of catharsis. I guess exposure therapy can be useful sometimes."

"And that's what they were trying to do with the sister?"

"I guess so. I'm not really clear on the details, myself. But then, I've never been through something like that. I imagine the trauma sticks with you. Poor Linda."

I watched him carefully, but unlike some people I knew, I wasn't much of a human lie detector. I knew this about myself. I had been fooled too many times.

Something occurred to me. "Last weekend you assured me the Murder House was vacant, full only of ghosts."

"That's true. I mean, every once in a while somebody stops by, but they don't live there. All's I'm saying is that if they want to sell that house, now's the time to get it fixed up so they can sell it when the new research campus goes in."

"What new research campus?"

"They're building right down there at the bottom of the hill. They say all our houses are going to double in value. Or maybe not double, but increase, that's for sure."

"*You're* not planning on selling, are you? After we just fixed up your house?"

He looked decidedly guilty. "No, of course not. That would be scummy, right?"

"Yes, it would be," I said, unconvinced.

"So, you're coming back tomorrow afternoon?" Monty said. I got the feeling he wanted to be rid of me.

"I'm going to try, if my schedule stays clear and I can get some help. I'll let you know."

Outside, I noticed Etta was working in her new vegetable garden. She leaned on her cane with one hand and dropped seeds to the tilled earth with the other. The process was slow and laborious, but even from a distance I could hear her humming to herself.

I crossed the street to join her.

"Hello, Mel! Beautiful day, isn't it?"

"Lovely," I said with a smile. "Could I give you a hand?"

"Oh, no, I'm fine," she said. "Thank you for the offer, but you've already done so much."

I looked at the vacant lot and wondered why it had remained empty for so long.

"Could I ask you something? Have you heard something about property values rising with a new research campus being built nearby?"

"Oh, I've heard the rumors," she scoffed. "But you know, these houses are worth a pretty penny anyway. San Francisco's an expensive place these days."

"True."

She waved a hand in the air. "Not that it matters to me anyway. What am I going to do—sell this place and move to a tropical island? What in the world would I do there?"

Etta's laugh was infectious. I smiled. She was right; it was hard to imagine her anywhere but here amid her things.

"Who owns this lot now, do you know?"

"I have no idea," said Etta. "Do you think it's terrible I'm using it? It seems a waste, just sitting here all these years. Perhaps the original family still owns it, but doesn't want to sell for some reason?"

"You said it was the site of the, um, 'drug house'?"

"Yes, Joe Jacobsen was the name of the owner. We were friendly enough at first, but he got worse the more he drank. Gerry and I had a few altercations with him over the years, but we made sure our fence was strong and ignored him, mostly. The saddest part was that he let his kids run wild. I knew a couple of them from school and tried to intervene, but there really wasn't much I could do. It was sad to see them grow up like that."

"What happened to the children, do you know?"

"The oldest was shot and killed in a gang-related shooting before he was eighteen. The middle wound up over in San Quentin, and the youngest eventually disappeared, but he was already on drugs, so who knows?"

"You mentioned the other day that Sidney Lawrence was fighting with Joe Jacobsen. Do you know what about?"

She nodded. "Sidney wanted Joe to rein in his second boy, Dave. He was worried that Dave was a bad influence on his daughter Linda."

"Dave's the one in prison now?"

She nodded. "A guest of the state, as they say. He was . . . well, I always felt bad about Dave. I truly believe he had a good heart, but there was no denying that he was dealing drugs. Attracting all sorts of characters to the neighborhood. It only takes one bad apple to destroy the sense of a place, and this whole block went from being a family-focused, friendly area to one where there were petty thefts, screeching tires at night, that sort of thing. Even the occasional gunshot."

"That must have been terrible to live with."

"It was. Gerry was not happy; I'll tell you that much. But our kids were already grown and gone, and we both worked so much, we weren't around that much for the drama. And it's possible we were more tolerant than some of our other neighbors."

"Like Sidney."

She leaned on her spade and shrugged. "When he and Jean found out that Dave was friendly with their daughter Linda, well . . . They found Linda with a joint one day and blamed it on Dave. And let's face it—it was very likely she bought it from him. So Sidney had words with Dave, and then with Joe."

"Did they respond at all?"

"They responded by harassing him more. The kids used to go bang that front door knocker all the time, just for fun. Now kids still do—they seem to think the place is haunted and they dare one another to run up and bang on the door."

The sound of the knocker reverberated through my head, sending chills up my spine. The way it echoed through the closed-up house . . .

"So, if Sidney and Joe were feuding, are you suggesting . . . that Sidney had something to do with Joe's house burning down and that Dave or his father went over that night and killed everyone in retaliation?"

"Oh, good heavens, no! Dave may have been dealing drugs, and he was running wild, but he has a good heart. I go visit him a few times a year, just to keep connected."

"Visit him? In San Quentin?"

"When I go up to the firing range. It's right there."

"The firing range is right next to the prison? Doesn't that seem . . . dangerous?"

"I don't see why. A lot of the guards practice there." Etta smiled and leaned toward me conspiratorially. "I'd wanted to go inside San Quentin prison for years. I was dying of curiosity, driving past it all the time. Is that terrible of me to say? When I'd heard that Dave was there, I thought I should go visit, for old times' sake. The cards were stacked against him from the start. Another kind of family, things would have been very different for him. He was always decent to me, caring in his own way. I can't blame young people for the sins of their fathers."

"Speaking of fathers . . . do you think Dave's father, Joe, could have done it?"

"Joe might just have been mean enough to go after the Lawrences, especially after the house burned. But frankly, he was so far gone by then, I don't think he could have managed. He had jaundice, the shakes, the whole nine yards. He passed away from liver failure not three months later."

I called Inspector Crawford to see if she had an update on Linda's case that she was willing to share with me and, more to the point, whether we were officially allowed to go back in the yard to finish the job on the weekend. The kind folks who had volunteered—including the fraternity boys—should have as much notice as possible; they hadn't signed up for two weekends in a row, after all. Plus, we needed to arrange for yet another Port o' Potty and Dumpster, and make sure the insurance was still in place.

"Yes, I'll be releasing the scene today. You are free to go back to work on Monty's house any time. In fact, that girl we caught? What was it, Crow?"

"Raven."

"Right. Knew it was a black bird of some type. Anyway, I scared her and told her she had to do community service with you at Monty's house tomorrow."

"Tomorrow?"

"I just got off the phone with Monty—he said you said you'd be working there tomorrow afternoon."

"I mentioned it was a possibility, but I didn't promise ..."

"How about you make it happen? I figured maybe Raven would learn a thing or two about giving back to her neighbors; I even told her she'd get extra credit for any other juvenile delinquents she might drag along with her, so with luck you might have a few volunteers of the Goth variety working with you. Let me know if she shows up, will you? Hope that's okay."

Funny thing about people who didn't manage volunteers was that they always assumed the more volunteers the better, which was actually almost never the case. If volunteers had no skills, much less a willingness to work, they were far more trouble than they were worth. Still, I reminded myself, a big part of the Neighbors Together philosophy was training people in basic skills and, like Annette pointed out, teaching them how good it could feel to contribute to their communities.

"Okay, I'll keep an eye out for her and any hooligan friends who might show up. Thanks."

"Also ... this is a little ... unconventional, but would you like to go talk to a man in Martinez with me this afternoon?"

"Um ... what kind of man?"

"The original inspector on the Lawrence family murders."

"Does he have information pertinent to Linda's death?"

"Not sure. That's why I wanted to talk with him. It's a long shot, but listening to his memories of the case might trigger something. You never know."

"This is one of the stranger things I've heard myself say . . . but yes, I'd love to go to Martinez to talk to a man about a mass murder. Thank you for thinking of me."

We agreed to meet at three at the Fourth Street parking lot in Berkeley. In the meantime, since I hadn't had much luck getting through to a human at Neighbors Together on the phone, I decided to stop by the office and let the staff know, in person, what had happened last weekend and about the change in plans.

Chapter Fifteen

There is something decidedly undignified about a grown woman begging for a Port o' Potty.

"I'm sorry, Mel," said Jennifer, the largely ineffectual director of the program. "But our budget just doesn't extend to—"

"I understand, Jennifer; I got that part the first couple of times." I knew she was vastly underpaid and even more well meaning—and *I* sure as heck didn't want her job—so I was trying to rein in my impatience. "But as you know, we didn't use up the entire weekend, so surely there was some leftover time? How can I finish up the project without a Dumpster and a Port o' Potty?"

"I can pay for it," said Ray Buckley from the doorway.

"I hate to ask for you to pony up more money, Ray," I said as I turned to him. His suit was wrinkled, as though he'd slept in it—but then I studied his face, which looked as though he hadn't slept for days, besuited or otherwise. "You've already done so much."

"The point is to fix up Monty's house, right? He is obviously in need, and I can give more. In fact, that's why I stopped by, to drop off a check for further projects."

"That's very generous of you," said Jennifer, "but we really can't take your money for Monty's house. The way our program is structured, all the money coming in now goes toward next year's budget—"

"Never mind; I can arrange for them on my own," I said, conceding defeat.

"And I'll pay for them," said Ray. "Seriously, a lot of us would like to do more good in this world. Projects like Neighbors Together have given me an outlet for just that. I don't have a lot of time, but I have money that I'd like put to good use."

"Thank you," I said. "That would be wonderful. I'll just ask you to foot the bill for the rentals. It won't amount to too much."

For that matter, I thought, I could have paid for the rentals through Turner Construction and written it off as a charitable expense, but I had thought Neighbors Together might be able to arrange for a special deal. Still, since Ray seemed so determined to complete his good deed for the year, I decided to let him do so. Ultimately, he was right: If you're wealthy, it's easier to give money than time.

Ray handed Jennifer an envelope with the check he'd already written to the program, and she invited him to come back in the fall, look through the files of eligible projects, and decide where he'd like his money to go.

"That makes it more personal," she said. "Otherwise, I'll just put it in the general fund."

"That's fine," said Ray. "Thank you, again, for all you do."

"You should come in early, too, Mel, and pick out your client for next year!" said Ashley, the recruiter who'd gotten me into this whole mess months ago.

"Um, yeah, maybe," I mumbled. It seemed to me a faux pas not to let volunteers forget their trauma before suggesting they come again next year. I had decided volunteering for a project like this one was like childbirth. You might need a few months to forget the pain and decide to do it again.

Ray and I walked out into a sunny but cool afternoon, where the breeze was carrying a slight stench from a stack of shiny black garbage bags spilling their dubious contents onto the street. Like a lot of nonprofits, Neighbors Together had its offices in a "transitional"—by which they really meant gritty—part of town, in the neighborhood dubbed "Dogpatch." There were a lot of artists' lofts and industrial arts groups that had found refuge here from the city's astronomical rents, and following them came cafés and restaurants. So it was a neighborhood in transition, but it was nevertheless notable for its urban grime.

"Could I buy you a cup of coffee, Ray?" As thank-yous went it was a meager offer, but it was a little too early in the day for a stiff drink, which is what he looked like he needed. He was gazing off down the street, a vague look on his face that reminded me of Hugh.

After what felt like a token protest, Ray agreed. I let Dog out of the car, put him on a leash, and we all walked to one of my favorite nearby restaurants, called It's For You. I tied Dog to the lamppost, where he had his choice of sun or shade and where I could keep an eye on him from the window.

"I'm telling you, I'm not a big one for breakfast foods

of any type," I said, "but they've got New Orleans–style beignets and strong, chicory-laced coffee here. A person could go far on food like that."

Ray smiled halfheartedly, taking his seat at a table next to the window overlooking Twenty-third Street.

We both ordered coffee, and I asked for an order of beignets over Ray's protests that his waistline would suffer.

"Seriously," I said. "These things are made fresh and then doused in powdered sugar. You really shouldn't live in San Francisco without having these once a year or so."

"I just can't stop thinking about . . . everything," Ray said, bringing an abrupt halt to my chatter about sugar-laden fried foods. He shook his head as he added cream and sugar to his coffee, stirring with one hand and with the other rubbing his knee absentmindedly.

"I'm so sorry about Linda," I began. "And I feel terrible that you had to learn about it like you did."

He shook his head. "It was upsetting, but hardly surprising. I know how harsh that sounds, but . . . Linda never managed to find a way to cope with what had happened. I felt so helpless through the years, never knowing what to say, how to help her move on."

"She was lucky to have people who cared about her," I said. "Hugh, and you. You can't . . ." What was I supposed to say? How would I feel if Caleb had suffered a similar trauma, and I couldn't help him get over it? Helpless. Heartbroken. Guilty. "You can only do so much," I finally finished lamely.

The beignets arrived, drowned in snowy powdered sugar, the sweet aroma wrapping around us like a fragrant shawl. I realized with a start that I hadn't thought of escaping to Paris when ordering the French delicacies.

Was this an indication of personal growth, or had I simply been too distracted by the resounding notes of sadness and resigned defeat in Ray's voice?

Neither of us moved to serve ourselves.

"'You never get used to what grief feels like,'" said Ray at long last. "That's what one of the therapists told me. You might make accommodations for it, adapt to it in order to survive, but you never get used to it. I guess Linda never was able to adapt; she seemed to live mired in it, day after day."

"You took in both Linda and Hugh after ... after what happened?"

"Just Hugh. Linda wanted to leave town, so she chose to live with her aunt in Palo Alto. I thought it was a good idea for the kids to remain in the neighborhood, to face their fears ... I don't know whether it was the right decision or not, in the long run. I'm not sure how happy Hugh is, ultimately."

"But at least he loses himself in his poetry, and his art contributes to other people's lives."

"Whereas Linda just lost herself in booze and drugs. I guess that's why Hugh was so hell-bent on exposing her to the house, like exposure therapy. He thought if she could face things ... But I guess it was all too late. She was determined to destroy herself, and she finally managed."

He played with the spoon, then continued.

"Do you know, it was one of the sweetest moments in my life when Hugh stopped correcting people when they assumed I was his father? I've never had children, so when he started calling me Dad ..." There were tears in his eyes. "I'm sorry; I'm not usually emotional. It's just ... that was such a hard time for him, for all of us. But he made it through — he didn't know his own strength. None of us do until we're tested. Not to change the subject, but . . . how well do you know Monty?"

"Just through the program. You probably know him better than I, since you're familiar with the neighborhood."

"I only saw him by chance when I was at Hugh and Linda's house once. But . . ." There was a long silence; Ray seemed to be pondering his next words. "I don't know how to ask, but does he strike you as a drug user?"

"I really don't know," I said.

"I thought he might have had pain pills, given his injuries . . ."

Our eyes met and held.

"I apologize," he said, sitting up and shaking it off. "I don't mean to insinuate . . . You know what? I'm going to let the police do their work and stay out of it. It's just that it's so personal, it's hard not to look for someone to blame."

He pushed up the sleeve of his nice wool suit and checked the time.

"I'm afraid I have to run," he said. "I have an appointment for a therapeutic massage."

"Everything okay?"

"Take my advice: Never get old. I gave up drinking and smoking decades ago, became a health nut. But there's no getting around age. Between my sciatica and this damned knee . . . somehow I thought surgery would solve all my problems, but it's never that easy."

"That's what my dad said — he had a knee replacement a few years ago, and I think it was the physical therapy afterward that nearly did him in."

"Listen to me complain, when we're talking about

Linda. . . ." He shook his head, his sadness palpable. "I'm so much luckier than most."

I forced a smile and watched him leave.

The beignets grew cold, untouched.

I took the beignets and two coffees to go, and Dog and I headed to San Francisco State University. Luz held office hours now, so I figured she'd be alone and in the mood to offer advice.

"He just seemed so sad," I said as Luz bit into a beignet. A soft shower of sugar sprinkled down on her black silk shirt.

"Híjole, 'mano," she muttered with a shake of her head. My rudimentary construction-site Spanish wasn't sufficient to translate that expression, but I gathered it had to do with being exasperated or upset. Whether the words were in response to the sugar or to my description of Ray and the situation, I couldn't be sure.

She and Dog appeared to be completely absorbed by the food. The fact that Luz remained lithe and willowy, while I gained a pound just *looking* at the beignets, was one of the mysteries of the universe. It said a lot about how much I valued Luz's friendship that I was able to get past it.

As for Dog, he was . . . Dog. He adored his people, and he adored his food. I thought it best for all concerned not to ask him to choose between the two.

"Hey, enough with the beignets already," I said at last. "I need you to put on your therapist hat. You should have seen Ray. And Hugh . . . That poor guy's been through so much."

"Sorry to interrupt your aberrant need to track down every killer in San Francisco, but signs here are pointing to an accidental-on-purpose overdose. Addicts often have a death wish, Mel. They may not consciously choose to kill themselves, but deep down they aren't too worried about floating away to the big crack house in the sky on a wave of drug-induced pleasure."

She took another huge bite. The phrase "floating away" reminded me of something Monty had said.

"You would understand better if you hadn't skipped the drug-experimentation phase of your rebellious adolescent years," Luz added.

"Hey, I rebelled plenty. Pot gives me a headache. And I don't like the smell."

"As drugs go, pot's more like alcohol or tobacco. I'm talking the heavy stuff."

"Pills scare me."

She nodded. "That's right—I remember you wouldn't even take the pain pills that time you dislocated your shoulder."

"I'd had a glass of wine already—seemed like a dangerous combination."

Luz waggled a finger at me. "Wine, schmine. You don't like to lose control; that's the real issue. You were afraid that if you were under the influence, you'd say something you'd regret."

I scoffed. "Not true. My life's an open book."

Luz snorted. "Everybody has secrets. Nothing wrong with it. Nobody needs to know what we're thinking all the time."

"Maybe so, but I've been very open about a lot of things."

"Even about Graham?"

I glared at her. "Why are we talking about me and my many faults?"

"Why do you frame it so negatively? You're a human being. We're faulty. It's part of our charm." Luz picked up another beignet. "Speaking of drugs, I think these beignets must be coated in an addictive substance. Oddly enough, I have no problem with that."

"It's just sugar, but I agree with you—it's addictive."

"Speaking of Graham, weren't you picking him up today? How was the big reunion?"

"He'd only been gone for five days."

"Uh-huh. That well, huh?"

"He was being bossy."

"About?"

I shrugged. "He's worried about the ghost thing. And the dead body thing."

"Gee, that sounds out of line. Why would someone who really cared about you be worried that you're once again involved in death and mayhem?"

I glared at her. "I thought we were talking about the Lawrence tragedy."

"Okay. The thing with this fellow Ray is he's sad about something real. It's a tragic situation. There's no way to reframe it or somehow see it in a different light. The original crime was horrific, and like all crimes it affected everyone it touched: certainly the family most, but also the neighbors, the first responders, even little kids who sing songs about it decades later. Some people, rare people, are able to respond to tragedy by opening up their hearts and giving . . . but even then, the hurt never goes away. Sometimes it consumes people."

"I hate that I think you're right," I said.

Luz shrugged. "Some things in life are just sad, Mel, and there's no way around it. That's why it's important to eat beignets."

"Walk me through that logical leap?"

"A key to emotional health is to balance sadness and stress with pleasure. Some people like to exercise. I prefer to eat sugar-coated, deep-fried pastry."

"Ah, it's all clear to me now."

"But speaking of being consumed by sadness ... If Linda really was murdered, you might look into who stood to gain from her death."

"That's always the place to start," I agreed. "Who had motive. But Linda didn't own anything except half of the house. I can't picture Hugh killing his sister just to gain complete control. Besides, he told me Linda had long ago given him power of attorney. What would be the point?"

"Power of attorney can be revoked, you know. And it doesn't take a lot to kill a desperate addict. Just hand her a bunch of pills that weren't what you told her they were."

I blew out a breath.

"Another thing," continued Luz. "Check out who would gain control of Hugh's assets if he's fifty-one fiftied."

I stared at her.

"It's code for committing someone against their will. You know, if they're cray-cray. And yes," she continued, "before you ask, 'cray-cray' is a professional term."

"You mean who would gain control of Hugh's assets besides the house? How do you know he has any? I don't know anything about the man's finances, but I can't imagine a poet makes a lot of money."

"Don't be so sure, my friend. This guy isn't your run-of-the-dive-café beat poet. He's Hugh Freaking Lawrence, poet laureate. People pay him good money to show up and read his poetry. Not to mention he wrote the lyrics for a famous rock song, and there was even an indie movie based on one of his poems. It wasn't bad, as far as that kind of thing goes."

"So you're saying . . . ?"

"Don't the police look to spouses first? Would Hugh's wife gain control of his assets if he's declared incompetent?"

"I suppose. But she seems genuinely concerned about him. She's urging him to write all about the experience, the grim stuff. Plus, she's a techie, so she probably makes decent money of her own."

"Never underestimate the power of greed. Some people will kill for what others would consider ridiculously small sums of money. Or maybe she just wants him to suffer for his art. Hugh's first book, the grueling, blood-fueled stuff, landed him on the literary map. His next published volumes were much less tortured, more about love and home and kittens, but that stuff doesn't sell. Maybe his wife wants him to be mired in the pain so he'll write more blood-and-guts poetry and keep on raking in the money."

"That's a terrible thought."

Luz had finished off the beignets and was now licking powdered sugar from her fingers. She shrugged.

"I'm just saying it's worth considering. Maybe his wife would be willing to sacrifice his mental health—and his sister—for the cash."

Chapter Sixteen

I got back to work for a while, making my usual rounds of the active jobsites, answering slews of telephone queries, and cajoling the clerk at the permit office to help me expedite the papers for a South Beach garage remodel. After going by the Bernini B&B and settling a dispute over the underlayment for radiant heat under the tile in the bathrooms, I met Annette Crawford at the designated parking lot in Berkeley.

Moments later we were zipping down the freeway in Annette's beautiful blue sports car. It felt freeing, doing this sort of thing on a workday. Annette's friend, the former homicide inspector, lived on his "ranchette" in Martinez, about twenty miles east of San Francisco, on the Carquinez Strait.

Martinez was one of those places I heard about in radio traffic reports but had never gone to. Though I was born and raised in the San Francisco Bay Area, I had only a vague sense of where Martinez was and what might be found there.

So I was impressed to discover that within twenty minutes' drive of San Francisco—without traffic—you might as well be out in the countryside, where men wore cowboy hats and boots, and horses and cows and sheep populated the pastures. The area around Martinez was typical for California: rolling hills lush with tall grass and dotted with majestic oak trees. Since it was winter, the hills were a bright green, rivaling the famous landscapes in Ireland. For most of the year, however, they were "golden," which meant the grasses were dry and dead. Still, the hills were gorgeous, a deep golden yellow shimmering in the bright sunshine, interrupted by the occasional lone oak tree. More than one California artist had attempted to capture their essence on canvas.

"So, what's this friend of yours doing way out here?" I asked.

Annette gunned the engine to show up a white Camaro with a red racing stripe, whose pimply driver glared as we passed. "A lot of homicide inspectors head to the countryside when they retire. Not because the rural life guarantees safety; we all know that. But because when you've worked homicide in the city long enough, you start to associate every neighborhood, every block, with its murders or suspicious deaths. You end up viewing the city not as a patchwork of distinct neighborhoods but as a series of zones strewn with corpses. It gets a bit gruesome after a while."

"A city of the dead, huh?" I never thought of that.

Annette nodded. "Not everybody feels that way, of course. But I guess getting out with the animals and the country smells . . ." She shrugged. "At least a person doesn't think about bodies all the time."

Now that I tripped over bodies with remarkable frequency, I was beginning to think more about the impact of the aftermath of violence on first responders. Whether paramedics or cops, we were all human and it was a lot to take in.

"Shel's always been an animal lover. Even back in the day, when he lived in a small apartment in the city, he had two dogs and a cat. Now he's on the board of the county's SPCA and works with a program that brings shelter dogs into prisons to be trained and socialized by inmates. Caring for the dogs requires the prisoners to take responsibility for someone besides themselves, which increases their capacity for empathy. It also gives them something worthwhile to do so they're not tempted to get into trouble. Meanwhile, the dogs are taught basic commands and good habits and are socialized so they'll be good family pets. It's a win-win situation."

"What happens to the dogs?"

"When their training is complete they 'graduate' and are placed in new homes with families on the outside. The prisoners start over with another homeless pet. The program's been a huge success."

That would be a good thing for my dad to get involved in, I thought, then caught myself. First I had volunteered Dad for Neighbors Together; now I was thinking he should volunteer for a prison dog–training program. Apparently, without realizing it, I no longer expected my dad to resume control of Turner Construction so that I could carry on with my oft-threatened plan to run away to Paris. And the odd thing was, I seemed to be okay with it. Turner Construction, which I had for so long seen as

an obligation and a weight around my neck, had somehow become mine, and I was feeling decidedly propri-
etary about it.

"Wow," I said as we sped down a winding road, emer-
ald hills on one side, an ancient walnut orchard on the
other. "So, this is Martinez. Who knew?"

"John Muir, the pioneering conservationist, was from
Martinez," said Annette as we drove. "So was Joe
DiMaggio. Bet you didn't know that."

"I surely didn't." It was embarrassing how little I
knew about local history, which just went to prove that I
was a true native. Only tourists and recent arrivals knew
factoids such as this. "How is it you know so much?"

"Years ago, when I first moved to the area, I did a lot
of exploring on my days off. I doubt I missed a single
historical marker. I should make time to do more of
that—I got a real kick out of it. It's a fascinating area."

There was a wistful tone in her voice. I had a number
of friends turning fifty and had noticed that for many it
was a time of reflection and introspection. I wondered
whether Annette considered giving up all this grisly homicide stuff in order to—I don't know—maybe take up
tending a herd of goats or weaving lumpy linen cloth on
a large wooden loom.

"Where are you from?" I asked.

"Alabama, originally, then I moved to San Jose."

"Seriously? You don't have an accent."

"You have any idea how hard I've worked to shed it?
Born and raised on a small farm outside of Selma, believe it or not."

"Wow."

"I know. I'm like the embodiment of the civil rights
movement, right? I'd like to say that my family marched

with Reverend King, but that would be a lie. They kept their heads down and worked their fingers to the bone to provide for us kids and to give us the education and opportunities they didn't have. But the legacy was there, and as soon as I was old enough, I followed. I remember the sensation, hearing about what was going on at school: I felt, quite literally, my chest puff up. As though I were taking a deep breath for the very first time. After that, there was no keeping this girl down on the farm."

Scratch the goatherding and handweaving.

Annette slowed, turned off the main highway, and passed through an open aluminum gate. We drove slowly another quarter mile down a dirt road, kicking up a plume of yellow brown dust behind us. We passed a fenced pasture where three swaybacked, scruffy-looking horses were contentedly munching on cropped grass. Beyond that was a mobile home surrounded by animal pens and cages holding a coyote and a variety of birds. A border collie and two dogs of dubious parentage raced toward the vehicle, barking.

A tall, slender man emerged from the mobile home and waved.

Retired San Francisco Homicide Inspector Sheldon Evans had embraced the rural life with enthusiasm. He wore a big tan cowboy hat, boots that had seen real labor, and an enormous belt buckle. A handlebar mustache dominated his face, as if tacked on during an out-of-control game of Pin the Tail on the Donkey. I gazed at him, fascinated that one person could embody so many western stereotypes.

Then I reminded myself of my own far-fetched outfits and told myself to stop being "judgy," as Monty would say.

Annette introduced us, and we shook hands.

"Do you do wildlife rescue as well?" I asked.

"Not really. There's a wildlife rescue station in Lafayette that takes them in and fixes their broken wings and the like, but a lot of them can never be released back into the wild. So they live here. Get room and board; all they have to do is look pretty and not eat each other. It's a pretty good deal, all things considered."

Dust on my boots, the smell of the grass underfoot, the wind through wet leaves, and manure. Country smells. It was a reminder to me how long it had been since I had taken a break, gotten out of town. I'm a city girl, by and large, but there was no denying that in a place like this, a person could breathe. I inhaled deeply, held it, released it in several beats like my Berkeley Buddhist friends were always telling me to do. It felt surprisingly good.

Since business was slow, perhaps I should propose a weekend getaway to Graham. It would be worth it just to see the shocked expression on his face. I couldn't help but smile at the image. That decided it. As soon as we nailed this murder down and I finished up the Monty project, I was going to take a weekend off.

I felt audacious and daring.

After a brief tour of the animals and introductions to his numerous dogs, Sheldon invited us into his double-wide mobile home, which was comfortable and surprisingly spacious inside.

"Have a seat," he said, gesturing toward the linoleum-topped dining table. "The wife's at Costco, so until she gets back the pickings are kind of slim around here, but I can offer you coffee or a beer."

"A beer sounds good," said Annette.

"Same for me," I said, to be sociable. I'm not a big beer drinker.

"PBR all around it is," Sheldon said, and set a cold can of Pabst Blue Ribbon in front of each of us before taking a seat.

We popped the tabs and took a sip, and while I tried to decide why anyone in their right mind would choose to drink beer, Annette and Sheldon got caught up with an exchange of shoptalk and "do you remembers." After several minutes, Annette asked Sheldon about the Lawrence murders.

"Like I told you on the phone, it seemed pretty clearcut," he said with a shake of his head. He stuck his chin out thoughtfully and stroked his mustache. "One of those heartbreakers, what with the teenager, and the other kids witnessing the crime and barely escaping with their lives."

"Was there any clue as to what led up to that night?"

"The father was having money problems. His company wasn't doing well, and there were rumors of embezzlement. Apparently he just . . . snapped. Or so it seemed."

"Was there any doubt that he was the one who did it?" I asked.

"Not at the time. Not officially."

Annette and I exchanged a glance.

"What about unofficially?" she asked.

Sheldon took a moment before replying. "That case always bothered me. Man had a nice wife, three good kids. Money troubles, but nothing he couldn't reasonably expect to recover from. The police had no record of incidents at the home. The neighbors said the Lawrences seemed like a nice family, no reports of loud voices or fighting. According to their teachers, the kids were good students, happy and polite, no acting out or signs of neglect or abuse. Usually in these kinds of cases there's *something*, some indication that all isn't well at home. But not this time. The in-laws had nothing but wonderful things to say about Sidney. They expressed no lingering doubts, no bitterness, no I-knew-something-was-wrong-why-didn't-I-say-something—nothing like that. Just stunned disbelief."

"Any other suspects?" asked Annette.

"All the usual suspects. We reconstructed the twenty-four hours leading up to the murder, then the previous forty-eight hours. We tried to avoid getting tunnel vision, seeing only what was most obvious. We looked into the wife, thinking maybe she'd had an affair. Nothing. We checked up on him; maybe he'd been seeing someone. Again, zip. The way his business was structured, his partner had nothing to gain from his death. The only financial motive was who would inherit and who got the insurance payout."

"The children?"

He nodded. "It was pretty far-fetched, but kids occasionally do kill their parents. It wasn't likely, but we had to look into it. We turned up nothing substantial. Linda, the daughter, made some contradictory statements, but ultimately we chalked that up to the shock of what she had seen."

"Which was?"

"Her father shooting her mother. On that point she was consistent: She heard a noise, came out of her room, saw her father at the foot of the stairs and her mother on the ground, reaching up to him. As Linda watched, her father lowered the gun and shot her mother in the head."

The nightmarish vision of Jean Lawrence on the floor at the bottom of the stairs, reaching out for mercy, flashed across my mind. I blew out a breath. So many lives destroyed.

"Did she see her father kill himself?"

"No. On that she was also consistent. According to what we were able to piece together, after seeing her father murder her mother, Linda ran to her little brother's room and blocked the door with a chest of drawers. Clever kid. So while they heard the shot, they were spared the sight of their father turning the gun on himself. Linda and her brother went out the bedroom window onto the roof, then managed to shimmy down the tree at the side of the house."

"Resourceful kids."

He tugged at his mustache. "I doubt it was the first time Linda had left the house that way—she was a bit of a handful."

"I thought you said there were no problems with the kids?" Annette asked.

"Didn't mean it that way," he said with a smile. "Hell, I snuck out my bedroom window once or twice when I was a kid; didn't you? I'm saying Linda wasn't the kind of kid to sit around and wait for her father to kill her. That's all."

We sat in silence for a long moment, nursing the dregs of our warm, flat beers. I couldn't stop thinking about how Sidney's actions were still claiming lives. Whatever violence had bubbled up that night had swallowed Linda, too; it had just taken a while.

"One of the older neighbors said something about a feud Sidney might have had with the neighbors across the street. She said the son was selling drugs?"

"Yeah, we checked that as well. Duct-Tape Dave, I guess you're thinking of."

I choked on my PBR. "Duct-Tape Dave?"

"That's what he called himself—he made these home-made silencers out of duct tape. Kind of clever, actually. The kid was a big talker, not a real player on the street. Sold some weed, but strictly penny-ante stuff. He had the nickname, but he never shot anybody 'til years later. Doing time now in San Quentin."

"So you don't think he could have been the shooter?"

"Nah. We grilled him good, but truth was he started blubbering like a baby. His girlfriend gave him an alibi, for what it was worth. Mostly I just didn't like him as the shooter. Just didn't fit. He was no stone-cold killer, and this was a brutal crime."

"Do you think Sidney Lawrence had something to do with the neighbor's house burning down?"

"Again, there were allegations. Most likely, that house burned down because they were cooking drugs or even dinner in there while they were high as kites. Or just as likely, they burned it themselves to get the insurance money. We never found any evidence that they had harassed the Lawrence family after moving, though, only beforehand. They were still living in the city, so I suppose it was possible, but as Inspector Crawford here would tell you, an experienced cop goes by his gut. I really don't think the kid did it. Like to think I'm not easily fooled."

"What about Dave's father?"

"He was a goner by then, sick as a dog. I just couldn't see it."

"Did you think Sidney Lawrence really did it?"

He held my eyes for a long moment, then glanced

over at Annette. Finally he leaned back in his chair, let
out a long breath, and shook his head.

"Nope."

It was on the tip of my tongue to ask him about ghosts.
I was trying to figure out how to phrase it when Annette
spoke.

"I know this is out of left field, but you ever feel anything weird in that house?" asked Annette in her typical
direct fashion.

"Weird how?"

"I'm talking ghosts here."

He smiled. "I suppose a place like that would be lousy
with ghosts, wouldn't it?"

"And did you ... feel anything?" I asked again, half
expecting him to burst into laughter. Instead, he was
quiet for a while.

"You know what I like about animals?" the retired
detective asked. "They don't question what they see.
They accept it. If something scares them, they hightail it
out of there, no ifs, ands, or buts."

"So ... you *did* feel something," I said.

"Not sure what I felt. The aftermath of a crime like
that, it can throw you for a loop. Tell you this, though: I
sure as hell don't think ghosts killed those folks that
night."

"Then who do you think did kill the family?" Annette
asked. "Any theories?"

"I was always under the impression it was a home
invasion of some sort. A robbery gone wrong."

"Was anything taken?"

"That was one of the frustrating things—we never
knew for sure. All we had was a pair of traumatized kids
who didn't know what might have been valuable. A

home safe was empty, but who knew if there was anything in there in the first place? There were no signs of
forced entry, no forensic evidence to suggest there was
anyone in the house who shouldn't have been." He
shook his head and smoothed his mustache. I was starting to think the purpose of the hair was to give him
something to do with his hands when he pondered.
"Nope, the boss said it must have been the dad, because
of the girl's testimony. So when I couldn't come up with
forensic evidence, much less a suspect for a home invasion, the case was closed."

"Just like that?" I asked.

He chuckled and squinted at me. "You probably
watch those TV shows where cops have the resources
and independence to go off and investigate crimes for as
long as it takes to discover the truth, right?" He gestured
toward Annette, who had finished her beer and was now
playing with a few grains of salt on the tabletop. "D'you
ever wonder why Annette's here on her day off?"

"Because the ME ruled it a suicide or accidental overdose," Annette volunteered. "But I don't believe it."

"A lot of times, you have to close a case even when
you don't feel good about it," continued Sheldon as he
rose from the table, gathered our cans, crushed them one
by one with calloused hands, and put them in a big blue
recycling bin. "That's just the way it is. Unless you're like
Annette here, and you're willing to go out on a limb, on
your own time, and risking your own neck. Want my advice?"

He leaned against the counter and faced us. "Both of
you? Stay out of it. The world has moved on. Some trag-
edies are meant to be endured, not understood."

Chapter Seventeen

As Annette drove us home, my phone buzzed. It was Caleb calling, asking whether he could come over tonight for a haircut. He was so standoffish lately that it made my heart happy when he asked me for things. Not for the first time, I wondered how that worked, exactly. I was guessing it was some hormonal mechanism that helped ensure we didn't eat our young.

"Sure, I'd be happy to. Want me to pick you up?"

"No, I'll get a ride, thanks. See you later."

I hung up and turned back to Annette. "So, you think Linda was murdered. Why?"

"I don't trust we know the full story of what she was doing there."

"You doubt her brother's account?"

"I don't think he killed her, if that's what you're asking. I find it hard to believe they were doing this exposure therapy, but then she stuck around and—what?—took a bunch of pills? And if so, why would she do it in the shed? It appears the body was moved, which would mean someone else was involved, and would explain the lack of forensic evidence. But I've had crime scene folks look through every part of that house, and they haven't found anything, either."

"The medical examiner determined Linda died of opiate overdose?"

"Yes."

"The guy who found her says it looked like she was allergic to opioids."

"How would he know?"

"I guess he'd seen a similar reaction in a frat brother once who was on pain pills."

Annette was silent for a few moments while she got on the freeway. "Thing is, people don't kill themselves by ingesting things they know they're allergic to. It's weird but true," she finally said. "And I think Linda Lawrence knew her way around drugs enough to understand what she was doing."

"That's what I was thinking as well."

"So let's say she was murdered by someone who gave her the pills. Could be a relative stranger, but it was probably someone she trusted."

"How do you figure that?"

"Ever try to give a pill to a dog or a cat? It's not easy to make someone swallow something. There was no bruising around Linda's face or mouth, so we can assume she took the pills more or less voluntarily. It could have just been a stupid mistake. Or maybe someone told her the pills were something else, or that they were a smaller dose than they really were."

"Okay, but we still have no idea who that person might be, much less why they wanted an apparently harmless woman dead."

"Let's approach this logically. Most people are killed for stupid reasons: a nasty comment in a bar, an episode of road rage over a parking spot. But those kinds of murders, which by their nature are spur-of-the-moment, usually involve weapons readily at hand: guns, knives, or blunt objects. Not pills."

"Fair enough."

"That means Linda's murder was planned. Let's assume we're not dealing with some kind of sociopath who kills at random to fill a sick need."

"Sure we can assume that?"

"It's a reasonable assumption. For one thing, serial killers are rare. And serial killers who use poison are rarer still. Since there are no other cases to suggest Linda's death was part of a larger pattern, I'm going to back-burner the serial killer explanation."

"Makes sense. Go on."

"So that leaves only a certain number of motives: greed, jealousy, covering up a crime."

"Did anyone profit from Linda's death?" I asked.

"Her brother, Hugh, inherited her share of the house. But Linda was happy to let Hugh make all the decisions about the place, and since he didn't want to sell it anyway, that doesn't seem like much of a motive."

"And it's hard to imagine Linda inspiring a passionate sort of rage—she hasn't been involved with anyone for years, right?"

"Not that we can tell."

"So, if greed and jealousy weren't the motive for her death, that leaves covering up a crime. And the only crime we know Linda was involved with was the family tragedy. Do you agree with Shel, that Sidney might not have been the killer?"

"I really don't know. But Shel's smart."

"It would explain a lot. For instance, no matter who I talk to, the neighbors or business colleagues, Hugh— none of them had any sense that anything was wrong with Sidney. They describe him as a loving father."

"Just to play devil's advocate," said Annette, "I'll say that it's not that strange. You must have seen all those scenes on TV, where some guy's been stashing bodies in his crawl space for thirty years yet all the neighbors report he was 'quiet' and 'seemed like a nice guy.'" She shook her head. "I don't think there are necessarily any outward signs."

"But the family would have seen his temper at least, wouldn't they? At some point? Wouldn't there be some evidence? Child abuse, spouse abuse . . . losing his cool with his coworkers, anything?"

"Usually you do see something, some sort of buildup; it's true. But people are often unwilling to speak ill of the dead. They might have seen flare-ups, that sort of thing, but not mentioned them to investigators just as a matter of course."

"Even after what he did?"

"In these sorts of cases, shock and horror set in. People don't always want to speculate on what was going on in the mind of a seemingly sane man that would lead him to such a thing—personally, I wonder whether people are secretly afraid they might one day snap under the pressures of work and family themselves, do something crazy. Besides, Sidney was fighting with the neighbors, remember? And there were the embezzlement charges looming against him."

Once again I considered what it must be like to be Annette and see the seamy underside of the world every day when you go to work. It made me ever more content to be dealing mostly with issues of molding choice. Even the really hard stuff, like the nitty-gritty of payroll and workman's comp and health insurance, was taken care of by Stan.

"Do you really believe that Sidney killed his family?"

Annette let out a deep sigh. "No. And what if Linda, the single eyewitness, was the only one who knew who did?"

Caleb sat up on a high stool, shirtless, while I snipped at his hair. Normally I cut his hair outside on the patio, but it was too cold tonight, so we laid down newspapers in the front room. Unfortunately, this was where his video-game system was set up.

"So, kiddo, I was wondering if you would do me a huge favor. I was hoping you could talk to a girl; she's a teenager, and she's been hanging around the Neighbors Together house, and it's possible she has some information, but she's not wild about talking to adults."

"What, like you want me to go up and ask this girl, like, if she wants to play?"

"Well . . . I wouldn't use those exact words. . . . I just thought that you might be able to talk to her, teen to teen." I cringed. Did that sound lame?

Yep, I was pretty sure it did.

Caleb stared straight ahead, mouth slightly ajar, intent on the video game in front of him. I was always amazed how my sometimes sensitive and apparently intelligent ex-stepson was turned into a grunting automaton whenever he spent time with his electronics.

But I reminded myself how my father sounded when he started going off about "how things were when I was growing up." Last thing I wanted was to start sounding like a middle-aged grump—like my dad—so I tried to clamp down on my impatience. Still, I couldn't stop the wave of nostalgia that threatened to engulf me.

I remembered, back when Caleb was little, how I would cut his hair outside and we let his dark tresses fall onto the broken concrete patio and waft in the breeze. Afterward we would watch from the kitchen window while birds swooped down and gathered up the soft material to line their nests. I loved imagining the fragile eggs nestled securely in fluffy beds made of Caleb's soft hair. I remembered how Caleb's shoulder blades would poke out of his tan skin like the fragile buds of wings; his neck had been so slender I wondered how it held up his head. But now ropy muscles were forming, his shoulders broadening, his neck thickening. Along with the whiskers, these were irrefutable signs that he was no longer a child but becoming a man.

At times I missed that little boy so much, I wondered how a biological parent must feel, having birthed this baby from her loins. His becoming a man was also a sure sign that *I* was aging, too. One thing about having a kid around: You can't deny the passage of time.

At long last Caleb put down his controllers and gave me his attention. Unfortunately, that attention wasn't focused where I wanted it to be.

"Are you planning on making that Murder House into a bed-and-breakfast or something?"

"No, not at all. Besides, I can't imagine anyone would want to stay in a house with such a history."

"Wanna bet? You can make a lot of money on stuff

like that," said Caleb with a tone that suggested world-weariness. At seventeen. "The Goths and other freaks, they're totally into it. But other people, too. They could totally open a bed-and-breakfast in that place, and people would pay to spend the night there with the recreations of the murder scenes."

"What are you talking about?" I asked, appalled.

"You ever heard of that Lizzie Borden chick?"

"Um . . ." I paused, wondering whether I should launch into a sermon about why we don't go around talking about every woman as a chick. But then I overcame it. And joined in. "Right, the Lizzie Borden chick. What about her?"

"They totally made her house into an inn. People, like, stay there. And sit right on the couch where she chopped up her father."

"Eh . . ." Ghosts were one thing, murder quite another. I don't care how long ago it took place; the Lizzie Borden story was still horrifying. I vacillated between appreciating that Caleb knew the story—it was part of basic U.S. history, after all—and worrying about how much violence he was exposed to through popular culture. "I thought it wasn't clear that Lizzie Borden even did it. Wasn't she found not guilty?"

He shrugged, his attention already veering back to the holding pattern on the screen in front of him. If I wanted to know the whole story about Lizzie Borden, I thought to myself, I could look it up. That was, after all, what the internet was for. I should use my time with Caleb for the important stuff, before I lost his attention completely.

"Okay, so you're saying that people want to stay in houses where murders were committed? Would that be a real moneymaker?"

"I don't know why you're acting so surprised. That last bed-and-breakfast you were working on had ghosts in it, and that was sort of like the point, right?"

"Yes, but those ghosts weren't murdered."

"*Somebody* was murdered." He twisted his head toward me and held my eyes for a moment. "A woman was killed while you were there. In fact, for someone so, like, weirded out by Lizzie Borden, it seems like you're around murder a lot. Like maybe you should watch your back a little."

Caleb never spoke like this. Could this be why he'd been acting so oddly toward me lately?

"Caleb, are you worried about me?"

He shrugged and turned back to his game.

"I'm not in any danger, you know," I said, clipping a few stray hairs. And then I thought how inane my words sounded, considering the situations I'd found myself in. "I'll be careful, kiddo, okay? I promise. I'm working with the police this time, so it's really not like before. I've got backup."

"Ungh," he grunted.

"And about talking to the girl, Raven . . . I just thought maybe you could ask her if she'd seen anything, noticed anything odd in the house, anything like that. She's coming to do some cleanup on Monty's house tomorrow. Would you be willing to join us after school? I could pick you up."

" 'Kay," he said.

And then he hit his controller, and something on-screen blew up in a burst of blood and fire.

I went upstairs to change out of my dirty clothes and take a quick shower.

When I started back down I could smell the homey scents of pot roast and caramelized onions, one of my dad's signature dishes. There was the clatter of dishware, and friendly chatter, and laughter. It reminded me of how much I had: people who cared about me, a warm, safe house, a loyal dog, and plenty of food. I gave myself a little talking-to about my recent treatment of Cookie. She was family. This was nice.

But then I heard a man's voice—not Dad, or Stan, or even Caleb.

Graham. What was *he* doing here? All my warm and fuzzy thoughts fled, and I fought panic. My hair was wet, and though I was clean, I was, once again, not looking my best.

Graham was recounting a funny story about people who call themselves "tree dwellers" and live in the top of an unthinkably tall redwood tree. Caleb kept asking questions about how they handled the bathroom situation. Stan was cracking jokes, and Dad was joining in while he cooked. Cookie was being generally adorable, of course.

Since I was pretty sure that everyone liked Graham better than me, anyway, what if I just slipped out the front door?

"Mel." I heard Graham's voice. He came out of the kitchen and joined me in the living room, where I'd stood waffling.

"Oh, hey," I said, playing it cool. "I didn't know you were coming."

"Your sister called and invited me."

"Oh . . . wasn't that nice?"

"I would have wound up on your doorstep one way or

the other, anyway. I wanted to apologize for this morning."

I shrugged. "No big deal."

"I acted like an ass. My only excuses are that I was tired ... and that I worry about you putting yourself in danger."

"Okay."

He studied my face, frowning slightly like he was trying to read my mind. I concentrated on remaining inscrutable.

"So, we're okay?"

"Of course." Liar, liar, pants on fire.

"Ah, I almost forgot." Graham pulled a book out of his bag. "I happened to stumble across this at Christopher's Books."

The dainty little sage green book was wrapped in a cover illustrated with a stark sepia-toned photo of an abandoned urbanscape. It was entitled, simply, *Grief: and Other Works of Poetry*. By Hubert Lawrence.

"How did you know?"

"I talked to Luz, and she filled me in on the whole story. She's worried about you. I have to say, I'm impressed that you're hobnobbing with California's poet laureate."

"You knew who he was?"

"Just because I'm in construction doesn't mean I don't keep up with the cultural life of our country."

I gave him the stinkeye.

He grinned. "Also, Luz told me who he was. Pretty interesting stuff there, though I'm not sure I understand it. It's a bit like rap to me. I'm pretty sure it's worthy and worthwhile, but can't comprehend enough to say for sure."

Twisting
driftwood memories Bent, cracked and gray
he is he, I am he
blood in the night
rooftop slick
we all fall down

"That's just plain depressing," I said.

"It's beautiful in its stark view of the world, though, right?"

"I guess I'm just not a poetry kind of gal."

"With an exception for Neruda?" he said with a wicked smile.

Graham had been wooing me for several months now, but I'll admit I hadn't been making it easy for him. I had moments of petulance and irritability, with selfishness and outbursts that Luz informed me were meant more for my ex-husband than for Graham. And yet he didn't go away. He didn't take my grumpiness seriously, which simultaneously annoyed and charmed me. Instead, he would smile an enigmatic, Mona Lisa–type smile and sit back, almost preternaturally relaxed.

So one unseasonably warm night, Graham had begged me to join him for a drive in the country. We had set out in his old truck, and he drove us to a spot he knew, deep in a redwood forest. Almost without a word he grabbed a packed picnic basket and a blanket, took my hand, and led me to a beautiful little clearing. Overhead was a thick blanket of stars, underneath the soft sponginess of the meadow. Crickets chirped and the full moon shone overhead.

He lay down a blanket and unpacked red wine, crusty

bread, stinky cheese, and fragrant nectarines from the farmer's market.

Along with a book of poetry.

"You've got to be kidding me," I'd said. "A bottle of wine, a loaf of bread, and thou?"

Graham smiled and handed me a glass of cabernet. "I'm romancing you. This is a courtship. Get used to it."

I had taken a deep drink of the wine, and gave myself a little talking-to. Why was I so sure of myself, so kick-ass when it came to construction, but so insecure when dealing with this sort of thing? Graham may or may not be the love of my life, but one thing was certain: He wasn't my ex-husband. I couldn't judge him on the same criteria. I should give him a chance.

And then he had started reading poetry. Neruda, to be precise.

Then I couldn't take it anymore. "Seriously, Graham . . . ? You're an employed, good-looking, interesting man in San Francisco. You're telling me that you can't get a date?"

He looked taken aback. "I can get a date. I happen to be on a date right now. What's your point?"

"Why would you want me?"

"You're impossible—you know that? I'm thinking you do better with action than with words," he said, leaning over to me, winding my hair in his hand, and kissing me.

And with that, we proceeded to do a few things that might have gotten us a ticket in the state park.

"You still with me?" Graham asked, interrupting my reverie and bringing my mind back to the smells of pot roast and the clatter of dishes.

"Um . . . sure. Sorry."

"So, Lawrence took his tragedy and translated it into poetry," said Graham. "While his sister tried to dull the pain with drugs and alcohol?"

"So it seems. Still, she was the one who saved Hugh that night. She saw her father shoot her mother but had the presence of mind to run to his room, block the door, and help him out the window."

"I can't even imagine what that must have been like. Is there anything more traumatic as a kid than to have something happen to your folks—and to see your father kill your mother, then himself . . . ?" Graham shook his head and let out a loud breath.

His own father had died when Graham was only five, so he knew the pain of growing up without a dad. In fact, I was sure that was one reason he felt so close to my own father, which occasionally made our relationship a little too incestuous for my comfort.

"Dinner's on!" yelled Dad, though a simple spoken announcement would have sufficed. We took our seats in the dining room tonight, since we didn't all fit at the kitchen table.

"So, Graham," said Cookie, "I am so *thrilled* to finally get a chance to get to know you. But you know, Mel is so tight-mouthed. She hasn't told me a *thing* about you!"

Cookie had been around when Graham worked for our father, back when we were in high school and college. But since she rarely spent time on the jobsites, she never interacted with him. I had kept my teenage crush to myself, thank heavens.

I stared at him across the table: *Don't say a word.* His lips curled up in a slight smile.

"I'm in construction, like Mel," said Graham. "But I specialize in 'green' techniques."

"Oh, like solar power? I have one of those emergency radios that runs off solar power. It's *miraculous*, isn't it?" said Cookie as she served herself a thimbleful of mashed potatoes and passed the dish along. I had to hand it to her: She was the only person I'd ever met who could eat just one potato chip—or one dollop of mashed potatoes—and then stop for fear of gaining weight. "I think it's so important to consider the future of our environment, don't you? Just the other day I was taking BART home from San Francisco and thinking to myself, If only we all thought about taking public transit rather than burning fossil fuels, just imagine how much progress we could make if we all pitched in."

Everyone nodded, mouths full. We were Northern Californians. We knew the drill.

When no one took up the conversational mantle, Cookie tried again. "Tell us more, Graham. I'm fascinated with green building."

"Mel's not so thrilled with it," he said as he served himself another slice of pot roast.

Cookie looked at me as though I'd suggested kicking kittens.

"It's not that," I said. "As Graham knows perfectly well, I use as many green techniques as possible within my projects. It's just that they don't always work with historical renovation."

"She's still smarting over installing solar panels over the decorative roof tiles on the Union Street Victorian," said Dad.

"And the new vinyl windows on that conservatory in Piedmont," offered Stan.

"Those weird water-saving showerheads didn't help," put in Caleb.

"Yes, thanks, everyone, for those examples," I said. I was all for the environment and included a lot of passive techniques in my work, but unfortunately applying green technologies to historic homes often meant sacrificing authenticity for the environment. I get it—the future of our planet and all that. Still, it made Graham a frequent thorn in my side. "But as I like to point out, renovating old homes is almost always much more environmentally sound than new construction. *Much* smaller carbon footprint. I just don't like it when people discuss green technologies with my clients outside of my presence."

Graham grinned at me. "Well, the shoe might well be on the other foot soon. My Marin County client wants to meet with you. He's building that inn out of historic bits and pieces he's bringing over from Europe—could be a real challenge."

"Mmm." I made a noncommittal reply and took a huge bite of broccoli casserole so I didn't have to answer. I was looking for future projects, and from what I knew of Graham's mystery client, I would normally give my toolbox for the opportunity to win the bid. But it would mean working closely with Graham for months on end.

That scared me.

I watched as Cookie did her best to be adorable. Was there any wonder men liked her? She smiled and cooed and acted interested in every word they said. As I watched, Cookie reached for the carrot sticks, and as she leaned forward her top gapped just enough to show a tantalizing glimpse of what lay beneath: something lacy, probably real silk.

I felt grumpier—and frumpier—by the minute. The truth was, my sister was charming. She made people—men especially, but often women, too—feel good about themselves. Whereas I went through life trying to get my work done and bowling everybody over with my efforts. And lately, of course, I spent an inordinate amount of time thinking about ghosts and untimely deaths. None of which was liable to improve my mood any.

While I was distracted, a forkful of mashed potatoes tumbled unceremoniously from my fork to my plate, spattering gravy all over the bodice of my dress.

I stared down at my chest.

Classy, Mel. Real classy.

I started dabbing at my neckline, and looked up to find Graham's eyes fixed on the low neck of my dress, now peppered with dark spots.

Our eyes met for a long moment. I forgot to breathe for a minute. *Maybe I should take a page out of my sister's book,* I thought. I sat up straighter, rolled my shoulders back, and looked down at my chest in what I hoped was a seductive move.

Cookie's high-pitched giggle shattered the moment. "Oh, Mel, *honestly*; I remember when you were little, you never could keep an outfit clean for more than ten minutes."

I excused myself from the table and hurried upstairs to change.

By the time I returned, clean dress on, they were all doing dishes, laughing it up, and having a great old time.

I couldn't face it. I ducked into the office and started catching up on paperwork. Though we did as much as possible on the computer, like most businesses, in construction we still worked with a lot of paper, from blue-

prints to permit forms to client contracts and change
orders put in writing.

"Your sister's charming," Graham said from the doorway twenty minutes later.

"Yeah, I noticed."

He came in and closed the door.

"I take it you two aren't close?"

"Not exactly, no."

He shrugged. "Not all siblings are best friends. You're
very different people."

"By which you mean I'm the opposite of charming?"

"I—"

"Well, if you stick around I think she might be available soon. She comes with two adorable children and a
pedigreed cat."

He chuckled. I continued to bang around the office,
slamming the filing cabinet and trying not to mutter to
myself.

"Hey, are you serious?" Graham grabbed me by the
arm as I tried to sweep by him. "What's gotten into
you?"

"I'm just saying . . . I am who I am. That's all. This is
me, no designer clothes—well, unless you count Stephen—
no blond hair, no entertaining little stories. I frequently
wear dirty coveralls and I'm grumpy and I don't particularly like to speak unless I feel I have something reasonably intelligent to say. So if you want someone more like
Cookie . . ."

"Why would you think I don't like you for who you
are? Have I ever given you that impression? I follow you
into ghost-infested attics, for crissakes."

"I just don't think . . . I'm not sure I'm ready for a
steady boyfriend. I wouldn't be good for anybody."

Graham held me at arm's length, hands wrapped around my upper arms. "Look, I know I pushed you a little bit before I left town. I'm ready. To be with you. But obviously you're not sure. That's okay; we don't have to rush this. We can back up a little, give you some breathing space. Just please stop trying to foist me off on other women."

"I wasn't foisting. I never foist."

He chuckled and drew me toward him. "How about this? We could have a strictly sexual relationship. Would that be more in your comfort zone, you modern woman, you?"

"You mean you want to be my boy toy?"

He kissed me on the neck. "Could be fun. I've never been anyone's plaything."

A gentle nibble on my earlobe sent shivers racing through me.

"Um . . . I suppose we could give it a try."

"Hey, you two!" Cookie opened the door without knocking. "What are you two up to? It's time for dessert!"

Graham and I shared a smile, and I took his hand.

"Come on, boy toy. Let's go sublimate with chocolate."

Chapter Eighteen

The next morning I gathered my papers, breezed through the kitchen, and waved good-bye, not even stopping for coffee.

There was no way in heck I was taking Cookie with me to prison.

After some thought, I had decided that the ideal person to drag to San Quentin with me was my old buddy Zach. Zach was several years younger than I, but there were times I felt a lifetime older. He was enthusiastic and fun, and usually up for odd things. He also tended to flirt with me, which is something my ego could use right about now. After dessert last night, Graham had asked me if I wanted to come to his place. But with Caleb and my sister at home, it felt awkward to leave. Besides, I had work the next day. Besides . . . I just wasn't sure. Unfortunately, Graham gave up too easily, leaving me dissatisfied but unable to put my finger on exactly why.

I didn't want to entertain the thought that maybe, just

maybe, I was calling Zach because I suspected that it would elicit a strong response from Graham if he knew. But he wouldn't know, right? So surely that wasn't the reason.

I called.

"Mel! I haven't heard from you in ages. How are the ghosts?"

"Oh, great, thanks. How's the life of crime?"

"Very funny. I've been on the straight and narrow for some time now, as you know. I've been a very, very good boy. So good it's boring, as a matter of fact."

"How about going to San Quentin?"

"I just told you, I'm a solid citizen these days."

"I wasn't suggesting you check in. I'm going during visiting hours and wondered if you'd go with me."

"San Quentin, as in the notorious state penitentiary?"

"Yep. So, pick you up noonish?"

"You're not going to tell me why you want to visit prison?"

"It's kind of a long story. I'll tell you on the way. And you really don't have to come if you have something more useful to do. Like making money, building your career, that kind of thing. I was just thinking about you, and I thought . . ."

"You needed someone to watch your back, and you're scared to go alone, and you thought I might be familiar with the penal code. I get it. Do I at least get lunch out of the deal?"

I laughed. "Sure."

"Just to be clear: No prison food."

"Agreed. I was thinking Larkspur Landing." It always seemed odd to me that San Quentin hulked on the shore of the bay, right next to quaint, prosperous Larkspur

Landing, which boasted a ferry terminal with commuter boats going to and from San Francisco. It was a strange study in contrasts.

We agreed to meet at eleven. That gave me a few hours to check on my current jobs and to pass by an old distillery in China Beach that some restaurateurs wanted to transform into a brewery/pub. We did a walk-through, and I took measurements and photographs so I could work up a written proposal. It would be a great project if we could land it. I enjoyed doing residential jobs, but it was good for the company's reputation to renovate public spaces from time to time. They often served as a source of client referrals.

A few hours later, I picked up Zach in front of the Palace of Fine Arts. I hadn't seen him in a while, and he surprised me, as always, with his good looks. He was tall with golden-brown hair, and must have been working out, because he had filled out since I first met him. Today he was dressed in jeans, boots, a sweater topped with a tweed jacket, and a hand-knitted scarf around his neck. He looked a bit like he was ready to tour Scotland.

"So tell me, Zach, what do you know about the drug trade in San Francisco?" I said as I drove onto the ramp that approached the Golden Gate Bridge.

"What, no 'Hello, Zach. It's been so long. How are you'?"

I gave him a look and then parroted in a flat voice: "Hello, Zach. It's been so long. How are you?"

"Ah, Mel, I do adore your social skills. Never mind. So, why would you think I would know anything about the drug trade?"

"You once told me you knew everyone in town."

"When did I say that? That's an asinine thing to say."

"I guess you were trying to convince me of how cool you are. Or maybe you were trying to throw me off the track of the fact that you were involved in a murder cover-up and attempted jewelry heist."

"Hey! I was in no way involved in that murder, and you know it." He paused. "Okay, you're probably right. That's probably why I said that."

"And you knew the Mafia-run girlie place, remember that?"

"Okay . . . Would it be too much to ask why you're interested in the local drug trade?"

I gave him an abbreviated version of what had happened, who we were visiting in San Quentin, and why.

"Hey, how come you didn't ask *me* to help on your volunteer project?"

"Would you have?"

"Of course."

"Do you have skills?"

He gave me a crooked grin. "Oh, baby, you have no idea."

"Cute. Tell you what—we're going to finish up the project this weekend. Care to join us?"

"Oh . . . *this* weekend? I'm not sure I can make it this weekend."

"I see how it is. All good intentions until I actually call you on it. How about this afternoon, then? I'm going to pick up Caleb after school and go over there to finish up a wheelchair ramp."

"Sure, why not? It's been ages since I've built a wheelchair ramp. Could I wear your coveralls?"

San Quentin sits at the base of the Richmond–San Rafael Bridge, right on the bay, with views of the bay and the Bay Bridge. Tens of thousands of commuters, I was sure, must daily share the thought that this was a prison set on some prime real estate. In fact, I kept expecting the place to be moved out to the central valley somewhere and the old Art Deco buildings to be converted to condos.

Decidedly eerie but expensive condos.

I was willing to bet there was a ghost or two—or hundreds—within those walls.

The tiny town of San Quentin had a little post office, an ice cream shop, and a few dozen cute little homes, right on the bay. If it weren't for some of the most violent offenders in the state living through the massive gates right down the street, one might convince oneself they were transported to a bayside version of *Mayberry R.F.D.*

Etta Lee had contacted Dave for me and helped me put my name on the visitor's list. So when I pulled up to the gates, I explained we were here for visiting hours and gave them Zach's name to add to the list. We were told where to park, then went through metal detectors and a quick check of our driver's licenses. We then joined dozens of people, mostly women and children, in a cavernous beige room, until our names were called and we were escorted into a room with glass separating us from the prisoners. We spoke by telephone.

I told Dave who I was, but apparently he and Etta had shared a lengthy discussion—he knew all about me.

"Yeah, of course I remember that girl. She was a kid, really, but then so was I. Older than her, but still a kid."

Dave was good-looking in a rugged way. His face was acne-scarred, his blue eyes intense in a dusky face. I studied him, trying to figure out what to say, how to ask the questions I needed answered.

"Did you . . . sell drugs to her?"

"Nah." His headshake was immediate, and he didn't break eye contact. "Like I said, she was just a kid, and to tell you the truth, I sort of had, like, admiration for her family. I would never have screwed around with those kids."

"What do you mean by *admiration*?"

I was surprised to see what looked like flags of red bloom high on his cheeks. Was this convict blushing?

"It was just that they were like . . . I mean the Lawrences were, like, practically *Leave It to Beaver*; you know what I mean? I mean, I never even seen that show, but I swear those Lawrences were like that, wholesome and loving and all that. I tell you what—it blew my mind when I heard what happened. I never would have believed it . . . I mean, I guess it just goes to show you never know what's going on behind closed doors, right?"

"So you never thought maybe they had something to do with the fire at your house?"

He waved me off, jerking back with a disgusted look on his face. "Oh, please. You're listening to neighborhood gossip? What was it, thirty years ago now? That house burned down because my dad fell asleep on the couch with a butt in his hand. Classic example of why you shouldn't smoke if you're a dumbass."

"Sounds like a great slogan for a new public health campaign."

He smiled. "That fire was probably the best thing could have happened to me—got me out of the neighborhood before I screwed it up for everyone. In fact, that kid, Linda? She's the one who saw the smoke that night. She probably saved our lives. She was always a special kid, real brave, sensitive."

"But you never supplied her with drugs?"

"I may have passed her a dime bag or two, maybe a joint now and then. Tell the truth, I can't really remember; it was so long ago. Her father was real uptight about it, not that I can blame him, looking back. But I never felt like he was the type to do something like that; he might call the cops—he *did* call the cops—and try to talk to my dad, that sort of thing. That was more his style. But I thought I was a tough guy back then; I ruled the neighborhood." He laughed and shook his head. "What a pathetic little nobody."

"Do you remember your, um . . . your people, knocking on the Lawrences' door?"

"Excuse me?"

"Etta mentioned that people would bang on that big knocker on the front door, then run away."

"You're here to talk about kids playing doorbell—'scuse me, knocker ditch? I don't know; nobody likes a nark. Why?"

"I just wondered . . ." Time to fess up about the ghosts or change the subject. I was a chicken; I chose the latter. "Etta tells me you've really turned your life around . . ." I trailed off, afraid to say "in prison" since it seemed so weirdly damning, even though it was stating the obvious.

"Yeah, well, it's sort of a last chance, if you know what I mean. In here, you don't have a whole hell of a lot of choices, and it sure does show a person how fu—'scuse me—*freaking* stupid he was on the outside. I had a lot of help; the pastor in here, he . . . well, he helped me see me how I lost my way. Now I reach out to dumbass kids like I was, help 'em turn their life around. I'm a living example of what they don't want to happen, if they have any smarts at all."

"That's a great thing to offer, though. You could really improve people's lives."

He nodded. "Knowing that, doing something for kids, that's the only thing that gets me through the day. That and the dog training."

"Dog training?"

"This program brings dogs in here, and we raise 'em and train 'em so they can get adopted by good families. They're mostly mutts nobody wants, not fit for human company when they first arrive. I don't have to tell you, there are a few obvious parallels 'tween them and us."

Again with the killer smile. I couldn't help think what Etta had said, that as a boy Dave had a good heart. That if only he'd had someone to care for him, perhaps things would have turned out differently. I admired that he hadn't once denied what he'd done, or tried to blame it on anyone.

"I adopted a stray dog," I said, "but he's not very trainable."

"They're all trainable, if you give it time and patience. On the outside it's hard to find those traits. In here, we got nothin' but time. Speaking of time, you been here fifteen minutes and I get the feeling you still haven't asked me the question you came here to ask me. You didn't brave the walls of this place just to ask me about some thirty-year-old house fire."

Now it was my turn to blush. "No, I . . . I wanted to ask you about what happened with the Lawrences. That night."

He shrugged. "I just told you—that whole thing blew me away. They always seemed like a perfect family."

"You were nowhere near the place that night?"

He shook his head. "I was living with a cousin out in the Richmond by then."

"I, um . . ."

He looked over at Zach, and they exchanged a "what's her problem?" look over my head. "You might as well come out and ask me," he said. "I'm in here, behind the glass. What am I gonna do?"

I took a deep breath, then jumped in. "I hear you go by the nickname Duct-Tape Dave?"

His blue eyes, so friendly and open an instant ago, shuttered as though a shade had been drawn. They were flat and hard, and I was very glad he was behind bars. Or glass.

"*Duct-Tape Dave* is the reason I'm in this hellhole for the rest of my life."

"Are you saying . . . ?"

"Yes. I was Duct-Tape Dave. Big macho nickname, right? I thought I was a big deal; had me some firepower, and I made homemade silencers to make myself look like a big shot. I never killed anybody, though, until that one night—drug deal gone bad. But you want to know something? I got nightmares about it, still. Guy I killed? He was scum, just like me. Still and all, I took his life, and ain't nobody supposed to take a human life 'cept God."

"So, just to be clear"—I mentally braced myself for his answer—"you didn't go over to the Lawrence house that night, for any reason?"

"Are you kidding me? You're accusing me of killing off that family? What, have you been talking to that detective, I forget his name? He always thought I knew more than I was telling about the Lawrence family. Hounded me for years; he was the one collared me for the real crime I committed. But he's the one got me into the dog training program, so I can't hold too much of a grudge against him." He put his palm up to the glass, the phone in the crook of his neck, and pulled down the neck of his orange jumpsuit to show me his tattoo of a cross. "I swear on all that is holy, on my faith in Christ, that I never hurt one hair on the head of anyone in that family."

"And you weren't seeing Linda Lawrence?"

"She was fourteen. I was almost twenty."

"I saw photos of her—she looked older than she was. Very pretty."

"Real cute. And I already told you, I liked and respected her, and her family, too much to even think about that sort of thing. She might have ... She had a little crush on me, and one time she came inside, and I gave her a soda, and she asked for some rum in it. I almost did it, almost gave in to the demons that told me to destroy her innocence, to take away her family's happiness. But I didn't. Even then I wasn't that lost. I told her to get going and not to come back. She was crying when she left. I felt bad, but I would have felt a damned sight worse if I'd given in to my base temptations."

I didn't know what else to ask. I wasn't even sure why I was here, in this grim place of desperation, other than the need to understand what could have happened, the strange neighborhood dynamics that seemed to exist back then and might have somehow contributed to what happened.

"I have nightmares sometimes," Dave continued, his voice quiet. "It's a pair of shoes, just the athletic shoes by themselves running down an alley, running away. No body, just the shoes."

I waited, not sure what to say.

"It's ... I think it's because, you know when people get shot, and the police are taking them away, they cover them with a blanket. But the shoes stick out the end. All's you can see of them are these white athletic shoes. Gets so the mothers in the neighborhood, they recognize their kids' shoes; that's how they know their babies are dead."

There were tears in his eyes. Either this guy was a truly great actor, or Etta was right: He had a good heart. He had made some terrible choices, but if he'd had a different start to life? He could have been so much more.

"Anyway, whenever I feel like, whatever, I'll just give in and try to screw everybody over like everyone else in here, then I think about those shoes. If I can do any good from inside, I will."

Chapter Nineteen

Zach and I walked silently side by side out of the meeting room, down the various corridors, and through the several lockdown doorways. When we were finally outside, the breeze was blowing in off the bay and the day was sunny and in the low sixties, one of those late winter days in the Bay Area that remind residents why they pay such a high price for the privilege of living here.

The snug little town of San Quentin seemed ludicrously charming after the grim reality of life inside the walls.

"Surreal," said Zach, giving voice to my thoughts.

"You can say that again," I said. Our boots crunched on the broken blacktop and gravel cul-de-sac, the dead end that was the prison, as we walked toward my car parked on the main street. "Do you believe him?"

"I'm no expert in this sort of thing," he said. "But he came off as pretty believable. And perhaps more important, I can't think why he would lie about it at this point."

"There's no statute of limitations on murder."

"True, but he's already a lifer. He had a criminal history and special circumstances of drugs and guns . . . life without the possibility of parole already. I suppose he might not want to be nailed for a triple murder. . . . But, I don't know; I guess I believed him. He admits to everything else so readily. And besides, didn't Linda Lawrence tell the police her father killed her mother? Why would she lie about something like that?"

"I was thinking that maybe he and Linda were seeing each other, and she didn't want to finger him for the crime. Or maybe she saw him that night but was so scared she didn't say."

"I suppose it's possible."

"Possible, but it's a stretch. Why would she blame it on her father, of all people? If she was lying to cover up the fact that she saw Dave, wouldn't she make up some other intruder or, at the very least, say she didn't see who did it? To finger your own father—that seems pretty extreme."

"It was worth following up on the idea, though, junior detective. And I've never been to San Quentin. One more destination to cross off my list of places to see in the Bay Area."

I smiled. "Also, you're now on a first-name basis with Duct-Tape Dave. That's got to be good for bragging rights at least, right?"

He grinned.

I clicked the remote to open the car doors but stood for a moment, just to savor the day. The bright sunshine warmed my back, seagulls called, and I basked in the knowledge that I was free to climb in the car and drive out of town, leaving the denizens of San Quentin in our dust—and relegated to the very back of our minds. Freedom felt like a sweet dream in comparison to the life that Dave—and all those other men condemned to San Quentin—were living.

"Where to next?" asked Zach.

"Have you ever been to a frat house?"

"Of course. I lived in a frat house when I was in a frat."

"You were a frat boy? Where was this?"

He smiled. "Oh, the things we don't know about each other. Let's grab some lunch, and I'll teach you the Greek alphabet."

I went to University of California, Santa Cruz, which was founded in 1968, and in an attempt to be progressive and nontraditional, the school had done away with things like competitive sports and the Greek system. In fact, prior to my lunch with Zach, I had been so unfamiliar with fraternity/sorority life that when I was studying anthropology in graduate school and was invited to a Greek party, I showed up in a toga.

But the University of California, Berkeley, wore its Greekness with pride. Several fraternity and sorority houses sat on one of the main streets through campus. What had once been beautiful homes for prominent families now sported huge wooden Greek letters and the occasional ratty couch on the front porches or bras hanging in the trees. Despite myself, I'd always wanted to check them out.

"I thought you saw the body yourself," Zach said. "Why question this guy about it?"

"I did, sort of. But to tell you the truth, I can't remember much. Weird, huh? It's like I couldn't hear, either. My ears were roaring . . . I think I may have been in shock.

But this frat boy discovered her, and I just thought maybe he could remember something, or it would jostle my own memory . . ."

"Besides, you want to check out the building."

"Aren't you curious?"

Parking is at a premium anywhere near the campus, so we were on our third loop around the block.

"I was thinking," said Zach. "Maybe you could develop some spirit pals on the other side, the kind who might make sure we have a parking space wherever we go. That would be mighty helpful."

"I'm not sure there are a lot of parking-valet ghosts. For that matter, it's not like they're just hanging around, waiting to do our bidding."

He shrugged. "I'm just saying . . . it could be helpful. You could probably make money off the service."

I urged Zach to take over looking for parking and meet me later.

"No way," he said with a chuckle. "I can only imagine what havoc you might wreak unattended in a fraternity house."

"What do you mean by that? I've got my steel-toed boots on; I can take care of myself."

"I don't doubt that when it comes to the boys. But knowing you, you'll accidentally attract some devilish spirit of a long-dead frat boy, and by the time I show up you'll already be embroiled in some kind of undead hazing. And you don't even have your ghost-busting stuff with you."

"Undead hazing?" I had to smile. "I didn't think you were much of one for hyperbole."

"If only it were hyperbole. Let's just call it an educated guess. And look, here's a parking space."

So a few minutes later, accompanied by Zach, I climbed the wooden steps up to the porch of the frat.

"Hello," I said to the young man who appeared to be asleep in a hammock. "Sorry to bother you. I'm looking for Jefferson Caster?"

"Yeah," he said, not opening his eyes or moving a muscle. "Inside. Upstairs, first room on the right."

Inside, the woodwork and original lines were still intact, demonstrating what a lovely house it must once have been. But at least it was being put to good use now, I supposed. Probably no one but the wealthiest would be able to live here if it weren't owned by the fraternity, and that wasn't fair. One of the problems with my profession: I wanted people to restore and live in beautiful historic buildings, but those people tended to be rich. And I didn't want to deal with only the rich. Why couldn't the rest of the world enjoy beauty as well?

"After you," said Zach, disturbing my reverie and sweeping his arm toward the stair in a gentlemanly gesture. But I wasn't fooled.

"Scared to go first?"

He grinned. I mounted the stairs, and he took up the rear.

The first door on the right was covered in posters and notes, many of which extolled the virtues of women's bodies and the like. There was also a whiteboard with various messages, including a rather ingenious dirty limerick.

"Look at that," said Zach. "This guy could give your poet laureate a run for his money. I didn't think anything rhymed with orange."

I tapped on the door. No response. Zach reached around me and banged caveman-style.

" 'S open," came the voice. Groggy, it came in that tone I was used to from my stepson and others who seemed to equate vagueness with coolness.

I opened to see a large room with several beds, all of which appeared disheveled as though the room had been tossed. But I wasn't fooled; I'd been to college, and Greeks or no Greeks, I knew what the average dorm room looked like . . . especially the average guy's dorm room.

Jefferson was lying on the bed, in approximately the same position and attitude as the guy on the porch. I reminded myself that these were UC Berkeley students, and Berkeley was one of the more competitive universities in California, or perhaps the world. Surely they were smarter than met the eye.

"Hey," said Jefferson, bloodshot eyes meeting mine. "Wait, weren't you the chick from the community service whatever?"

"Yup, that's me. The chick from the community service whatever. I wanted to ask you a couple of questions."

"What's up?"

"Could you walk me through how you found the, um . . . ?"

"The body? Dude, that's all I can think about. I mean, you don't come across something like that every day— you know what I mean? It's not like I'm a doctor or whatever."

"You should go into the construction business," murmured Zach. I elbowed him and heard a muffled *ooofh*.

"I'm, like, an architecture major," Jefferson answered seriously, not getting Zach's joke. "That's sort of the construction business."

"It is, sort of. So, about the body?"

"I mean, seriously? It makes a person think about, like, mortality or whatever. And the fact that we don't really deal much with death in this society. It's, like, all handled by doctors and whatever behind closed doors."

"True," I said, shifting my attitude. Like my stepson, Jefferson had a certain mien that distracted from his thoughtfulness. "I know it was hard for you. Do you think you could walk me through it?"

"I already told the police, like, a few times."

"I know, but I'm looking into it for a friend, for her brother."

"Dude, her brother? What a drag for him. Is it true he's, like, a totally famous poet?"

I nodded. "Yep. Poet laureate. It's a pretty big deal."

"Yeah, I told it to my girlfriend—she's a lit major— and she was all, like, that guy's a genius. Poor guy."

"Yes, he's dealt with a lot. So when you found the body . . . ?"

"Okay, so like I said, I was just pushing in the door to the shed, but it wouldn't really budge. And then, like, I saw hair, so I knew it wasn't good."

"Did you see anything else, anything that seemed out of place, anything like that?"

"She had, like, vomit on her. And what really bothered me—I don't know why exactly, but what bothered me was she was all swollen."

He was right; Linda had looked terrible. Not much of a surprise. After all, she was dead.

As though reading my mind, he went on: "I mean, she looked bad because she was dead; I get that. Kind of a weird gray color, not the normal color. But what I keep thinking is, dude, you kill yourself with painkillers because it's like a sweet way to go, right? No pain, just ride right on out of this life. But dude, what rotten luck that you'd be allergic and instead of just having a nice trip to the beyond, you blow up and get all itchy and weird. You know? But if you don't know your pills, I guess you wouldn't know."

But Linda *did* know her pills. She had been using one thing or another—Hugh had mentioned prescription drugs specifically—for years. Wouldn't she have known she was allergic to opioids? Jefferson was right—it would be surprising for someone to knowingly dose herself with the sorts of drugs that would cause her such discomfort on the way out.

So did that prove that someone else was there, that someone gave her those pills? And whether she had taken them willingly or not we might never know . . . unless we could figure out who that person was, and he—or she—told us the truth.

"Oh, one other thing? One of the sorority girls told me she saw a lot of vials of pain pills in Monty's bathroom. Maybe she got into those somehow?"

We picked Caleb up from school and headed to Monty's house.

Caleb remained silent in the back seat. When we pulled up and Zach got out, Caleb leaned forward. "So, like, are you with Zach now?"

"Of course not," I said. "I'm not 'with' anybody."

"Oh. 'Cause I sort of, like, invited Graham—"

Just as he was saying it, I saw Graham emerge from his truck, glaring at Zach. For his part, Zach held his hands splayed out as though he was surrendering. They didn't have the best history.

But no fistfights broke out, and everyone got to work. There was no Port o' Potty or free food, but our little group seemed like a nice echo of the huge weekend crew. All of us here, working together for a good cause.

Kobe came wandering by shortly after we arrived. He was without his entourage today. I introduced him to everyone and asked if he wanted to join us, even without the enticement of cookies.

"C'mon, you could do a good deed. No one would have to know, and you'll see how good it feels."

Kobe shrugged. Caleb rolled his eyes. Apparently I no longer knew how to speak to the youth.

Graham handed him a hammer. "Come help me finish up this ramp. I'll teach you how."

To my surprise, Kobe followed him across the yard but then asked, "Why I wanna learn how to build a ramp?"

"Build a ramp today, build a skateboard park tomorrow."

"Why I wanna build a skateboard park?"

Graham shrugged as he started to set out his tools.

"I guess a person who could build a skateboard park might be able to do a lot of things. Build things, start a business, be his own man. On the other hand, maybe you want to stay in school and study and go to law school or something like that; not everyone's cut out to work with his hands. Or I guess you could join your buddies down the street and sell drugs." Graham took some measurements and studied the drawings for a moment. Perhaps it was because he didn't make eye contact with Kobe that the boy seemed rapt, waiting for him to finish. Finally, Graham continued. "Problem with that, as far as I can tell, is that most of the money goes to the guys in charge, while the kids out on the street get busted or shot. In fact, I guess a person might want to learn to build a wheelchair ramp in case he gets shot in the back sometime and needs to use it for the rest of his life."

It was clear there was no need whatsoever for me to intervene. Graham was casting a much more powerful spell than I could ever muster with my self-important "help the community" line. Graham was speaking to Kobe with respect and laying out the truth of the world without judgment or opinion.

Our eyes met. I felt another little piece of the ice around my heart slough off in the heat.

Raven showed up half an hour later, standing on the sidewalk and rocking from one foot to the other. In the harsh afternoon sun, she looked much younger than she had the other night. I almost felt bad about pinning her to the floor with my boot.

I gestured to Caleb. "That's Raven. I'll introduce you, and then you could get her a pair of work gloves, and maybe you two could clean up the path between the houses?"

It was still littered with junk from old furniture to stray nails, from our interrupted work on the weekend.

"Okay," he said, clearly dubious. "But it's awkward."

"I know. I owe you one. Or lots of ones."

Speaking of awkward . . . Hugh was now standing on the sidewalk in front of Monty's house. Again, he had such an ethereal look about him that he appeared almost like a specter himself.

"Hi, Hugh," I said. "What are you doing here?"

He shrugged. "I was just—I don't know—just looking at the house. My house. The Murder House."

Once again it struck me that this was not a useful way for Hugh to spend his time; I was no therapist, but dwelling on the place that had housed so much tragedy didn't appear to have helped his sister, and I wasn't sure Hugh would fare any better.

"If you have some extra time, we could use all the help we can get," I said.

"Really? I'd love to help. It's about the only useful thing I can do. My dad was handy; he taught me."

As was predictable, at his own mention of his father, Hugh's attention wandered. His lips moved slightly, as though working on yet another poem. But since he didn't have Simone with him, there was no one to translate for him.

"Thank you, Hugh; that would be great. We're trying to finish up this ramp while we still have the light."

As I led him over to the ramp, he kept his eyes on the house next door.

"Have you seen anything else happening at the house?" he asked.

"Not really, though I haven't gone back in, so . . ."

"Tomorrow is the anniversary," said Hugh.

"I know."

"Have you . . . you mentioned once that you might be able to arrange for a séance?"

I wish I knew what was best in this situation; in a way, a séance seemed like the smart move, since ideally we could keep things under control, and with luck we could actually ask questions of the spirits. And according to Olivier, Hugh's presence there would help by boosting the connection to the family. But I worried about his mental health.

"Yes, I think we can do that," I said. "But are you sure you want to be part of it? We could do it without you and let you know what happens."

Hugh fixed me with a look that was suddenly focused and intense. "I know I seem fragile sometimes. But I'm not. I want to understand what happened. I need to talk to my father. If you can't do it, I'll find someone who can."

"Okay," I said, taken aback. "I understand. I think you're right; we should have a séance tomorrow night and see if we can get to the bottom of all of this. I'll see if I can make it happen."

We joined the group working on the ramp, and I introduced Hugh around. Monty came out briefly and asked if someone could fix the curtain rods in the front windows. Hugh volunteered to go in and see what he needed. Monty didn't seem interested in interacting with the ramp crew; it made me wonder about what Stan had said, about Monty's lack of involvement in the ramp's construction.

While the others were busy, I called Olivier and asked about the séance. He had made contact with Meredith, and it was set to move forward. "We need six people besides Meredith. Three women, three men. I'll be there, and Hugh, and you and Hugh's wife? Do you know another man and woman who would be willing and able to come?"

"Sure, I'll find someone," I said, looking over at Zach and Graham. Once the posturing and power struggle between Graham and Zach settled down, and it was clear Graham was in charge, everyone had relaxed, and the work was progressing well.

I still felt a bit defensive about the whole ghost thing

in front of Graham, and I realized a good part of it was that I cared what he thought of me. With Zach I felt more at ease, because I didn't care as much. But if I asked Zach to the séance instead of Graham, I would never hear the end of it.

As for a woman to invite? Luz was petrified of anything ghostly, but my friend Claire, the landscape designer, was pretty kickass. She might well have plans for Friday night, but it couldn't hurt to ask.

The sound of sawing and hammers banging was like a lullaby to me, calming and soothing. It was enough to make a person forget about ghosts and murder for a bit.

Kobe was using a drill with a Phillips-head bit to screw a sawn plank onto the support below. Graham, I noticed, was working nearby but acting as though he wasn't watching; it wasn't irreparable if Kobe did it wrong, after all. The boy was applying himself with concentration; tongue curled around his lip, he held the drill with both hands and pressed down firmly and steadily as he'd been told. The screw went in a little crooked but adequately.

He released the mechanism on the drill and stood back to admire his own handiwork, a pleased look coming over his face.

"Not bad," I said. "Not bad at all."

He seemed to catch himself and shrugged. "Yeah, no big deal."

"Could be a very big deal if it makes the difference between a man being trapped in his house or getting out independently."

Another shrug.

"Hey, could I ask you a question? Where would a person get drugs around here?" I felt like the worst kind of old person, the sort that asks kids about "newfangled" telephones and the like. Did people even call drugs "drugs" these days? Did you say "score some dope"?

Kobe gave me a decidedly disapproving look. "Don't you think there are better ways of handling your problems? Lady, like, you should have, like, resources or whatever."

"Thank you, Kobe. I appreciate your concern. But I wasn't looking to buy anything for myself. I'm trying to find out who Linda—the woman we found here?—who she might have been in touch with before she died, and you mentioned you had seen her hanging around here. She had some problems."

"She a user?"

"I think she was, yes."

"What was she into?"

"I'm not really sure. Alcohol, definitely, but drugs, too."

"Alcohol's, like, totally a drug."

"Yes, I realize that."

"Worse than a lot of drugs."

Little Kobe was a real stickler for public health issues, it seemed.

"I agree with you," I said. "All of it can be dangerous stuff if it gets out of hand. But there's one big difference: Alcohol's legal. For grown-ups, anyway."

He pondered this as though it were news.

"Anyway," I continued, "I know it's a long shot, but I'm trying to help out the folks who used to live here." I glanced over at Hugh, who I could see through the front windows adjusting the curtain rods. "The boy who escaped, he's a man now, but this sort of thing can haunt a person."

"No shit, Sherlock."

"Hey, what's with the potty mouth?" I couldn't help myself.

He gave me yet another scathing look.

"I would like to talk to whoever deals around here, just to see if they knew her and can give us any information." It dawned on me that this was precisely what Graham was worried about—that I really should leave this sort of thing to the police. In fact, Annette might already have spoken to the local suppliers. But then, I imagined Kobe would know things that others might not.

"Have you ever heard of a guy that used to live around here a long time ago, dealt some drugs, named Duct-Tape Dave?"

"Duh."

"He must have been before your time," I said, unconvinced.

"Well, yeah, but he's a legend around here. He was a great businessman, but he had heart."

"He went by Duct-Tape Dave."

"That was because of his homemade silencers."

"Yeah. I think that was sort of my point. If you go by an assassin's moniker, I'm not sure I'd say you qualify for the crook with a heart of gold."

"What's a 'moniker'?"

"It's another word for your nickname or your handle."

"Why you don't just say that, then?"

I shrugged.

"Dave gave money away sometimes, though," Kobe continued. "He gave money to the lady lived next to him, old Ms. Lee."

"No kidding? Hey, this was decades before you were even born. How do you know so much about this guy?"

He shrugged. "I'm sorta like the local historian; that's what people say. I like the stories, so I'm always asking my mom and the neighbors, and they tell me stuff."

"And Ms. Lee told you Duct-Tape Dave gave her money?"

"Not exactly. I heard that from—I dunno—maybe one of the runners? Can't remember. It's just the word on the street. Dave's still kind o' like a legend."

I looked down "the street." It sure didn't look like the urban mean streets that one might see in certain parts of the city, in the Bayview or West Oakland—or even in the Fruitvale, where I lived. No abandoned vehicles or houses—with the notable exception of the oddly majestic Murder House, of course—no trash, not even in the empty lot next to Etta's house. It could be called a bit down-at-the-heels, but the yards were tended, and there was a sense of community and history—even if that history was focused on the most successful drug dealer in the neighborhood. But it sure didn't seem like much of a Mean Street.

So if the street of thirty years ago was anything like it was now, I could only imagine how a drug-dealing house went over with the neighbors.

"Hey, Kobe, do you go knock on the door of the house over there?"

"The Murder House?"

I nodded.

He twisted his mouth and looked away. "Um . . . maybe. Sometimes. Can't back down on a dare."

"Well, knock it off. Or I'll sic Ms. Lee on you."

He looked at me, startled. "Don't even joke about that. She knows people. She knows people who *know* people."

I laughed, but I noticed he didn't join in. Was this nervousness around someone who knew his mother, or could the energetic, oh-so-understanding Ms. Etta Lee be more involved than she might at first appear?

The ramp came together well and quickly; Kobe had become Graham's shadow, listening intently to every instruction. Hugh spent the whole time inside with Monty, rehanging drapes and earthquake-proofing bookcases. Caleb and Raven had begun chatting, and I heard more than one giggle ring out as the Goth girl let slip her sullen facade.

In fact, the teenagers were getting along so well, I started to get a little nervous. I had asked Caleb to befriend her, but I wasn't sure I was ready for him to bring Raven around for dinner.

The sun set a little before six, cloaking us in the orange rays of dim light. Next door, I noticed several lights clicking on. Monty was right—that house seemed to have a life of its own. As I looked toward the lit windows, I wondered whether the resident ghosts were carrying on their routines, walking through their strange afterlife . . . and condemned to reliving the crimes of that terrible night.

Chapter Twenty

"**E**nough already," said Graham that evening as we were putting away the tools. The ramp was finished and solid. There was still plenty to do this coming weekend, but at least now Monty had complete access and egress to his house. He came out and rolled up and down a few times, to our applause.

"Enough what?"

"I get the point."

"What are you talking about?"

"You think I was flirting with Cookie last night, so you spent the day with that boy to drive me crazy."

"Zach's not a boy."

"Yeah. I guess that was partly my point. Enough with the flirting with Zach."

"I have no idea what you're talking about."

"Okay, 'flirting' might be too strong a word in this case, because you really suck at flirting. But admit it: You're trying to make me jealous."

"Whatever do you mean?" I winced at my own wording, which put me in mind of *Gone with the Wind*, which my father insisted on watching the other day, blaming it on my dear departed mother.

"Come off it, Scarlett." Apparently Graham noticed the same tone in my voice. "Have dinner with me; give me a chance to win you back."

"Um . . ." While I was trying to think of an excuse, Graham rested his hand on the back of my neck, then scrunched my hair up in his fist and gave a gentle tug while looking deep into my eyes. It was a signature move that made me melt. "Okay. But first we have to take everybody home. And then you have to go with me to talk to a guy about a thing."

"Oh, boy. Who is this?"

"Just a guy Kobe told me about. It'll be real quick."

"Mel . . ."

"Look, you said you were worried about me, so I'm asking you to be my backup. If you don't want the position, I could always ask Zach to go with me. He's remarkably accommodating."

"I'll just bet he is," he grumbled. "Let's go."

We dropped Raven off at her home with the promise to tell Inspector Crawford she had fulfilled her community service. I noticed she and Caleb traded digits on their phones, which worried me. I'd wanted him to snoop around a little for me, not get involved with kids who performed rites over Ouija boards in empty houses.

Then we dropped Zach at his car. I got out to hug him good-bye and to thank him for being my escort today. He gave me a wink, saluted Graham, and was gone.

"Did you get any information from Raven?" I asked

Caleb as we drove him to his mom's place near Pacific Heights.

He shrugged. "Sorta."

"Like ... ?"

"I don't know if it really relates to what you were looking for. I mean, it's not really about the dead body. It's just, like, kinda weird."

Graham gave a mirthless chuckle. "Like anything about this case isn't."

"What is it?" I asked Caleb, pointedly ignoring Graham.

"Raven says she, like, totally saw Monty walking around one night."

"Around where? At the Murder House?"

"No, I mean like, not in his chair."

"Out of the wheelchair? You're saying he can walk?"

He nodded. "You don't think ... like, if he could walk, maybe he could have been part of what happened to Linda? And maybe he'd be worried now about what you might do if you figure it out?"

I tried to process this information. "Even if he can walk, that doesn't mean he had anything to do with Linda's death. Among other things, the police still think she killed herself or that it was an accidental overdose."

"Yeah, but you think someone killed her," he said, his dark eyes unusually sharp and focused on me and my response. "Don't you?"

We pulled up in front of a tall building where Caleb lived with his mother in the penthouse suite. The front doorway was decorated in ornate concrete tracery formed to look like a stylized face, with its mouth as the entrance. It was the sort of thing people did in the old days: They tried to make a splash, design something unique and special.

"I . . . um . . ." I stumbled as I tried to gather my thoughts. I didn't want to scare Caleb, but there wasn't much point in denying the obvious. And after all, this was why I asked him to speak with Raven. "I'm still not sure. I guess it seems sort of suspicious to me . . . but I haven't figured it out."

"Anyway, Raven says Monty's totally, like, a crook." said Caleb as he gathered his heavy backpack full of schoolbooks. "Promise you won't go over there alone anymore."

"I . . ." I was about to protest that I would be fine, but realized how stupid that sounded. If Monty was able-bodied, he could well have been involved with this somehow. At the very least, it was suspicious behavior, and I needed to be better about my safety. Last time I was involved in something like this, I landed in the hospital.

I locked eyes with Graham, who was studying me.

"Okay, I promise."

I forced Caleb to accept a kiss and a hug—which I held too long for his liking—and then Graham and I watched as he was swallowed up by the mouth of the apartment building.

"You see," Graham said in a low voice. "I'm not the only one worried about you."

"I know. You're right. So, let's go talk to Monty."

He gave me a pained look. "I thought we were going to talk to some mystery guy, then going to dinner."

"We are, but it's still early. The fellow I want to talk to isn't far from Monty's house. You'll be my backup."

"Okay, so go over this whole thing for me one more time, will you?" Graham asked. As we drove back across town, I gave him the lowdown as far as I knew it. It was helpful to hear myself talk aloud about the situation. As I spoke, I thought about what Kobe said about Ms. Lee receiving money from Dave, and how he'd reacted when I mentioned telling her about his behavior. And the gun, and how the house that burned was right next to hers . . .

We pulled to a stop at the corner of Noble and Dover streets. Graham remained silent. I looked over at him and realized he was trying not to chuckle.

"What?"

Now he let loose with a little whoop.

"*What*?"

He held up his hands in surrender. "Hey, far be it from me to second-guess the crime-solving, ghost-catching queen of the construction trade. But little old Ms. Lee, the retired schoolteacher? You seriously think she masterminded some sort of drug-payoff/murder scenario? This is the woman with the model railroad in her illegal add-on porch? The one with the three-legged cat?"

I could feel my cheeks flame.

"I'm just trying to keep an open mind," I mumbled. "I may be a crime-solving genius, but if you've noticed, so far my genius pretty much arises from accidents. I haven't actually guessed the perpetrators before they, you know, try to kill me."

Graham looked suddenly serious. "Yes, that part I've noticed."

"Anyway . . . if Monty can walk . . . maybe he really was part of this. I don't even know what to make of that."

"You drive me insane, you know that?"

I did my best to channel Cookie, copping what I hoped passed for a coquettish smile. "In more ways than one, I hope."

He reached out and pulled an unruly corkscrew curl. It bounced back immediately. It annoyed me, which he knew perfectly well.

"Let me assure you," he said as he pulled me into the circle of his arms, which pushed the annoyance right out of my consciousness. "You drive me crazy in any number of ways. This one happens to be my favorite."

We shared a long kiss.

When I finally pulled away, he started to lean in for another kiss, but then pulled back with a resigned look on his face.

"You're plotting, aren't you? Fess up. While I'm getting carried away kissing you, you're thinking about your next move in whatever crazy investigation you're conducting. Might as well tell me what it is."

"It's not that big a deal, really. I just want to talk to the local drug dealer. Real quick. Kobe told me where I could find him."

We were in a dicey neighborhood. There was a group of young teenagers sitting on the steps, and I thought about Ms. Lee saying that kids as young as ten were sometimes recruited by gangs.

A young boy, no older than Kobe, came to the passenger-side window. Graham leaned over me and spoke to him.

"Have you seen this woman?" I handed out the photo of Linda.

"We're not cops, and we don't care what you're doing here," said Graham as he handed him a twenty. "We're just friends, looking for this woman. There's another twenty in it for you if you take the photo to your friends and ask them about her."

After a few moments an older teenager approached the car. He walked cautiously, approaching the vehicle sideways, his hands down at his sides, as though ready to pull a piece if he needed to. He grabbed the money.

"Yeah, I seen her," he said. "A regular. Not for a while, though."

"What did she buy from you, do you remember?"

"All she bought was oxy and pot. She wasn't what you'd call hard-core. Just, like, a user."

"Well, that was a bust."

"And I'm out forty bucks," Graham commented.

"I'll pay you back."

"What did you expect to learn?"

"Just what she was on, I guess. And to be sure she really was an addict—you never know. Everyone keeps saying that, but I didn't feel like I knew for sure. Oxy isn't an opioid, is it?"

"I have no idea. This isn't my area of expertise."

"You seem to know how to get dealers to answer questions."

"I've seen TV. And offering money comes in handy in a lot of scenarios. So, now we go to dinner?"

"First I'd like to speak with Monty. Do you think he really could be a crook?"

"Anybody could be a crook. Especially in your orbit, I've noticed. But even if he's ripping off everybody doesn't mean he murdered Linda. What would have driven him to something like that?"

I shrugged. "Annette keeps telling me murder is usually committed for stupid reasons. Maybe she saw him out of the chair, and he panicked that she'd tell."

"And he feared that Neighbors Together would shun him? That doesn't seem like much of a motive. On the other hand, disability-insurance fraud might have been enough of a threat. But then why leave the body there, where it wasn't much of a stretch that you all would find it?"

I thought of Monty shouting from the porch that we were cleaning out the wrong shed.

"Again, all I can think of is stupidity. Or arrogance. Or both."

We parked in front of the Murder House and mounted Monty's steps. I looked at the just-completed ramp, and my heart sank at the idea that Monty might have been taking advantage of the kindness of all those volunteers. Of course, the possibility that he might have been involved in Linda's death was pretty awful, too, but there was something so . . . conniving and dispiriting about pulling a scam on a charity.

There was no answer to our knock. I called out; still nothing. He had to be home; he was always home. But then, that was back before the ramp, and when I thought he couldn't leave his house unassisted. If he was able to get around, I supposed he could go out when he wanted.

I peeked in through the front window, where the drapes were drawn and the light was on. I could just barely see through a crack in the curtains.

Monty was out of his chair.

But he wasn't walking. He was lying on the floor, covered in blood.

Chapter Twenty-one

The door to the kitchen was still swinging, as though someone had just run through it.

While I called 911, Graham ran down the steps and out the back, hoping to intercept the attacker.

The front door was unlocked, so I rushed in to kneel by Monty, phone still to my ear.

Blood streamed from a head wound, but he was conscious.

"Monty! The paramedics are on their way."

"No, cancel the call," said Monty. "Seriously, I'm okay. Someone came up behind me and hit me. It's a bleeder, but I've had worse. Then you knocked—I think you may have saved my life."

"They didn't say anything?"

He shook his head, then cringed. I was still on the line to the 911 operator, who fed me instructions.

"Try to lay still. You might have a concussion." I ran into the kitchen and got a hand towel, which I told him to press gently to his wound to stanch the flow of blood. Head wounds always bleed a lot, but by and large our skulls can take a beating. Luckily for Monty. This was no little tap on the noggin.

"He says he doesn't need the ambulance," I told the operator. "He's up and talking and making sense. We'll take him to the hospital."

I heard someone at the back door and looked up to see Graham, panting. In answer to my unspoken question, he shook his head.

"He ran into the neighbor's yard, and I lost him. How's Monty?"

"I've had worse," said Monty.

"Did you see who it was?" we asked in unison, Graham asking Monty while I asked Graham.

"Nah, man," groaned Monty. "He coldcocked me. I was reading *Wuthering Heights*, and someone came in here and coldcocked me from behind."

"Did you see anything?" I asked Graham.

"I'm not sure ... but whoever I was chasing had a walker and a three-legged cat."

I gaped at him. He laughed and shook his head. "No, unfortunately, I couldn't see anything more than a shadow slipping past the old shed. By the time I got down there, there was nothing. No one."

Monty's eyes grew huge. "Maybe it was one of the ghosts!"

"It wasn't one of the ghosts," I said. "Be serious."

"They've been threatening me ..."

"What are you talking about?"

"The ghosts have been, like, threatening me. They sent me notes. You don't believe me?"

I shook my head. "I don't think they work that way."

He pointed to a volume labeled *Notable Quotables* and asked me to take it down off the shelf and look inside. There was a square cut out of the pages, the perfect hiding place. And in it were two folded pieces of paper.

"The blue one," said Monty.

The note was written on sky blue parchment and made up of letters cut from a magazine, kidnap-style. The letters spelled out:

Don't tell. Or else.

"Monty, I'm pretty sure whoever sent you that note was human, not a ghost." I thought back to the slogan of Ghost Hunting 101: *Ghosts are people, too.* Now I have to learn to be politically correct about ghosts, of all things. I rolled my eyes. "I mean, a currently viable human, as opposed to a dead one."

He looked at me, uncomprehending. I tried again. "Ghosts don't write notes."

"What about spirit writing? What about the Ouija board?"

"Um, okay. True. But . . . Okay, I really don't know whether it's technically possible or not. But in this case, anyway, I don't think the ghosts sent this note. It's like a kidnap note. What is it referring to?"

"Maybe . . . something about the body?"

"Monty, tell me the truth. Were you involved in Linda's death?"

"Not in so many words."

"In what way, then?"

"I may have moved the body."

"Are you kidding me?"

He shook his head glumly.

"You can't mess with a murder scene! Where did you move her from, exactly?"

"I didn't mean anything by it! She was down in my back bedroom, on the basement level. At first I thought she was hurt, so I went to help her. But then ... I saw that she had, um, passed. But she was on my property, and you were on your way with a million volunteers, and I didn't want it to be a problem. ..." He trailed off. "I really didn't mean ... I was going to call the authorities; right after you all finished, I was going to call them. I just assumed she was a junkie who had wandered over from next door."

"So you moved her from your basement floor down the hill to the shed."

"I didn't mean anything by it."

"So, then, it's true: You're able to get around just fine. You don't need the chair."

Monty looked like a kid caught with his hand in the cookie jar.

"Are you *kidding* me?" I ranted. "How scummy do you have to be to cheat a community organization? All these volunteers who worked their butts off to make you a comfortable home, for no gain of their own but just to help ..."

"That's what I'm saying," said Monty. "They feel so much better about themselves afterward. Really, I'm just presenting them with the opportunity to know they've done a good thing."

"Oh, *please*. There are plenty of people in real need out there, Monty. These volunteers can feel good about their services to any one of them. As it is ... if any of them find out, they'll feel like idiots and become cynical about charity work. This is a seriously slimy thing to do."

"Okay, okay. You're right. It was wrong. But it has nothing to do with the body in the shed. And now I'm afraid if people find out about this, it will make me a suspect. If people think I'm capable of something like this, they might wonder about other things, too. It's like that book by Camus."

"You're referencing literature now?"

"We're big readers in my family," said Monty, a defensive tone in his voice. "There's nothing weird about it."

I had trusted Monty despite my instincts, I realized, because all of his crammed bookshelves made me think he was different.

Which he was, I supposed. Different in the sense of being scum of the earth willing to rip off an organization that ran on a shoestring budget and the kindness of strangers. Which made me realize he was right: I wasn't going to shout this to the rooftops, for fear of putting people off this sort of project altogether.

"So . . . what about Camus?" I asked, coming back to the rather esoteric subject at hand.

"You know that book, *The Stranger*. The main character is convicted of murder because people didn't like the way he reacted to his mother's death. People are very judgy."

"Somehow I think scamming a charity organization isn't quite at the level of Camus-like existentialism. But okay. I get what you're saying. The police know you're scum perpetrating a fraud, they'll look at you more closely. But like I said, if you didn't do anything, there would be no other evidence to indicate that you were involved."

He didn't answer. Maybe I was being judgy, but this guy was getting on my nerves.

"Let's get you some medical attention," said Graham, the voice of reason. "We can work all this other stuff out later. You think you can walk at all?"

"Nah, man, I'm disabled."

"For heaven's sake," I said, annoyed. "Just get up and walk. Enough with the whole ruse."

Graham took one arm and I took the other, and we helped him stand.

"I try to keep consistent so I don't forget and screw up in front of people."

"Well, the gig is up, Monty. Seriously. And speaking of that—this is a pretty tight neighborhood. How'd you manage to keep this a secret?"

"The accident was real, and I did land in the hospital for weeks and had a wheelchair to get around at first. Then I thought I should just keep it up, for the reasons we just . . ." He trailed off when I glared at him. "Anyway, I'm remarkably consistent. And the truth is, most people don't look at you that carefully when you're in a chair. They don't like to meet your eyes or look too close. It's sad, really."

We maneuvered him down the new ramp, since it was easier than the stairs, then got him into the back seat of my car.

"Listen, we have to call the inspector," I told Monty as Graham drove us toward St. Luke's hospital.

"I told you—she'll blame me."

"She's smart," I said. "She'll know whether you're telling the truth. And believe me, in a situation like this, it's best just to come clean with what you've done."

"But . . . there's more."

"I can hardly wait."

"I found this other note with the body. She was holding it in her hand—I think she was planning on black-mailing me. You can't tell where you got it from, though, okay?"

"You're in no position to ask for any favors," growled Graham before I got the chance.

I put my palm out, and he handed it over.

The script was feminine and erratic. It read: *I know the truth. Bring $50,000 tomorrow, or I'll tell.*

"What truth?"

Monty shrugged.

"When was 'tomorrow'?"

He shrugged again. "I think maybe she was trying to blackmail me because she saw I could walk."

"I thought you said you didn't know her?"

"I'd seen her hanging around the Murder House once or twice. I thought she was just some junkie, but maybe she saw me. I might have forgotten to draw the shade in my bedroom or whatever."

"Would it have been worth fifty thousand dollars to you to keep it quiet? Do you even *have* fifty thousand dollars?"

He shrugged.

I realized I kept thinking of Monty as a needy member of society, but maybe he had rolls of hundreds or stacks of gold coins stashed away in yet another fake book. He might have been defrauding countless governmental and charitable institutions, for all I knew.

I called Annette and gave her the lowdown. She said she would meet us at the emergency room.

"Oh, I'm really sorry about trapping you in the shed that time. I was just sort of freaking out. I mean, you can imagine, right? I didn't know what you were after, what you might find. . . . The police had already looked, but I got the feeling you were seeing ghosts at the Murder House, and what if you met one in the shed and it talked to you?"

"You're the one who pushed me in there? You really are scum in so many ways." I fumed, looking out at the darkened streets and thinking of all those duped volunteers.

"I know. You're right." He held his head in his hands for a moment, then looked up at me with pleading eyes. "Don't repossess the ramp, though, okay? Maybe somebody will need it. Somebody 'worthy.'"

"Don't you dare play all hangdog with me. I don't feel sorry for you; you hear me? You should get off your keister and do something with your life. People like you make people like me feel foolish for giving our time and resources to charity, and that's unforgivable. The only way you're going to make it up to me, to any of us, is to turn your life around and do good deeds."

"I'm going to. I swear. I just wanted to get my place fixed up a little so I could sell it when the prices rise." He shook his head, to which he still held the bloody towel. "All I ever wanted was to be left alone to read. I never catch a break."

A tiny part of me could relate. For years I'd wanted a similar thing, albeit in a Parisian garret. I had wanted to be left all alone so I could do nothing but read and feel sorry for myself. I would never have gone to such nefarious lengths to attain the dream, but part of me understood the sentiment.

"You know," I said, "Ray mentioned he was financing a workday down at the youth center this weekend. If your wound's not serious, you should go help, start making it up to the world."

"Really? I will. You'll see. This weekend, at the youth center. I'm starting to turn my life around, from now on."

Graham and I hung around, explained everything to Annette, and waited to hear about the outcome of his injury. The X-rays showed that while Monty had sustained a serious contusion and a major lump, there was no concussion. I was glad to leave him in Annette's hands. I wondered whether he'd be up on charges for moving Linda's body or for fraud against the charity or disability insurance . . . but in any case, I felt confident that Annette would make the right call. And I hoped that he might provide her with some shred of information that could help her solve the case.

"You seriously think Monty's going to show up to help at that youth center project on Saturday?" asked Graham as we left the emergency room. "I tell you what, Mel, for someone who describes herself as a misanthrope, you sure do have a lot of faith in people."

"I doubt it, but it's worth a try. I don't know how he could even begin to make something like this up to society."

"He might well have to pay the price by doing time. Fraud is serious. As is disturbing a crime scene in order to sustain that fraud."

We walked out into the brisk night and lingered for a moment in the parking structure. I looked down at myself: encrusted in dirt, blood on my skirt, and I could only imagine what my hair was doing.

"Graham, seriously. Why would you want to go out to dinner with someone like me? Look at me."

He released a deep breath, put his finger under my chin, and lifted my face to his. "I'm just as dirty as you are."

"It's not just that. Dad says I'm like Typhoid Mary. Trouble follows me wherever I go."

He smiled. "And I'd be better suited with, say, someone like Cookie?"

I punched him lightly in the ribs. "Oh, by the way: Are you free tomorrow night?"

"I thought you'd never ask."

"Don't get too excited . . . I was going to invite you to a séance. At the Murder House."

He let out a bark of laughter that reverberated in the cavernous parking structure. He shook his head. "I cannot *wait* to see your sister at a séance."

"Cookie is *not* coming along."

"Sure about that?"

"Absolutely."

Chapter Twenty-two

"Why *can't* I go?" Cookie whined. "You always think you're the only one that can do anything."

"It's not a game, Cookie. This is serious."

"Come on, Mel. Really, you're saying you *talk* to ghosts? Like they were *people*?"

"It's not that simple. But...don't you remember Mom sort of...knowing things she couldn't have known?"

"Well, sure. But that's called being a mother." She didn't even try to keep the smugness from her voice. "You would know if you had children."

"I do have a child. He was here for dinner last night, remember?"

"Caleb's a doll, but he's your stepson. It's not the same."

"Wanna bet?" As someone who had adopted—more or less—her stepson, I realized that few people could understand the level of my love and connection to the boy. My feelings toward Caleb were so deep that it was shocking when others assumed my bond with him was less than a parent's. But that wasn't the point of the argument here.

I tried again. "All I was trying to say was that Mom knew things; she saw things in the houses we were flipping. Just ask Dad. Mom was able to intuit and communicate with spirits or ghosts, whatever you want to call them. Apparently I am, too."

"You always did think you were Mom's favorite. Just because you took off and had your fancy life all over the world while the rest of us settled down and raised families, you think she admired you the most."

"I . . . What are you *talking* about?" As was so often the case when speaking with my sister, I was shocked to learn how thoroughly we misunderstood each other. What "fancy life" was she *talking* about? Hadn't she noticed that I'd been mired in divorce and post-divorce pain and petulance for the past several years?

I didn't know how to respond. She was so off the mark that I couldn't think what to say in rebuttal. Not to mention that it had nothing to do with what I was trying to explain to her.

"I would love to go to Paris and Rome and London and wherever else it was you and Daniel were always jetting off to all those years while you were married. But I had responsibilities at home. I had children and a husband who works so much I scarcely see him. Do you know I don't even have a passport? I've never needed one because I never go *anywhere*!"

I was stunned at her interpretation of the "glamorous" life I had led with my now ex-husband, Daniel. Most of what I remembered about those trips was exploring on my own because Daniel was busy giving papers at conferences and meeting with publishers and giving lectures at foreign universities. Cookie and I had rarely talked during those years, so she had no way of knowing that all was not what it seemed. "So get a passport. Take a trip with Kyle. Nothing's stopping you."

"He won't want to."

"Have you asked him?"

"My marriage is none of your business, Mel."

"Fine. My work is none of *your* business, Cookie."

"What's goin' on in here?" Dad demanded as he walked in, and Cookie immediately turned to him for support.

"Why does *Mel* get to go to séances? How come *she's* the only one able to talk to ghosts? Maybe *I'm* a ghost talker, too. I tell you one thing: I'm way cuter than that ghost whisperer on TV. I'll bet I could have a reality series!"

"There already is one," I grumbled.

"I'm way cuter. Seriously, Mel. I saw that show when we were at Olivier's shop."

"Why'd you take your sister to the wacko's whaddayacallit? The ghost store? You gave her ideas."

"*You* said I had to, remember?"

"All I want is to go to one lousy séance with my sister," said Cookie. "I really don't think that's asking too much."

"Take your sister with you, Mel. She won't hurt anything."

"All right, all *right*," I conceded. "If you want to come so badly, fine. Just don't come crying to me if you get scared." With luck, maybe Cookie would get the you-know-what scared out of her. Maybe she'd be a little less snide about communicating with ghosts. "But I'm not kidding, Cookie—you have to go into the situation with an open mind and follow instructions."

"Oh, yay, let's do it!" cried Cookie. She wrapped one arm around me and posed for my father. "Look, Daddy, we could be the next prime time ghost-hunting sister act!"

Dad and I snorted in unison.

I was really beginning to worry about myself.

Friday was the twenty-fifth anniversary of the incident at Murder House. I awoke with that knowledge firmly lodged in my head, and the idea didn't leave me at any point during the day. Not while I was working on a sewer-pipe issue at the Bernini B&B, not while I was trying to explain to the Neighbors Together staff that any and all resources allocated to Monty's house for this coming weekend should be steered over to the youth center instead, not when I was canceling the Port o' Potty and the Dumpster that Ray had financed, not while I was pondering Monty's health and level of criminal scumminess, and not even while I was consulting with Olivier as to what to expect at a séance.

"The crimes took place a little after nine in the evening," said Olivier. "So we should arrive no later than eight fifteen so we can arrange ourselves and be prepared."

"Okeydokey," I said.

"Do not be nervous, my friend. Meredith has agreed to work with us. I assure you she is an excellent medium."

I met Meredith a long time ago, when I was working on Matt's house—which was also where I encountered my first ghost. Or, rather, where I was first *aware* of seeing a ghost. It was dawning on me that I might have been seeing ghosts for a long time but not registering them as such.

It sort of weirded me out, thinking like that, and I had to force myself not to go over memories and scenes of life in my head, trying to ferret out who might have been spectral. But it was a bit like one's tongue worrying a sore tooth; it was virtually impossible to leave it alone. The little boy who was my "imaginary friend." The young woman in sixties garb I saw one time in the high school locker room and no one else seemed to see. A watermelon vendor in the Mission with an old-fashioned stand that I thought was so cute and retro until Luz pointed out that no one else could see him.

It was disconcerting, to say the least, but I was learning to deal. Whether they were hanging around because of trauma, or stubbornness, or habit, or unfinished business . . . sometimes I could help put them to rest.

Meredith was not what I had expected from a medium, but my expectations were fueled by Hollywood— and the people I'd met at Olivier's shop—so I always expected scarves and gypsy earrings.

But Olivier swore she was good. As did Brittany, the Haunted Home Realtor to the Stars.

"Well, super," I said in a high-pitched voice. I noticed that the more nervous I got when dealing with ghost business, the more I spoke like a perky cheerleader. Like, well, Cookie, in fact.

Okay, now I was *really* beginning to worry about myself.

We arrived at eight that night and headed for the dining room where, according to the police reports, no one had died. We ringed the table with seven chairs for me, Meredith, Graham, Olivier, Hugh, Simone, and Cookie. Annette would witness the séance in the event something useful was revealed, but would not be part of the circle. Monty's deposition had helped Annette get Linda's death ruled a homicide, but the killer remained a mystery.

"This is excellent," said Meredith as she walked slowly through the first floor, sensing the vibrations by holding her hands out to her side the ways mediums always did on TV.

"You almost never see this: the original furniture, the original fixtures," said Olivier.

"Does that help?" asked Hugh. He and Simone were following Meredith and Olivier around, watching for signs of . . . what, I wasn't sure.

"Oh, yes," said Meredith. "Most definitely."

"I don't know about this Olivier fellow," Graham said to me in a low voice. "He seems more like a used-car salesman than a ghost specialist."

"Yes, he's very different from you," I said. "He's charming."

"Cute."

"You just don't like his fashion sense. Whereas I can appreciate a coat like that."

Graham smiled. "How about if I let you dress me from now on? That way we'll look like the cast of a postmodern production of Les Misérables."

"You've never heard me sing, have you? For now, would you mind making a fire? Simone said she had it cleaned so we could use it tonight."

Cookie looked bored and appeared surprised that we were taking this so seriously. I'm not sure what she expected—perhaps some version of Disney's Haunted Mansion.

Soon a fire was blazing on the hearth, offering warmth and, along with the candles on the mantel and the table, the only source of light in the room. Hugh set a family portrait, taken the year of the murders, in the middle of the dining room table.

We all started at the sound of the door knocker. Two taps, and the door opened. Inspector Crawford.

"Sorry I'm late," said Annette. "Are we a go for the séance?"

"Looks like," I said.

As time passed, Meredith appeared increasingly nervous. Her wide eyes darted around the room, and she rocked back and forth on her small feet. She even began wringing her hands.

"Well then, let's get started, shall we?" Meredith said, and everyone took a seat at the table except Annette, who leaned against the wall near the fireplace. Cookie sat on my left, and Graham sat on my right. Meredith cleared her throat, and when she spoke, her voice wavered a bit. Still, she spoke with authority. "We are trying to reach out to the souls who were taken from this world. I will call them, but we don't know if they will respond to me, or to Mel, or perhaps to another in the group. No matter what happens, try not to respond with panic or fear. We are merely communicating, trying to understand what happened that night.

"Concentrate your thoughts on the beautiful family in the photo before us. Try not to speak, no matter what you hear. Anyone have any questions?"

"Will the ghosts appear to us?" Cookie asked.

"We're not sure what will happen," Meredith replied. "They might. If they do, do not break the circle and do not speak to them. And dear God, whatever you do, don't scream."

"Oh." Cookie looked a little deflated, and I wondered if she was starting to regret coming here tonight.

"Everyone ready?" Meredith looked at each of us in turn. One by one, we nodded.

"Now," she said. "Let us hold hands."

Cookie's hand was limp and warm. Graham's hand was strong and cool. Each was reassuring in its own way. Meredith bowed her head, and the only sound in the room was the crackling of the fire. After several minutes my mind started to wander. Was Cookie actually jealous of *me*, the younger sister who lived with her father because her life had imploded? Was Cookie, to whom the fates had been extraordinarily generous, unhappy with her life? I glanced at my sister, who was staring into the candlelight, and wondered what she was thinking.

Then the door knocker began rapping.

Bam bam bam . . . *bam*.

Meredith kept her head down, and though one or two of us—okay, me and Cookie—sneaked a few peeks, no one responded.

Then the knocking started in earnest.

Bam bam bam . . . *bam*.

Bam bam bam . . . *bam*!

Bam bam bam . . . bam!

Annette got up and opened the door. The knocker was raising and lowering by itself, as though possessed.

Annette jumped back and swore a blue streak.

"There is an angry spirit here," intoned Meredith.

I imagined little Kobe saying: *No shit, Sherlock*.

The screeching of chairs pushing back from the table now rang out as we broke the circle and got to our feet.

"What is *that* about?" Cookie demanded.

"Could it be Morse code?" I said loudly. It was hard to talk over the continuous pounding. "Like an SOS?"

"No, SOS is three dashes and dots," Cookie said. "We learned that in Girl Scout Camp, remember, Mel?"

"It's not Morse code," Graham said. "It's just a door knocker."

"Everyone, please. Sit down and re-form the circle," said Meredith. Though her wide eyes looked scared, she remained calm. I was impressed. "This is a good sign. They are open to contact. Take your seats."

One by one we sat back down, held hands, and bowed our heads. Cookie's hand was a bit damp now, and I imagined mine was as well. Meredith began mumbling, but I couldn't make out the words.

The flames in the fireplace suddenly surged, then receded, and I thought to myself, *What next? Moans and groans and rattling chains?* A candle blew out, and I stifled a nervous laugh. Could the ghostly behavior be any more clichéd? Then I thought, *Maybe ghost stories are based on what people have seen and heard.* So perhaps it wasn't cheesy so much as accurate.

I stared at the fire so long, I saw green marks when I closed my eyes. The dark of the rest of the house seemed to close in on us. I shut my eyes, just for a moment, feeling the sting of weariness, enjoying the brief respite from the tense séance gathering.

I had to force myself to open them.

When I opened my eyes the room was cheerful and

warm, the lights were ablaze, and the table was set for a meal. When had we put out dishes and silverware? I struggled to make sense of what I was seeing, my mind muddled, as vague and disconnected as Hugh always seemed. I heard voices swirling around me, but they seemed far off, unintelligible.

The light in the room was strange ... blue and flickering, like an old home movie.

A woman was in the kitchen. I could hear the clatter of dishes, the sound of water running, the radio playing "Hotel California."

The door knocker rapped. Bam bam bam ... *bam*!

The woman called out:

"Bridget, get the door, will you please?"

No response. The banging continued.

"Bridget?"

Drying her hands on her apron, the woman headed for the door. I recognized her from the photos: Jean Lawrence.

"All right, all right, I'm coming!" she called out.

A teenage girl came down the stairs. "What, Mom?"

"Too late now," said Jean, the exasperation in her voice belied by the smile on her face at the sight of her daughter. "I wanted you to answer the door. Your father must be out in the shed."

"He's packing," said Bridget. "I heard him whistling out there earlier."

"Ooh, is that the new dress we bought?" Jean said, reaching for the doorknob. "Come here and let me see it in the light."

Bam bam bam ... *bam*!

As though in slow motion, her eyes still on her daughter, Jean opened the door, not even looking to see who it was.

Bam bam bam . . . *bam!*

"*Mel!*"

I snapped out of it.

Seven pairs of eyes were on me. Olivier was, predict-ably, amused. Meredith seemed wary. Graham and An-nette looked concerned. Hugh's face was ashen, Simone's puzzled.

Cookie looked appalled. She was standing, and I was willing to wager it was she who had shouted my name, breaking the contact and destroying the circle.

"What happened?" I asked, my voice strange in my ears.

Graham rose and came to stand behind me, placing warm hands on my suddenly cold, stiff shoulders and massaging gently.

"You left us there for a few minutes," he said.

"Are you all right, Mel?" Annette asked.

"I'm fine. Really."

"What did you see?" Cookie asked.

"I thought . . . I could see what was happening. I saw the mom, Jean Lawrence, in the kitchen, the daughter Bridget coming down the stairs." I looked at Olivier and Meredith. "I think I was there, that night."

"The spirits were eager to speak with you," said Mer-edith. "They recognized you; they have been waiting."

"Well, that's seriously creepy," Cookie said.

"What else did you see?" Olivier asked.

"Someone was knocking on the door."

"Like earlier tonight?" Olivier asked.

I nodded.

"Who was it?" asked Annette, sitting up eagerly.

"I didn't see," I said. "I came out of it just as she was opening the door."

"Wait, wait, *wait*," said Cookie. "I thought the *dad* killed everybody. Why do we care about who was at the door?"

"Because Sidney Lawrence didn't do it," I said.

Hugh gasped, and Simone held him to her chest.

"Are you certain of that?" Annette asked.

"No. But I know how to find out. Let's do this one more time," I said. "Everybody take a seat and join hands."

"Are you sure you want to do this?" Annette asked.

"I have to," I said.

"Are you *kidding* me?" said Cookie with a tone of outrage I hadn't heard since the time Daphne and I used her junior prom dress for an art project. "This is dangerous! If the dad didn't kill his family, then whoever did could still be around! And if Mel sees who it is, she could be . . . I mean . . . What's to keep him from coming after her?"

"Me, for starters," said Annette.

"It's okay, Cookie," I said. "This is what we're here for."

"It most certainly is *not* okay, Melanie Ann Turner. You should have seen yourself. It was . . . it was as if you weren't even *here*. What's *wrong* with you people? Graham?"

"Gotta say, I'm siding with your sister here, Mel," said Graham.

"Cookie," said Olivier, coming over to take her hand. "You must understand, your sister is very gifted. She might be able to tell us what happened that night, be able to help Hugh understand his family's tragedy. Maybe discover a killer. It is very noble, what she does. You understand?"

"No, I don't understand," Cookie said flatly. "I don't care about Hugh's family tragedy. Sorry, Hugh, but I don't. Not if it means risking Mel's safety."

"If I can help solve a murder and clear an innocent man's name, Cookie, then it's something I have to do."

Cookie glared at me for a moment, then let out a shaky breath.

"Fine." She looked around at the group. "But I want to make one thing perfectly clear: If anything happens to Mel, anything at all, each and every one of you will answer to *me*. Do you understand? We'll give this séance one more try because Mel insists, but the moment it's over I am taking her home and we're ordering Thai food and watching a DVD on the couch under the quilt Mom made. That is it. Period. End of story."

And with that she flounced back to her chair, plopped down, her back ramrod straight, and held her hands out, palms up. "Well? Let's get this party started."

Chastened, we did as we were told. I hid a secret smile. My big sister had stood up for me.

We held each other's hands and bowed our heads. Meredith began her incantation ... and just like that I was back again.

This time Jean was in the kitchen, chatting with someone I couldn't see.

"I always know it's you by your knock," she said. "It's been a long time."

Why couldn't I see who she was talking to? I felt the urge to go into the kitchen, but my body felt strange, not my own. It wouldn't respond to my commands. Nightmarelike, it was as though I could run forever and yet never move. I walked—or was I walking? It felt like floating. No one saw me, no one noticed me as I moved into the foyer, and then into the parlor.

As if *I* were the ghost.

Bridget was in the front room, humming, looking at her reflection in the mirror. She turned around and looked over her shoulder, to see herself from behind.

She glanced into the hall, then picked up a man's plaid jacket from the brocade loveseat. She patted it down and took out a pack of cigarettes, then frowned as she felt something else. She pulled it out: a gun.

She whirled around, the gun held out in front of her.

"Why do you have a *gun* in your ja—"

There was a brief struggle. The log came down . . . and Bridget fell, banging her head on the fireplace hearth.

"*Bridget!*" Jean screamed from the doorway. "My baby! *My baby!*" She reached for her daughter, then reared back, her eyes wide with fear. She turned and ran. A shot rang out. And another.

A dark stain marred Jean's white shirt, and she collapsed at the bottom of the stairs. But she was still alive, looking over her shoulder.

"*Sidney . . . ,*" she whispered, then screamed, "*No . . . Sidney!*"

Another shot.

And a child's gasp. At the top of the stairs was Linda. She wore a white T-shirt and faded jeans shorts, her unkempt hair curling around her pretty face, her arms and legs thin and long. A girl on the brink of womanhood.

"*Daddy! Daddy shot Mommy!*" She screamed as she ran down the hall.

Sidney burst in through the kitchen, running to tackle the shooter.

"*Nooooo!*"

More gunshots. *Boom, boom.*

Sidney fell near his wife. The killer put the gun in Sidney's hand, wrapped his fingers around it, held the barrel to Sidney's temple, and pulled the trigger.

Boom.

Chapter Twenty-three

"**W**hy couldn't she see the killer?" asked Annette.

"An excellent question," I said. "It was incredibly frustrating."

"I was afraid of that," Meredith said, shaking her head. "But I was hoping they would say a name, or in some other way identify the killer. You remember anything like that?"

I shook my head. "You knew this would happen?"

"I didn't *know* it would happen, but I'm not surprised. What you saw was not a replay of the actual event, but a reenactment of sorts. You couldn't see the killer because he or she did not die here that night. The ghosts manifested because they are here, connected to this home, in these walls. But he is not. He is still alive."

"I knew it," Hugh said. He held his head in his hands, rocking, and his voice was raw. "I *knew* it. It never made any sense. All these years . . . and it wasn't my father after all."

I shook my head.

He leaned back in his chair, looked up at the ceiling with tears in his eyes. Simone stood behind him, hugging him gently.

"Well, that's just great," I said, disgusted. "So does this mean we're back where we started?"

Meredith shrugged. "A vision like the one you experienced can be like a dream, vague and just beyond conscious grasp. But you may remember more when you sleep. Or something you encounter during the course of your day may spark a sudden picture. Don't try to force it."

"Fine, fine," Cookie announced, her arm wrapped around my shoulders. "We're leaving. Thai food and movies at our place. Everyone's invited, but only if you promise not to talk about ghosts, goblins, witches, werewolves, or things that go bump in the night. I've had just about enough of this."

And with that, Cookie grabbed my elbow and steered me out the door.

"So does this mean you're giving up your plans to star in a reality TV show about ghost busting?"

"Don't start with me, Mel. Just don't start."

The next morning, I was running late. Despite our movie marathon—three romantic comedies, back to back—I had had trouble sleeping. I kept dreaming about the events I had seen and heard at 2906 Greenbrier. Jean answering the door, the log slamming down on Bridget's head, the finger pulling the trigger. The sound of the knocker, over and over. *Boom. Boom. Boom.*

But no matter how hard I tried, I couldn't see who was behind the door.

As I stumbled downstairs and made my way to the kitchen, I heard Cookie on the phone in the living room, giggling.

"Who's she talking to?" I asked Dad, who was sipping coffee at the kitchen table.

"Kyle," Dad said. He held up crossed fingers.

"Did she call him or did he call her?"

"I didn't hear the phone ring, so she must've called him."

"Interesting," I said, pouring a cup of coffee.

"Don't say anything to screw it up."

"Why would I screw it up? I like Kyle. And as much fun as Cookie's visit has been, I'm thinking this house is no longer big enough to house three Turners. We're a strong-minded bunch."

"You get that from your mother," Dad said.

"Yeah, sure. *Mom* was the stubborn one."

"I don't know what the hell kind of crazy party you dragged Cookie to last night, but I guess it knocked some sense into her."

"It was a séance, Dad; you know that. You insisted I take her, remember?"

He ignored that. "You got plans today? I gather you're not working on Monty's place anymore."

"You can say that again." That reminded me: I should call Annette and see where things stood with Monty.

Just then, Cookie sailed into the room. She kissed Dad on the cheek and poured a glass of orange juice. "Morning, Mel! Did you sleep okay?"

"Kind of fitfully, actually. You seem in a good mood."

"Guess what!" she said.

"What?"

"Kyle and I are going on a cruise!"

"Really? Well, isn't that nice?" Dad said, looking pleased. "Your mother and I really enjoyed the cruise we took that one time. The Panama Canal was sensational."

"Sounds like you're going to need a passport," I said. She beamed at me.

"And the cruise is just the beginning. Maybe next summer we'll rent a house in the Italian countryside, you know, like in that movie we saw last night? The whole family can come!"

"A Turner family reunion?" I asked.

"Better make sure it's a big house," Dad said.

"Well, I'm off to make a few phone calls. Kyle's hoping I can catch a plane tonight. I've been away too long!"

She sailed back out of the room.

Pleased that the crisis between Cookie and Kyle had blown over, Dad prepared to make a celebratory breakfast. I was explaining to him that I wasn't in the mood for eggs and grits when my phone rang. I looked at the screen to see that it was Monty calling.

"I wanted you to know that, even though I'm injured and all, I'm going to work at the Tubman youth center today. I used my one phone call from jail to talk to Ray Buckley. I told him none of this was your fault, that you were acting in good faith. I came clean about everything."

"Oh, that's . . . um, great, Monty."

"He's a really good guy, not judgy at all. I thanked him for what he tried to do for me, and he said that if I made bail, I should meet him at the youth center for workday today so I could make it up to him and to society. So you see, I'm not such a bad person after all."

"I appreciate that, Monty. I think you have a lot to offer." I wasn't going to ask about the whole disability fraud part of this equation. I imagined Annette was on top of that.

"So, that's what I wanted to say. Oh, one more thing. Since you aren't going to be working on my house today, your weekend must be free. Maybe you could join us at the youth center project? I'm meeting Ray there in half an hour. I even recruited Kobe and some of his friends."

"I don't really . . ." I wanted a day off. Just one day off. But tomorrow was Sunday, so I could lounge around then. And the thought of Kobe and his friends having a youth center to call their own appealed . . . "Okay, sure. I have something to do this morning, but I should be there by eleven."

My dad's eyes were on me as I hung up.

"Let me guess: Monty wants you to do something else for him? That guy's got some nerve."

"Not for himself this time. Believe it or not, he's trying to make it up to me—and society, I guess—by volunteering at the youth center."

"I didn't hear you saying no."

"Well, I was going to work at his place today, and since that's no longer happening, I might as well use the time at the youth center. And he's volunteering with a head injury. You have to give him a little credit."

"Oh, I give him exactly as much credit as he deserves."

"Speaking of volunteering, weren't you going over to Etta's today to work on that model train set of hers?"

I was itching to return to the Murder House. Now that I was no longer frightened by its ghostly residents, I wanted to see if they would speak to me directly. But it would be nice to know I had backup right across the street.

He grunted. "Yep, leaving in a few minutes. By the way, Graham mentioned you thought Etta was a murderess at one point. Does that mean you were trying to set me up with a murderess?"

My cheeks flamed. "I think he must have heard wrong," I fibbed. "Anyway, I'll stop by Etta's this morning, too, but we'd better drive separately since I'm going to the youth center afterward. I'll take Dog with me. You can have Cookie."

"See you there."

On the way to Murder House, I couldn't stop thinking about last night's visions. Also, I was hoping Dad wouldn't say anything to Etta about my wild conjecture. I had been trying to keep an open mind, but it did seem absurd the more I thought about it. It was just that she was armed and able today, so I could just imagine her twenty-five years ago. And I knew better than to think that only men killed.

One thing about last night's visions: I was now sure the murderer was a man. Or was I? I saw a man's plaid jacket, but a woman could wear a man's jacket.

Still . . . something about the vision made me feel that the killer was a man.

Gee, that narrowed it down.

A man with a plaid jacket. A lot of people wore plaid jackets. Like that photo Hugh had shown me, where he and his dad and Uncle Ray were wearing matching plaid hunting jackets, holding up their freshly caught trout with pride.

I thought of those pictures, taken so long ago. Sidney and Ray could have been brothers; they had similar coloring and build. I remembered Ray saying how touched he was the day Hugh called him "dad."

Little Linda told the police she had seen her daddy at the base of the stairs that terrible night.

And when the adult Linda went back to the house last Friday, she thought she had seen her father's ghost at the bottom of the stairs ... but it turned out to be Hugh.

My heart started to pound.

Could Linda have realized on Friday, as she stood at the top of the stairs, that it wasn't her father she saw that long-ago night? That it was someone who had resembled him in the dark, violent night?

Could it have been Ray? Ray, who always stopped to knock, even though he was part of the family? Ray, who treated the children as his own, who bent over backward for them? Could he have been guilty of the embezzlement, rather than Sidney? Ray had no money problems, and he kept the company books. If Sidney was out of the way, Ray could blame everything on him, even while vociferously defending his old friend.

But why would he have killed Bridget and Jean? I kept turning it over in my mind. Jean was supposed to have taken the kids to the seaside that afternoon, and Sidney was to join them the next day, but Hugh got sick. Would Ray have expected Sidney to be alone, perhaps expecting to blame the breaking and entering on the local drug trade? Was he surprised by finding them at home, and so struck out in a moment of panic?

The vision came over me again.

Bridget turning ... *Why do you have a gun?*

The sight of the log coming down.

The bang of the gun, the mother running, screaming.

Calling out, *Sidney!*

But Sidney had been in the yard, in the shed. Whistling happily while he gathered items for their delayed outing.

My heart raced, my breath sped up. It seemed impossible, didn't it?

Ray Buckley was such a good guy. Not judgy, as Monty said. Committed to all sorts of good deeds.

Almost as though he was plagued by a guilty conscience.

I parked in front of Murder House, and brought out my phone. I tried Monty. No answer, but I left a message on his machine. "Monty, don't go anywhere with Ray alone," I said. "He . . . he may have been the one who attacked you yesterday."

I had guessed wrong before. If I was wrong this time . . . I would have a lot of 'splainin' to do.

Next, I tried Ray. I had no idea what I would say if he picked up, but all I could think was that if he was with Monty and planning something . . . I had to come up with something that might change his mind. No answer, again.

Finally, I called Annette.

"Listen, I think it's Ray. I think he thinks Monty saw him with Linda's body. I think he's the one who attacked him yesterday. Ray might be out to shut Monty up permanently."

"You saw him in your vision?"

"No, nothing like that. But I think Ray is responsible for everything, and I'll explain it all right after you send a car over to pick him up. He's over at the Tubman youth center meeting with Monty. Neither of them is answering their phones. I'm worried for Monty."

Annette agreed, then called me back a few minutes later.

"Okay, I'm listening. Run this whole thing past me. Why would a respectable businessman like Ray Buckley go after Linda?"

"I think when they did that walk-through of the Murder House together, he realized that Linda was putting it all together in her mind, that maybe she had seen Ray—who looked a lot like Sidney—rather than her father. What if she tried to blackmail him and he killed her? He had knee surgery recently, so he probably had access to prescription painkillers. Maybe he offered them to her and lied about what they were, or . . . crushed them and put them in a drink of some kind?

"And then Monty moved the body and screwed up the crime scene forensic evidence."

"But Ray was investigated at the time of the family murders. He had no financial motive. The cops found him credible at the time."

"You've met him. He comes off as very credible. Very empathetic."

"We still don't have motive. Why would he have done something so horrific?"

"The accusations of embezzlement." I said it before I had fully fabricated it in my own mind. "What if Ray was the one embezzling? That's why he was so well-off financially. After Sidney's death, Ray blamed everything on him, and the external investigation was dropped."

"And the rest of the family?"

"Things got out of hand. Ray expected Sidney to be alone that night, remember? Maybe he was planning on taking him out, assuming it would be blamed on the neighborhood violence. But he abandoned the idea when he realized the family was home. Then Bridget was snooping in his jacket for cigarettes and pulled out the loaded gun. He lashed out to keep her quiet but wound up hurting her. He didn't know his own strength."

Again, I remembered Ray's words: *He didn't know his own strength. None of us do, until we're tested.*

"Then the mom ran in, and he shot her to keep her quiet. She was crying out for Sidney, who was out in the shed."

"The shed where we found Linda."

"The very one. And when Sidney ran in, Ray shot him, too. Realizing Linda thought it was her father who'd done the deed, he made it look like Sidney had shot himself. But then, last week, Linda sees Hugh at the base of the stairs and thinks it's her father's ghost. Maybe it clicked then, and she realized it had been Ray."

"So Ray killed Linda to keep her quiet, and figured he'd stash the body in the basement floor of Monty's house, since he thought Monty couldn't go down there in his wheelchair."

"Right. And he made a point to sponsor Monty's house, I guess, in a kind of secret apology. But when Ray realized Monty could walk, and Linda's body was found down in the shed, he figured Monty moved it — but also thought maybe Monty had seen him earlier with Linda's body. Ray must have been a nervous wreck, wondering if and when Monty would say anything."

"All right, we don't have enough evidence to hold him, but I'll bring him in for questioning."

We hung up. On the plus side, it looked like I really did now have a friend in the SFPD. Unfortunately, it was for all the wrong reasons.

I remained in the car for a moment, petting Dog and gazing at Murder House.

It was overwhelming. Could a trusted family friend

really carry out such atrocities, then go on with his life, just like that? And never kill again?

Actually . . . he *had* killed again. Linda. She realized it had been Ray she saw at the base of the stairs, rather than her father. Foolishly, she thought to blackmail him rather than running to tell the world what he'd done. She was no foe for a man already saddled with such sins.

Do you believe in demons? Ray had once asked me.

I was beginning to.

Chapter Twenty-four

The blue knocker lay still and foreboding against the front door.

These knockers used to remind me of Paris, but I feared from now on they would carry a different association for me.

I reached out, wrapping my fingers around the cold metal of the hand. Lifted it up, banged it down. *Bam*. Twice more: *Bam. Bam*. And then a pause, one more *bam*.

I had no idea what I was doing, but perhaps the ghosts would recognize their own knocking pattern. I wanted some time alone with these ghosts. Perhaps, if I was right about Ray, I could let these ghosts know that he had been discovered and finally lay them to rest. That justice would be done, at long last.

Dog stood behind me, growling from some deep place in his furry chest.

The door swung in slowly. Dog immediately raced past me, running up the stairs, barking.

I crossed the tiled entry and stood on the spot where Jean Lawrence had died, calling out for her husband. Feeling nothing, I walked over toward the fireplace, where poor Bridget had fallen.

Nothing. No cold spots, no sounds, no eerie, blue-gray scenes unreeling like an old home movie.

"I want to talk to you," I said, my hand reaching for my grandmother's wedding ring hanging on a chain around my neck. I wasn't afraid of these ghosts, not anymore. I was afraid of how they died, of the rage and cold ambition that could push a seemingly normal person to do the unthinkable. I didn't want to know something like that was possible.

But the more I thought about it, the more sure I was. Ray was "part of the family," but he always knocked. Jean recognized the pattern as his. Bam bam bam ... *bam*. He had knocked that night. Was that why the sounds rang out, over and over?

"Dog?" I whistled. "Come here, sweetie."

More barking from upstairs was my only response.

It was possible Dog was chasing spirits. It was also possible he was chasing dust motes. Like most animals, he was more tuned in to spirits than were humans. But like a lot of dogs, his attention wavered. And Dog wasn't all that bright.

But then I heard a yelp and a panicked canine cry.

"Dog?" I ran up the stairs and down the hall. "Dog, come here, boy!"

The door of the second bedroom was ajar. I stopped short in the doorway.

Ray had Dog by the collar. He held a gun to my pet's head.

I swallowed hard and tried to steady my hammering

heart with a deep breath, which I let out slowly. We all, even Dog, seemed to freeze: a strange tableau.

"I thought you were meeting Monty at the youth center," I said inanely.

"Change of plans," said Ray.

The knowledge that I was right about the man before me was small comfort when I realized that I was here with no backup save the four-footed variety now in the clutches of the very evil I had been contemplating. My dad would be pulling up at Etta's soon. My mind cast around for some way to make enough noise to get his attention.

"What are you doing here?" My hand went toward my pocket, hoping I might be able to surreptitiously hit the panic button on my car keys and set off the alarm. It would annoy the neighbors and attract attention.

"Uh-uh—keep your hands up."

Ray shook his head, looked at me with tears in his already red-rimmed eyes. His skin had a gray cast, haggard. He looked like a man on his last legs.

"You already figured it out, right? I mean, it's not like I gave myself away right this second, what with the gun and everything?"

I shook my head. I don't know why it would comfort him to know the gig was already up, but I played into it.

"We all figured it out," I said, hoping that now that all was said and done, he would let me go. "It's over, Ray. Time to get it off your chest, move on."

Unfortunately, my two-bit psychology wasn't enough to get this madman to put down his gun. Dog squirmed and wriggled, looking at me with imploring eyes, certain I had everything under control. Such trust felt like a burden under the circumstances.

"I can't . . . I can't go on like this."

"Of course not. Ray, you never intended for this to happen; I know that. I can see what happened that night."

"I wondered if you could. Why didn't you turn me in then?"

"I couldn't see you clearly . . . but the events of that night played out like one of Sidney's home movies."

He let out a mirthless chuckle. "He loved that damned vintage movie player. I bought it for him, you know."

"You two were good friends, weren't you?"

"Best friends. People thought we were brothers."

"You really were Uncle Ray. You never intended to hurt anyone, did you?"

"Oh, I meant to kill Sidney."

So much for assuming good intentions. "Why?"

"I had to. He was just about to figure out what was going on, that I was skimming funds from the company. There was an independent review scheduled. But . . . I really don't know if I could have done it. Really. I'd been drinking that night, and I had it in my mind, but even when I was knocking, I thought, *I can't do this.* And then the family was home. . . . They weren't supposed to be home."

"I know. They surprised you." I remember Annette telling me how it sickened her, to have to pretend to empathize with killers, be their pal, so she'd gain their confidence and they'd tell her what happened. I understood that now, at a visceral level, as my guts roiled in my belly.

"It was Bridget at first. She found the gun; she was about to make a stink. I didn't think, just picked up the closest thing to shut her up. But then Jean came running out of the kitchen, screaming at me, calling out for *'my baby, my baby. . . .'* It was horrible."

I nodded because I didn't trust my voice to speak.

Dog tried to move away, but Ray yanked him back, and he let out another yelp, tail wagging frenetically as he stared at me as if to say, "Get me out of here, please?" I tried to relax, hoping that would ease his anxiety.

"And I had to keep her quiet, too, so I shot her. She didn't die right away, though. She fell at the foot of the stairs, whapped her head so hard on the tile I thought she'd be out, but she kept trying to get up. Kept calling for Sidney. He was out in the shed, of course, tinkering like he always did. He must have heard the gunshot, because he came running in. He was in the kitchen, yelling for Jean, when I looked up and saw little Linda at the top of the stairs. In a flannel nightie. White with pink roses. I . . . I couldn't do it. Couldn't shoot her. I shot Jean again because she wouldn't stop screaming; it was too horrible. . . . Then I was going to shoot myself. I swear I was. But then Sidney was there, running toward me . . . and I shot him as well." He shook his head. "I didn't . . . I haven't touched a drop of alcohol since, I'll tell you that much."

"Ray, you didn't mean for any of it to happen like that; I can see that. Let's just get you to someone who will understand—you don't have to keep this up. Now let me have my dog."

"He tried to bite me. I was about to shoot him, but then you showed up. Do you have any idea how easy it is to shoot someone? Or some . . . dog? Too easy."

I shook my head again. Ray looked down at the wriggling dog with cold, distant eyes.

"You're okay, though, right?" I asked. "I mean, now Linda's gone, no one can tell on you. No one needs to know the truth."

"*You* know."

I tried to laugh. It didn't sound natural, but I was hoping it would fool Ray. "Hey, who's going to believe *me*? I'm just a nosy general contractor. Really, you should see my track record—I'm always wrong. You let me leave with my dog, and it's my word against yours, right? What am I doing to say, that I saw you commit a murder during a séance? No prosecutor in his right mind would put me on the witness stand—if he even believed me. There's no proof you were even here that night. There's no evidence of anything, Ray: nothing from the long-ago crime, and Linda's body was moved, so there wasn't any forensic evidence from that, either."

"That was a stroke of luck, right? I guess I was born under a lucky star."

Yeah. I wasn't going to engage in *that* conversation.

"I thought little Linda would run and tell. Fully expected her to. But she said it was her daddy. I guess she was so traumatized by what she saw, she couldn't tell fact from fiction anymore. And then I realized: I *should* be her daddy. Those children needed someone to take care of them. I took their parents away; the least I could do was take care of them. And now that Sidney was gone, the embezzlement charges evaporated, and I could take good care of them financially as well."

"That was good. You did well by them. You've done a lot of good things, Ray. Anyone can see that. You've given a lot to the community. Let me have Dog, and we can get out of here, okay? This house . . . It isn't good for anyone."

There was a long pause. My mind raced, trying to think of what to do next. There was nothing within reach to defend myself with, and he had a gun. Even my cell phone was downstairs, in my purse.

"You're right—this house is bad. *Evil.*" In one fluid movement, Ray released Dog and brought the gun up to his temple. Dog whipped around and sunk his teeth into Ray's thigh with a ferocious growl.

Ray cried out, and when he tried to strike Dog the gun flew out of his grasp.

I launched myself at the deadly hardware, landing on my stomach on the floor, my fingers wrapping around the cold steel.

I felt Ray try to grab it from me, but we rolled on the floor, tussling. Dog flung himself into the fray, snarling and spitting, sinking his teeth into Ray's neck and shoulders. I heard Ray cry out in pain, and as he reared back to push Dog away, I scrambled to my feet and pointed the gun at him.

"Dog! Stop!" I yelled. "C'm'ere, boy!"

Dog released Ray and came over to my side, though he continued to growl and bare his teeth in warning.

"Don't move, Ray," I said. "My dad gave me my first gun when I was eight years old, so you better believe I know how to use one. I don't want to shoot you, but I will."

Only a few moments ago, Ray had held the gun to his own head, but if he had been truly motivated, he would have had time to use it. I was betting the drive for self-preservation was strong enough to overcome his rash actions.

Ray saw the gun in my hand and stayed on his knees, blood flowing from the wounds on his thigh, neck, and shoulders. "Is he a police dog?"

"As a matter of fact, he's a retired member of Oakland's K-9 Corps, a highly trained canine weapon," I said, lying my head off. In the entire time I had known him,

Dog had never shown the slightest aggression toward anyone except when I was being threatened. Heaven knows we hadn't trained him to attack; we hadn't even trained him to sit on command. Dog spent almost all his nonsleep hours (there weren't many) begging for food or barking at squirrels. This was a whole new side of him: WonderDog.

"Let's go downstairs. And Ray? No sudden moves. Though it would be fitting if you were to die here, with the others."

Although I was reasonably confident I would shoot Ray if he tried anything, I really didn't want to find out.

"Just keep that dog off me," he whined.

"Do what I say and you won't have to worry about Dog. Now start walking."

Ray headed for the stairs. I followed. Dog took up the rear, now trotting jauntily behind me as though we were out for a picnic. He was pretty Bay Area Zen about the whole thing, living in the moment.

When we reached the top of the stairs, Ray halted abruptly.

For a moment I thought I was seeing Sidney's ghost.

Hugh stood there, pointing a gun at Ray. Seems I wasn't the only one who had figured things out.

"It was you!" Hugh said, tears streaming down his face. No longer seemingly detached from the world, Hugh's anguish was piercing. "All this time, all these years ... And you ... you were the one who did it!"

"Hugh," I said. "It's okay; I've got this. Put down the gun; I've got one, too. Ray's not going anywhere."

"I'm going to ... I'm going to kill him! Let him die right here, like the rest of my family. My *whole family*. You've destroyed us!"

"Hugh, *don't*!" I was willing to bet Hugh hadn't spent much time at the gun range, and I didn't fancy the idea of Hugh accidentally shooting me or Dog. Besides, although Hugh would no doubt find killing the man who had caused him so much pain to be cathartic, I feared the guilt would finish him off for good.

"Listen to me," I continued. "You're right; he's responsible for all of this. But you're a better man than he is; you know that, don't you? So much better. If you kill him, it'll be murder, Hugh, not self-defense. You'll go to prison. And then he would have truly destroyed the Lawrence family. Express your emotions in your poetry instead. Your words offer beauty and insight to so many."

"I'm useless," said Hugh. "He's made me useless. I can't even take care of myself. . . . All I can do is write poetry. Simone says I would be of no use in the apocalypse."

I almost laughed; it seemed like such a bizarre thing to say under the circumstances.

"Well heck, no one will be of much use in the apocalypse. I think that's why it's called an apocalypse. In the meantime, your poetry is worth a great deal, Hugh. You have the power to touch perfect strangers with your words. Don't you understand how rare and precious that is? Don't put it all at risk now—you can't be Ray's judge, jury, and executioner. No one has that right."

"Judge, jury, and executioner . . ." Hugh repeated in that vague way of his, and stared off in the direction of the window. I got the impression he felt a poem coming on.

I pressed the muzzle of my gun into Ray's back, just in case he thought I was getting distracted. But he really did appear to be a broken man; the fight seemed to have drained out of him.

"Hugh, call 911, will you? And Ray, walk very, very slowly down the stairs."

"Yes, right." Hugh patted himself down, looking for a cell phone.

"Let's go, Ray. Walk slowly down the stairs, one step at a time. No sudden moves, you understand?"

It happened so fast I couldn't stop it. I would never know whether Ray's bad knee gave out or if he purposefully threw himself down the stairs. But down he went.

He tumbled down with a series of violent grunts and thumps until he landed at the base of the stairs, right where the tile had been taken up. Exactly where he had killed Jean Lawrence, on the spot where he stood over her body while he looked back up at young Linda at the top of the stairs.

Ray landed on his back.

His eyes grew huge, and he reached above himself.

Then he started screaming.

I watched, horrified, as bluish figures surrounded him, one, two, three—and then a fourth joined in. They hovered over him, rose up in the air, and came back down as if performing a dance of death. The ghosts of Murder House, come to escort their killer to the next world?

Ray's screams cut off with a sudden gurgle, and then he stopped breathing. His eyes remained open and fixed in an expression of sheer terror.

Chapter Twenty-five

A week later I was working in the Murder House, starving and caffeine-deprived, but I couldn't stop thinking of that last scene at the bottom of the stairs.

The final autopsy report stated Ray died of a coronary obstruction: a heart attack, in laymen's terms. I guessed when it came right down to it, it was the best outcome for everyone concerned. I wasn't sure how Hugh would have fared through the long slog of a trial.

Somehow, the atrocities Ray had committed were made so much more terrible by his allowing Hugh and Linda to blame their father all these years. That he could have looked into their young, innocent faces and led them to think they were children of a monster . . . but there was no sense in going over this anymore.

Hugh was seeing a psychiatrist on a daily basis, and Simone told me he was coming to grips with everything that had happened, now that the truth was finally known. I was happy that at the very least he had reconciled with the memory of his father. When I stopped by their apartment earlier in the week, several family portraits hung on his walls, images of a happier time, quarter of a century ago, before death came a-knocking.

Hugh had decided to sell the house on Greenbrier Street after all. But first, he wanted to have it redone, renovated, and decorated in the style it deserved, Art Nouveau. And luckily, he happened to know a top-notch contractor who was perfect for the job. We had sold or given away all the usable furniture, clothing, and linens — much of which was snapped up by vintage shops — and now my demo crew was ripping up shag carpet, removing outdated appliances, and steaming off several layers of flowered and flocked wallpaper. It was deeply satisfying to see the vestiges of that terrible crime disappearing room by room.

Following the aftermath of Ray's shocking dive down the stairs, there appeared to be no lingering ghostly presence in the house. No more pale faces in the windows, no more whistling in the shed. As far as I could tell, the spirits were quiet or had departed entirely. According to Olivier, a traumatic event connected to the death might silence spirits for a time, but they could return. So far, however, the demo work was going well, with nary a bump in the night *or* the day.

Or . . . maybe not. I jumped when I heard a loud sound. *Bam bam bam . . . bam!*

I moved gingerly toward the front door, and looked out the peephole. Nothing. But as I swung the door wide, I could see it was Kobe, too short to be seen from the peephole.

"I seen your car outside," he said. "You still willing to teach me how to build things?"

"You willing to work hard and not complain?"

He gave me the stinkeye; then, finally, with a twist of his mouth, he held his hand out to shake.

"Tell you what," I said. "This is a professional job, but this weekend I was going to check on the progress at the youth center. I'll bet they could use your help down there. My stepson Caleb's going to be there."

"Will they have snacks?"

"I'm pretty sure they will," I said. "Plus, there's a fraternity there, doing some community service. Maybe you could meet a big brother."

"Okay. Plus, your dad said something about working on Mrs. Lee's train set. That would be cool."

"Look, there they are now." Across the street Etta and my dad were out in her garden, chatting while my dad secured a rose vine to a trellis. "Let's go say hi and see if my dad needs some help on that model train."

Dad looked up from his task as Kobe and I approached. "Ah, there she is now. Etta, did I ever tell you my daughter thought that you might be a murderess?"

I felt my face flame as Etta and Kobe stared at me, surprise in their eyes.

"It was just that . . . Kobe mentioned Duct-Tape Dave sent you money, and I . . ." I trailed off with a shrug of embarrassment. "I was just trying to keep an open mind. Kobe seemed wary, and he's a smart kid. And you had a gun, and . . . anyway . . . I apologize."

Etta laughed, her blue eyes crinkling attractively. "Dave once sent me money because a few of his customers trampled one of my prizewinning rosebushes—I told you he was always a good boy down deep. And I believe Kobe's wary because I know his mother, and he knows better than to act up around me. But please don't be sorry—I do believe that's the most interesting thing any-one's assumed about me in quite some time."

"Mel?" I heard one of my workers calling me from across the street.

"I'd better get back to work," I said. "But I believe Kobe wanted to volunteer his services with that train set."

"Do you, now?" said my dad to Kobe, slapping him on the back. "Well, let's go to the porch and take a look, shall we?"

"How lovely," said Etta, trailing them into the house. "This is a dream come true. Two handsome men, work-ing on my train set . . ."

"Smells like cookies in here. Do you have any snacks?" I heard Kobe ask as Etta closed the door be-hind them.

"Hey, boss lady." I turned to see Graham had arrived. He pulled something out of the cab of his truck that looked suspiciously like a picnic basket. "Time for lunch?"

"Did you bring poetry?" I asked, raising my eyebrows in doubt.

"Nope. Just sushi. But I could try to come up with a limerick or two, if you like."

"What's the occasion?"

"Just thought it would be nice to have lunch with my favorite cranky contractor. And besides, I was hoping to convince you to meet with my Marin client. The ob-scenely rich one. We need you."

"This is the corporate mogul set on importing an en-tire building from Scotland, to make it into a hotel?"

He nodded. "It's several buildings, actually, all from an old monastery. We're having a few problems with the architect, and the permits, and the building department. . . ."

"Code issues?"

"You know how historic buildings are. Nothing but trouble."

"Sounds right up my alley. Besides, you had me at 'obscenely rich.'"

"I thought so."

I flipped open the top of the picnic basket to see Graham had filled it with enough takeout containers to form a sushi feast, everything from miso soup to dragon rolls. And best of all, there was a thermos of hot coffee.

I opened the thermos and took a deep whiff. Really good coffee.

"You, Mr. Graham Donovan, are a man after my own heart."

"Yes, I am."

"I just have to check in with my crew, and then I'm all yours."

"No fair, making empty promises."

"Speaking of empty promises, weren't you supposed to be my boy toy?"

He ducked his head and smiled a slow, sexy smile. "That I was, boss lady. That I was."

Read on for a preview of Juliet Blackwell's

A Vision in Velvet
A Witchcraft Mystery

Available from Obsidian in July 2014

Sometimes it's hard to distinguish between an antiques dealer and a hoarder.

Sebastian's Antiques was a tiny shop on a narrow side street off San Francisco's Jackson Square. The place was so crammed with furniture, paintings, carvings, mirrors, rugs, dolls, miniatures, and tchotchkes that it was hard to know whether its proprietor, Sebastian Crowley, was the owner of a vast treasure trove or simply the unfortunate overseer of a musty, oversized closetful of junk.

Not that I was pointing any fingers. After all, my primary motive for opening Aunt Cora's Closet, my vintage clothing store, was to indulge my love of fabulous old garments . . . some of which no doubt qualified as junk to those who didn't share my passions.

"Course, the trunk alone is worth a fortune," said Sebastian Crowley as we inspected a very old, very damaged wooden chest.

I was skeptical. The chest's metal hinges were so cor-

roded with rust that I doubted they could withstand repeated openings, while the wood sides, bottom, and lid
were pitted and crumbling. "It came across the country
on the overland route, all the way from Massachusetts.
Back with the pioneers who came to settle the new
land."

"Was this during the gold rush?" Like many newcom-
ers to the West Coast, I was a little fuzzy on California's
history. For such a young area of the country, it had a
colorful and tumultuous past.

Crowley frowned. "Yeah, um . . . not sure 'bout that.
As I was saying, the trunk's a beaut, but it's what's *inside*
that's gonna knock your socks off."

He heaved open the lid to reveal two neatly folded
stacks of clothing.

I drew back as my nostrils were assailed by the inter-
mingled odors of mothballs and cedar. One quick glance,
and my heart sank. It didn't take a close inspection to see
these garments had fallen victim to the vicissitudes of
age that combine to ruin cloth materials: rot, moths, and
moisture. I keep a seamstress on retainer at Aunt Cora's
Closet to address the minor repairs needed by many of
my vintage acquisitions—small tears, lost buttons, frayed
cuffs—but at the end of the day I stay in business by
selling clothes my customers can actually *wear*. The
items in this chest should go to a museum-grade clothing
conservator . . . or straight into the trash can.

Sebastian lifted a simple white shift and shook it
open. The aged, yellowed cotton cracked and split along
the folds, sending small poofs of dust into the musty air.

"Well, I'll be *danged*," Sebastian murmured, studying
the shredded garment with a furrowed brow.

It was an expression I'd already grown familiar with.

In the half hour we'd spent together Sebastian's expression had been a mixture of surprise and confusion, so perhaps that was simply the way he viewed the world. Tall and gaunt, the antiques dealer was in his late sixties, with a weak chin and raised bushy eyebrows that reminded me of Ichabod Crane, a character in one of my favorite childhood books, *The Legend of Sleepy Hollow*. He dressed well—I had to give him that: a nice white linen shirt under a tweed jacket. But his wire glasses had a tendency to slip down his large, hooked nose, and he had a habit of pushing them back up. Since everything in the shop was covered in dust, his nose was now covered in grey and brown smudges. I tried not to stare.

"They looked fine when I bought the trunk. . . . I didn't think to inspect them. I'll be *danged*."

"Cloth is tricky," I said sympathetically. "If it's not preserved properly, it falls apart with age. Antique pieces were made of natural fibers like cotton, linen, wool, or silk. Eventually they break down and return to the earth. Dust to dust, and all that. It's rather poetic, in a way."

The sour expression on Sebastian's face made it clear that he did not share my appreciation for poetry. He shook his head. "That pretty little thing sold me a trunk full of worthless clothes. Son of a *gun*."

I wondered how much he had paid for the trunk and its contents, but refrained from asking. I'd been burned once or twice myself. It isn't a pleasant feeling, but it happens in our line of business.

"Tell you what: How 'bout you give me seventy-five bucks for the whole kit 'n' caboodle," he suggested, his voice regaining a touch of the salesman's swagger. "Get it out of my way."

"I'm sorry, Sebastian," I said with a shake of my head.

"I'd like to help you out, but I can't use these. The fabric is just too compromised."

"Nip here, a tuck there, it'll be right as rain. You'll see."

"It would take a lot more than a nip and a tuck, I'm afraid. Maybe a professional conservator could help . . . but for my purposes they're beyond repair."

"*Humpfh.* Try to do someone a favor, and what do I get for my trouble? Ripped off, is what." Sebastian made a face as if smelling something unpleasant, and said in a falsetto: " *'My uncle needs money. He's selling off all his antiques. Can't you help him out?'* Sweet young thing comes in here and twists me around her little finger. I'm just too nice a guy, is what."

Next time, try thinking with your brain, I thought but did not say. We stood for a moment, staring at the open trunk.

That's when I felt it. Something emanating from beneath the stack of linens.

Vibrations. Strong vibrations.

I have a special affinity for clothing. For textiles of all kinds, actually. It's hard to explain why or how—I'm not sensitive to what most psychics are, such as metal and stone, though maybe that's because I'm not a psychic. I'm a witch. A powerful witch, too, though I'm not always on top of my magical abilities—I never finished my formal training in the craft, so I'm learning as I go along. I can brew with the best of them, but divination and most psychometrics escape me.

But clothes? Clothes, I can read. They absorb the vibrations of the people who have worn them and emit a wisp of that human energy. Before moving to San Francisco and finding a community of friends, I had lived a lonely and isolated life. The sensations I picked up from cast-off clothing had offered solace and connection to others, and old clothes had become not just a passion but a profession.

Even given my particular sensitivities, though, I wasn't normally able to hear a piece *calling* to me.

Sebastian slammed the lid shut, muttering under his breath. "Worthless piece of—"

"*Wait.*"

His eyes flew to mine.

"Mind if I take another look?" I asked.

"Why, surely. You take all the time you need." A calculating gleam entered Sebastian's watery blue eyes as he lifted the trunk lid with a flourish. "Don't see specimens like this every day, am I right? Work a bit of the ol' magic on them, they'll be good as new."

I gave a start of surprise, which I turned into a shrug when I realized the "magic" he was referring to was just a turn of phrase. And frankly, I could have brewed for a week nonstop and still not have reconstituted those decaying threads. Even my strongest magic didn't work that way.

But when Sebastian opened the trunk, I heard it again. Something was in the trunk, calling to me. I heard it, *felt* it, deep in my gut . . . and in a tingling in my fingertips.

"May I?" I asked.

"Just don't hurt anything or you bought it. Like the sign says." He jabbed a finger in the direction of a large sign, grimy with age, hanging above the register: YOU BREAK IT, YOU BOUGHT IT.

It wouldn't take much more than a gust of wind to damage these pieces, I thought. Gingerly, I lifted the top garments from the trunk and set them aside: men's clothes in one pile, women's in another. My practiced eye recognized that the yellowing white cotton shirts, petticoats, and bloomers had once been fine-quality garments, but now were all falling apart. The linens beneath them were in somewhat better condition, but still too far gone to sell. Taking care to disturb the clothes as little as possible, I dug a little deeper.

My fingers touched something soft and fine, like the coat of a baby bunny. I peeked in: Velvet.

"What's this? Do you know?" I asked.

Sebastian shrugged. "I didn't look through it, tell you the truth. The girl who brought it in said her uncle was desperate for cash, and the whole trunk came across from Boston back in the day, with the pioneers. Probably some cockamamie story. Tell you what: I have too big a heart — that's my problem. She sold me a few decorative items that might be worth something, so I just took this as part of the deal."

"Would you mind if I examined this velvet piece?"

Sebastian rubbed his hands together. "How 'bout you buy the lot, and it's yours. Think about it — this trunk came from Boston with the pioneers! Just imagine the history, the stories it could tell. There's bound to be something really great in there."

"I thought you said that was a cockamamie story the seller made up."

"Doesn't mean it's not true."

I shook my head. "So if the trunk came across the prairies all the way from Boston, how come it's still packed? Why wasn't it opened, and the clothes worn?"

"The owners died en route."

I glanced up at him, surprised.

"Leastways, that's what the gal said." Sebastian stuck out his receding chin. "She said the way she heard the story, her relatives were in a party of wagon trains coming overland, and this trunk and a few other items belonged to a family who died before they got here. Buried somewhere along the way. I guess their stuff was picked up and carried the rest of the trip by other relatives and eventually ended up here in San Francisco. Listen, I tell you what I'm gonna do: seventy-five bucks and the trunk's yours, contents included. You can't beat that."

I hesitated, calculating the available floor space at my store. The shop was already jammed with rack upon rack of dresses, coats, skirts, jackets, and blouses, and shelf upon shelf of hats, gloves, purses, and shoes. There were umbrellas and parasols, shawls and scarves, and a sizable selection of secondhand jewelry. I also had a weakness for antique kitchen gadgetry, which meant a growing collection of vintage cooking items now crowded a cupboard in one corner. Much of the inventory turned over quickly, but the quirkier items collected dust in nooks and crannies and display windows. So crowded had the shop become in the past few months that my friend and coworker, Bronwyn, had threatened to pack up her herbal stand and leave.

Which was why I sympathized with Sebastian Crowley. Honestly, if left to my own devices, my shop would look as bad as his.

"I can't take the trunk, but I'll take the clothes." It was possible we would be able to salvage something from the shattered garments: a few buttons or bits of lace. We might even be able to copy some of the designs to make recreations. And there was something about that velvet item. . . .

"Hundred bucks."

"You said seventy-five!"

"That's for the trunk and its contents. Contents *without* the trunk are a hundred."

"That's ridiculous."

"Hey, you know how this works!" Sebastian was referring to auctions, where patrons bid on numbered "lots" that contained numerous items. If you wanted one particular item, you had to take the whole lot. Afterward, you were stuck figuring out what to do with the rest of the stuff. The problem was that few of us junk hounds were able to toss the worthless items into the nearest Dumpster. "One man's trash is another man's treasure" were words we lived by, which explained why so many of our shops resembled Sebastian's Antiques.

"These clothes really aren't worth anything, Sebastian. Let me give you fifty for the clothes, and you keep the trunk."

"Seventy."

"Fifty-five."

"*Sixty*-five, and you help me carry this beautiful, historic trunk out to the curb. Tomorrow's trash day."

I studied the chest one more time. If it really had come across country on the overland route—and it certainly looked old enough—it seemed wrong for it to meet its end in the gutter.

"Oh, fine," I said with a sigh. Giving in to the inevitable, I handed him three twenties. "Sixty, and you help me carry it out to my van."

Sebastian beamed. "Pleasure doing business with you, Lily Ivory."

About the Author

Juliet Blackwell is the pseudonym for a mystery author who also writes the Witchcraft Mystery series and, together with her sister, wrote the Art Lover's Mystery series as Hailey Lind. The first in that series, Feint of Art, was nominated for an Agatha Award for Best First Novel. As owner of her own faux-finish and design studio, the author has spent many days and nights on construction sites renovating beautiful historic homes throughout the San Francisco Bay Area. She currently resides in a happily haunted house in Oakland, California.

CONNECT ONLINE

www.julietblackwell.net
facebook.com/julietblackwellauthor
twitter.com/julietblackwell

ALSO AVAILABLE

FROM

Juliet Blackwell

Murder on the House
A Haunted Home Renovation Mystery

Contractor Mel Turner has the chance to restore a coveted historic house. The new owners hope she can encourage the ghosts that supposedly roam the halls to enhance the paranormal charm of their haunted bed and breakfast. The catch: Mel has to spend one night in the house. But during the spine-chilling sleepover, the estate gains another supernatural occupant—when the former owner is murdered. Now Mel must coax the resident spirits into revealing the identity of the killer—without becoming a casualty of the renovation herself.

Also in the series:

Dead Bolt
If Walls Could Talk

**Available wherever books are sold or at
penguin.com**

facebook.com/TheCrimeSceneBooks